PRAISE FOR WILLIAM BERNHARDT AND THE DANIEL PIKE NOVELS

"*Court of Killers* provides a mind-teasing investigation, vital courtroom conflict, and multiple perspectives on an issue that permeates all of our lives."

— RICK LUDWIG, AUTHOR OF *PELE'S FIRE*

"[*Court of Killers*] is a wonderful second book in the Daniel Pike legal thriller series...[A] top-notch, suspenseful crime thriller with excellent character development..."

— TIMOTHY HOOVER, FICTION AND NONFICTION AUTHOR

"[*The Last Chance Lawyer* is] a brisk tale with a surprisingly sympathetic protagonist..."

— *KIRKUS REVIEWS*

"Bernhardt is the undisputed master of the courtroom drama."

— *LIBRARY JOURNAL*

"William Bernhardt is a born stylist, and his writing through the years has aged like a fine wine...."

— STEVE
COT

COURT OF KILLERS

COURT OF KILLERS

COURT OF KILLERS

A Daniel Pike Novel

WILLIAM BERNHARDT

BABYLON
BOOKS

dedicated to the Oklahoma Center for the Book
with gratitude for all it has done for Oklahoma writers

"All human beings have three lives: public, private, and secret."

— GABRIEL GARCIA MÁRQUEZ

THE BURNING QUESTION

CHAPTER ONE

"How much would you give for one moment of perfect pleasure?"

"A great deal."

"Would you give anything?"

"Anything. Everything."

"Do you mean that?"

"Can you deliver?"

"I can."

"Will it hurt?"

"Doesn't pleasure always hurt? In the end?"

────────────

SHE HELD HIS HAND AS THEY WALKED DOWN THE NARROW hallway of Crislip Arcade, a testament to nostalgia and commerce, just as they were. Was his grip somewhat tentative? Obligatory? Under the circumstances, she was astounded he was willing to touch her at all. Perhaps this was attributable to the enormity of the promise she had made. Who wouldn't take a chance to obtain the elusive butterfly they had pursued their entire life?

"Look," he said, pointing to the display in one of the shops. "Can you believe it? Old-style vinyl records. Everything old is new again."

"Vinyl probably seems more romantic if you weren't there for it the first time around," she replied. "All I remember are the skips, scratches, and hisses."

"But still." He picked up an album. "Some of these are seriously old, not reissues."

"The owner only carries classics. Nothing later than 1985."

That caught his attention. "You've been here before?"

"Oh yes. More recently than you might imagine."

"Should I be jealous?"

"Why bother?"

"So true. Life is too short."

She just smiled.

They continued strolling down the hallway. A sudden gust of wind brought a chill and he slid in closer, taking her arm. He was hers now, she knew it. Their shoes clicked on the Cuban floor tiles, creating a syncopated soundtrack to their long day's journey into twilight. The tall ceilings, the iron chandeliers, the retro vendors, conspired to create an ambience suggesting all things were possible, failure could become success, and what seemed most hopeless might yet hold promise.

"Oh no. It's her."

They stopped. The soundtrack ceased.

"Who?"

"*Her.*"

At the far end of the walkway, someone attracted a small crowd.

"Did she spot us?"

"I don't know. She's turning this way."

"Run!"

They pivoted and bolted, still clutching one another's arm.

They burst through the crowd, carving a path through strollers and scooters and gangs. They spun and twisted, moving like ballerinas, maintaining poise while desperately fleeing. They panted and gasped and even laughed a little, not sure if they should be amused or terrified, happy to feel either emotion or both, delighted to feel anything at all.

They passed through the tall iron gates onto Central Avenue, breathless and sweating and fully alive.

"Do you—Do you—" He could barely catch his breath. "Do you think she saw us?"

"No."

"Should we leave?"

She shoved him against a brick wall, pressing close. "No." Their lips were barely an inch apart, eyes locked tightly together. She spoke a language he could translate with ease.

"We…don't want to attract attention," he said, not breaking her gaze.

"I know a place. Thirsty?"

"Very."

She pulled a small metal flask out of her jacket pocket. "Take a long swig of this."

He did, then winced. "That stings. What is it?"

"Brandy."

"There was more in it than brandy."

"I enhanced it."

"With what?"

"Paradise."

She led him to a bakery, currently closed. The doors were shut and the windows were shuttered. It looked as if it had been sealed for some time, but scaffolding nearby suggested some kind of work was about to commence.

"I don't think it's open."

"I can get us in." She slid a key into the lock. The door complained but ultimately yielded. She closed the door behind them and secured it.

The interior was dark and fusty. A bit of sunshine trickled in from the skylights, but not much. She could see the counter where the bakery once sold its goods, and tables of various sizes where people consumed them.

"How long has this place been closed?" he asked.

"Not that long. The machinery still functions. New management is revamping." She grabbed his butt cheeks and pulled him close. "Are you ready for that moment of perfect pleasure?"

"What, here?"

"Why not? Don't you feel it? Stirring inside you? Something new, something exciting. An aching from the core. A yearning." She pressed her lips against his, hard and rough. "You want me."

"I do." He swung her around, slammed her against the wall and hoisted her skirt.

"Not like that." She swept the napkin holder and salt-and-pepper shakers off a table, clearing it. "Here." She lay down on top and invited him in.

He ripped off his trousers and climbed aboard. Once they connected, he gasped. "Oh. Oh. Yes."

"Tonight will be different. Like nothing you've ever done before." She rocked her hips, pulsing. He moaned in rhythm. "Starting now."

She flipped him around and in an instant, she was on top of him, astride and in control.

The thrusting was urgent and furious, but not fast, not fleeting. His eyes rolled back into his head. She could read his thoughts. He had never experienced anything like this, never felt anything so intense in his entire life. This *was* perfection, this was the sanctuary he had sought for so long. This was worth the danger, perhaps enhanced by the danger, being with her again, putting everything on the line, throwing caution and common sense to the wind. This was being alive.

When he finished, it was not so much a release as a full-body nirvana. He cried out, loud and unrestrained.

"Was it all you hoped it would be?" she asked, snuggling beside him.

"More. Much more." He laid his head on her chest, ready to rest.

"One moment of perfect pleasure?"

His eyelids fluttered and closed. "So good. So hot."

She patted him gently till he fell asleep, which did not take long. She knew he would be out for at least an hour. Enough time to accomplish her next task. While he slept, she bound his arms and legs and lowered him onto a sheet so he would be easier to move.

You thought that was hot? She was unable to suppress her pleasure.

Wait till you see what comes next.

"What's going on? Why am I tied up?"

"So you can't leave, obviously."

"Why am I here?"

"You said you'd give anything. Everything. Now you will."

"What is this?"

"The moment of perfect pleasure."

"We already had that."

"No. You had yours. Now I'm going to have mine."

CHAPTER TWO

DAN BOUNCED A BIT AS HE APPROACHED THE WITNESS STAND. His Air Jordans always gave him an extra lift, and he would need that to bring off this cross-examination. His client, a twenty-year old USF student with no record, was accused of assaulting a police officer and resisting arrest. The charges hung on this witness. If he discredited the witness, the charges would disappear. If he didn't, her college career would be interrupted, probably derailed, by a three-year stint with the Florida Department of Corrections, no chance for parole.

A video screen stood at the edge of the courtroom, on the jury side. Currently turned off.

He scrutinized the witness. Crewcut. Duty uniform. About fifteen pounds overweight. Pale white skin. Nervous.

He started the cross-examination. "One thing I don't understand, Officer Porter. What caused you to interrupt that pool party on Burlington Avenue?" The party was in the 801 Conway neighborhood, a downtown district that in recent years had become a haven for young urban professionals. "I assume you weren't invited."

Porter cleared his throat. "I heard screaming. So I pulled over, left my vehicle, and investigated." His words were even and measured. He was taking no chances, using the time-honored "just-the-facts-ma'am" approach. Police officers were trained to avoid the smart-aleck attitude you sometimes saw on television shows because real-life jurors found it off-putting. "I immediately saw signs of illegal activity. Fighting, plus illegal drug use."

"You could tell from a distance that the drugs were illegal?"

"When you see people passing a bong, you know they're not sharing Marlboros."

"Was my client, Grayson Grant, using drugs?"

"I didn't see that. I first saw the defendant when she challenged me, suggesting that I had no right to be there. Threatening me."

He scrutinized Officer Porter carefully. Many years before, his favorite law professor had told him he could learn everything he needed to know if he watched people carefully. That had become his mantra. Any time he saw someone, he gave them a head-to-toe scan, carefully drinking in as much as he could. Often those initial insights proved useful—if not immediately, then later, when his subconscious connected the dots, made the smaller observations add up to something larger.

"What did my client say that was threatening?" This was important. Contrary to what people thought, assault was not physically striking someone. That was battery. Assault was putting someone in apprehension of being struck. Hence the phrase "assault *and* battery."

"It wasn't what she said. It was more…her manner. She didn't want me to be there."

"Is that surprising? You crashed their party and pulled out your gun."

"I did not draw my weapon until I saw signs of imminent danger."

"Which were?"

"I already told you. Screaming. Fighting. A young woman

behaving in a confrontational manner. With many friends backing her up."

"I don't doubt that you attracted their attention. But is it possible you imagined the threat?"

"I was seriously outnumbered."

"So you were intimidated. But that's not the same as being threatened." He paused to let the jury soak that in. "Was the fact that most of the party guests were African-American a factor?" Out the corner of his eye, he saw the prosecutor, Jazlyn Prentice, raise her head. He'd known Jazlyn for some time. She wouldn't let him accuse an officer of being racist unless he could back it up.

"That had nothing to do with it," Porter said.

"Didn't heighten your fear? Cause you to overreact?"

"I didn't overreact. I acted to defend myself, as St. Petersburg police officers are trained to do. As you know, the defendant did in fact tackle me. Knocked me to the concrete."

He was tackled by a much younger woman half his weight, which is probably what really got his dander up. "My client did that after you pulled your gun. You looked like you were about to shoot her friends."

"I posed no threat to anyone obeying the law. But when attacked, a police officer has no choice but to respond. We are the thin blue line. We serve and protect. People depend on us."

"I agree that we need police officers, and most do their difficult job well and honor the rules. The question is whether you were thinking clearly at this pool party."

"Objection," Jazlyn said, rising. Slender. Mid-thirties. Shoulder-length brown hair. Ballpoint pen in left hand. "Motion to strike. That's not a question. That's argument."

"Sustained." Judge Petersen had little patience for showboating. "If you're out of questions, counsel, please sit down."

He didn't argue. This would be the wrong time to get crosswise with the judge. He needed to bring this witness down, and he needed to do it quickly. "Officer Porter...you like firing guns, don't you?"

He could feel Jazlyn's hesitation. She wasn't sure whether to object or to let the witness handle it himself.

"I never draw my weapon unless I must. It's a last resort."

"But when you're off-duty. You like to shoot. For fun, right?"

He could see Jazlyn's eyes narrow. She wasn't sure where this was going. But she knew it was going somewhere, probably somewhere she wouldn't like.

"I like to target shoot, on the weekends. Keeps my skills up."

"Do you personally own any weapons?"

"Yes."

"Several?"

"Yes."

"Semi-automatic weapons?"

"No."

"What exactly do you do on the weekends? Skeet shooting? Trap shooting?"

"When I can. I don't have that much spare time."

"And of course you're a member of the NRA, right?"

"Okay, now I have to object," Jazlyn said. "I was willing to give Mr. Pike some latitude, but now he's just prying into the witness's private life and raising matters that are not relevant and potentially prejudicial."

"Not true," he rejoined quickly, before the judge could speak. "This all goes to understanding the officer's motivation for pulling his weapon at a kid's pool party."

"Very adult kids." Judge Petersen frowned. "I suppose I'll allow it. But I expect you to tie this up fast."

"I will, your honor." He proceeded. "I noticed the ring on your right hand, officer. That's a collector's item, isn't it? An NRA Collectors ring?"

For the first time, the witness looked uncomfortable. "So?"

"So you're a member of the NRA. Are you in any other…organizations?"

"Like what?"

"Rifle clubs? Survival groups? White supremacist associations?"

"Absolutely not."

"But you're a hunter, right?"

"Objection," Jazlyn said. "Being a hunter hardly proves he's a white supremacist."

"And I never suggested it did." But thanks for suggesting that association to the jury. The more extreme the witness appeared, the better. "My goal is to understand the officer's thinking, so we can understand why he reacted as he did at the pool party."

"Not liking it," Judge Petersen grumbled. "But the witness may answer."

Officer Porter replied. "I like to exercise my Second Amendment rights."

"And the Second Amendment, of course, relates to *militias*." He laid the heaviest possible emphasis on the word. "Do you hunt for food or for sport?"

Porter hesitated a moment. "Both."

"What do you like to hunt for?"

"Ducks. Deer, when they're in season. Usually whitetails."

"Anything else?"

"That's about it."

"You're sure."

A frown line appeared between the officer's eyes. "Yes. I'm sure."

"What about this guy?" With a dramatic flourish, he pivoted, grabbed the remote control, and activated the video screen…revealing an enlarged, grainy photograph of a hairy humanoid figure, apparently out in the woods. "Ever seen him?"

The witness squinted. "Is that…Bigfoot?"

"Sasquatch to his friends. Ever seen him?"

Jazlyn shot to her feet. "Your honor, this is outrageous. I give Mr. Pike some latitude—and you see what happens. His legendary courtroom shenanigans have no place in this trial."

Judge Petersen looked angry. "Can you explain yourself, counsel?"

"I'm just inquiring into what inspires the witness to pull his gun."

"Surely you're not suggesting—"

"If I'm wrong, your honor, the witness need merely say so. But I have a duty to ask."

"Do you? Do you really?"

"Really."

The judge raised a finger. "One minute. I want to see this going somewhere relevant in one minute."

"I'll do my best." He stepped closer to the witness. "You believe in Bigfoot, don't you?"

"I…try to keep an open mind about things."

"That's very evolved of you. But there's no convincing evidence that Bigfoot exists, is there?"

"Wild animals don't usually mug for photos."

"But still you believe."

"There's a lot of evidence. Abandoned campfires. Carrion. Nests."

"If a tree falls in the forest and no one hears it—it must be Bigfoot."

"It's worth investigating."

"You realize science says this is a myth."

"They laughed at Columbus, too."

"You've gone hunting for Bigfoot on more than one occasion, haven't you?"

"I…may have done." Behind him, he saw Jazlyn's head drop.

"And you've shot at the big guy a few times, too, haven't you?" He bounced back to the defendant's table and withdrew a police report from his backpack. He preferred backpack to briefcase—easier to travel fast, less strain on the shoulders. "Like on October 21 of last year in a field not far from Tallahassee. Would you tell everyone about that incident, please?"

Jazlyn rose. "Your honor, I don't see the relevance."

This time, the judge waved her down. "No, I want to hear this."

Officer Porter spoke slowly and carefully. "I was hunting and I…erroneously fired my weapon."

"Or to put it differently, you nearly drilled an innocent bystander." He offered the document into evidence. "According to the police report, your bullet came within a foot of hitting a long-haired, bearded Nature Conservancy intern who was collecting deer scat. And in explanation, you told the police that you thought he was Bigfoot. And apparently, any time you think you see Bigfoot, you shoot at it."

Officer Porter frowned. "He should've worn reflective clothing."

"So he wouldn't be mistaken for Bigfoot?"

"If he'd worn bright orange, there wouldn't have been a problem."

"But if he's a bearded guy in dark clothing, he might be Bigfoot."

"Look, I made a mistake."

"And you got a misdemeanor firearms charge that you did not report to your department chief, which is a violation of St. Petersburg PD policy."

"It was an honest mistake. And it has nothing to do with my police work."

"Are you sure? Because every time I read your report, I asked myself the same question. Why did Office Porter rush into the pool party? Why did he pull his gun? And now I know the answer. Because you thought you saw Bigfoot."

Porter's jaw tightened. The cool demeanor disappeared. "I heard screaming."

"And you thought that was unusual? At a pool party? They were having fun."

"I thought there was…more."

"Like Bigfoot."

"No."

Time for the finishing stroke. He pulled a photograph out of his backpack, then passed it to the bailiff, who passed it to the witness. He put the pic on the video screen for the jury. "This shot was taken at the pool party shortly after you arrived. One of the college kids took it with his iPhone. I notice the backyard has trees on both sides of the pool. I believe those are American arborvitae, sometime used around here to create a privacy screen. What I thought interesting was…well, with the tall shoots and jutting branches, how much they can look like a big hairy animal." He pointed. "See, doesn't that look like a face? Especially if you're driving fast and don't look too closely." He peered at the witness. "That's the real reason you invaded that pool party, isn't it? You thought you saw Bigfoot."

"I got confused, that's all." Porter leaned forward. "Look, someone has to be willing to investigate these things. The government has hidden the truth for decades, about this and a lot of other stuff. Not all knowledge comes from colleges."

"Just to be clear, is that what you were doing when you raced into my client's party? Tracking Bigfoot?"

Sweat dripped down the side of Porter's face. He was squirming, apparently having trouble sitting still. "No."

"Thank goodness you didn't see the chupacabra. The kids might all be dead."

Jazlyn shot up. "Objection."

"Sustained."

Porter's face flushed. He was breathing hard. "I didn't hurt anyone."

"No, luckily, but answer the question. You drew your weapon because you thought you saw Bigfoot, right?"

"You're trying to make me sound crazy."

"You're doing that just fine on your own."

"My job is to protect people."

"So is mine. Answer the question."

"I didn't do anything wrong."

"You ran into that party because you zoomed past those trees and thought you saw Bigfoot, so you raced in to take him down. Isn't that true?"

"I wouldn't exactly—"

"Tell the truth for once, officer." His voice rose. "Didn't you run in there to shoot Bigfoot?"

"*Well, wouldn't you?*"

The sudden outburst reverberated through the courtroom. He let that hang in the air for a long time before he spoke again.

"Just one more question. Ms. Prentice—would you consider dropping the charges against my client?"

CHAPTER THREE

OUTSIDE THE COURTROOM, DAN WATCHED HIS CLIENT, Grayson Grant, shiver with excitement.

"OMG. OMG." She pressed her hand against her chest. African-American. Nose piercing. Comb in hair. Bright multi-colored sweater. "Thank you, Mr. Pike. I've been so worried. I can't believe you pulled that off."

"Even after I told you about his Bigfoot obsession?"

"Oh, so what? I've heard people say weirder stuff than that."

"Police officers?"

"Especially police officers. Maybe a white boy like you doesn't get it, but in my world, cops are trouble. A lot of them have serious issues, and the best thing you can do is stay out of their crosshairs." She clasped his hand. "When I got arrested, I thought my life was over before it had begun. I really appreciate you taking my case."

"That's what I do."

"For no charge?"

"Sometimes. Glad I could help."

She tilted her head slightly and a sly smile crept out. "Some way I can thank you?"

"Yeah. By making the most of this and having a great life."

She pointed a finger at him. "You got it. See ya when I see ya."

After she left, he considered what to do with the rest of the day. He didn't have any pending cases. Mr. K, his boss, had been quiet for several weeks. This might be a perfect opportunity to get in a little kitesurfing. Or maybe it was time to give zorbing a try. He'd heard there was a place outside town that rented inflatable balls.

"Basking in the afterglow?"

He glanced up. Jazlyn made her way toward him, swinging her briefcase.

"Forgive me, but that sounds a little sexual."

"I think you get a bigger charge out of winning cases than you ever got with a woman."

He arched an eyebrow. "Care to test that hypothesis?"

"Hard pass. Got another hearing in fifteen minutes."

He wasn't normally all that friendly with prosecutors, but Jazlyn had earned his respect and admiration. Despite usually being on opposite sides of a case, they'd become friends. And he wouldn't object to becoming more. "Pity. Something big?"

"Extremely. And don't bother asking, because I can't talk about it. Totally hush-hush DA stuff."

"Got it." Probably something political. Those cases always produced the tightest lips. "By the way, thanks for agreeing to the dismissal."

"My case was shattered and you know it. Why didn't you tell me about Porter's...eccentricities?"

"I did tell you he was an unreliable witness. I strongly recommended that you not put him on the stand."

"Which was impossible, since the whole case depended upon him. But if you'd told me about the Bigfoot thing, I might have thought twice. How did you find out about that?"

"Garrett unearthed the Tallahassee police report. Turns

out Bigfoot hunting is at an all-time high, especially in the alt-right community."

"I don't see the connection."

"They link Bigfoot with freedom from government restraint and living by instinct, in tune with nature. Searching for Bigfoot gives them a taste of that freedom. And there's an anti-intellectual aspect, particularly popular with people who don't have much formal education. Knowledge about Bigfoot doesn't come from books."

"That's for certain."

"They associate it with explorers and survivalists. The pioneer spirit. They even have tours. And television shows. *Finding Bigfoot* ran for eleven seasons—even though they never found anything."

"Like *Ghost Hunters*."

"Exactly. Apparently the whole thing began back in the fifties when a prankster named Ray Wallace planted fake footprints. He later admitted it was a hoax, but no one was listening. Someone else staged the famous film footage—obviously a guy in a suit. And no footage since, despite the fact that everyone on earth has a smartphone in their pocket."

"I suppose there's no harm in allowing yourself to believe in a little fantasy."

"Except there is. This anti-intellectual, unscientific fuzzy thinking is becoming all too prevalent and leaves people susceptible to crackpots saying the moon landings were faked. Or climate change is a myth. We need less romanticism and more critical thinking."

"You didn't answer my question. Why didn't you tell me about the Bigfoot connection before we got into the courtroom?"

"That would've been previewing my case to the prosecution. Which would be extremely stupid, and probably malpractice. You should've dropped the charges."

"Well, as it turned out, I did. And Sheriff Pike gets

another notch on his gun belt. Another villain vanquished in his eternal quest for justice."

"I don't like the government railroading people, if that's what you mean. I don't like innocent lives ruined because someone was in the wrong place at the wrong time."

"I think you have a problem with cops."

"I don't. I respect and appreciate cops. Just not this one."

"We charged five people at that party. Why did you take this defendant's case?"

"I couldn't represent them all. Potential conflicts of interest."

"But why her?" She gave him some serious eyeball. "Because she was the skinny pretty one?"

"Because she was the one who had the guts to tackle the screwball cop."

"I think you took her case because she's a hottie. Men always want to save the damsel in distress. If she's hot."

"Don't try to turn me into some chauvinist stereotype. I've always supported equal rights."

"Doesn't mean you're not kinda sexist though."

"Did you come over here to question my stance on gender politics?"

"No. I came to invite you to a party."

"Not a pool party, I hope."

"As if I could afford a pool. No, Esperanza turns ten this weekend. She wants you to come to her celebration."

A few months earlier, Jazlyn adopted a young El Salvadoran émigré he had helped with her immigration problems. "Would this be me and a bunch of grade-school girls from St. Teresa's?"

"And me."

"Count me in. Enjoying motherhood?"

"Surviving motherhood. Let's just leave it at that."

"Aw, come on. Esperanza's adorable."

"Yes, but parenting is still an enormous amount of work. I

had no idea. Plus the DA keeps increasing my workload. I'm working twelve-hour days and I can't afford an au pair." Her voice dropped slightly. "I'm beginning to wonder if this adoption was a mistake."

"You're a terrific mother and Esperanza is lucky to have you. And she knows it. Give it more time. You'll find your groove."

"Thanks. I needed to hear that. I suppose you're right. But still—" She exhaled heavily. "That business about women having it all? Not possible. I think Gloria Steinem owes me a refund."

"Hey, maybe after the party we could go out to dinner. Just you and me."

Jazlyn twisted her neck. "I...don't think that's such a good idea, Dan."

"We went out once before. What's the problem?"

"The problem is, I'm a prosecutor. You're an extremely high-profile defense attorney. Some would say notorious."

"Some would say fabulous."

"Certainly you would. Yes, you're the miracle worker, the Annie Sullivan of the courtroom. You've tanked more of our prosecutions than all the other defense lawyers in town combined. Which is a good reason for me to say no to dinner."

"Ok, how about a Sunday spin in my boat?"

"*The Defender?*"

He lived on a forty-foot sailboat moored in the bay. "The one and only. I thought I'd take her out, maybe chug down to Tampa. The weather is great. I'll cook."

"Now this is actually tempting. Maria tells me you're a fine cook."

"Some would say fabulous."

She took a step back. "Let me think about it. Ok?"

"You've got my number." He felt a vibration in his pocket. "Speaking of which." He pulled out his iPhone.

"Looks like I'm wanted back at the office. Mr. K has a new case."

Jazlyn shook her head. "Isn't that whole arrangement... kinda creepy?"

"What? Taking assignments from someone I've never met? Who only appears as a disembodied Skype voice? What's unusual about that?"

She swung her briefcase around. "Different strokes for different folks. I just wonder about his motivation."

"I know his motivation. He wants to help people. And he has an unerring knack for finding the right clients."

"The slim minority who are actually innocent?"

"The ones who genuinely need assistance and can't get it through the usual channels. They need the Last Chance Lawyers. You know, if you'd like, I could put in a word for you with Mr. K."

"Thanks, but I've already got a boss."

"Till he runs for mayor."

"We already have a mayor."

"Word is she wants to move up in the world and your boss wants to take her place."

"Then I'll get a new boss."

"Or maybe you'll run for DA and be the new boss."

"Stranger things have happened. I'll get back to you about the boat."

He nodded. "Could be just what you need, Jazlyn. Basking on the deck. Contemplating life's mysteries. Like *Life of Pi*."

"With you at the helm?" She waved as she cut a path down the hallway. "More like Mr. Toad's Wild Ride."

CHAPTER FOUR

HE WOKE TO UNBEARABLE HEAT. HE FELT AS IF HE WERE melting, as if his flesh were dripping from his bones.

He couldn't move. He couldn't see, he couldn't hear, and he could barely move. He was helpless. And melting.

What happened? All he could remember was being with her, strolling through the arcade, then the sudden run and rush, adrenaline pumping, excitement, she smelled too good to resist, she was on top of him and—

Why couldn't he remember anything after that? He'd fallen asleep in the afterglow, but so hard and so fast and — and then that weird conversation he could barely remember…

Where the hell was he? Sweat poured down his face. His clothes clung to him like a second skin. The heat was so thick he imagined he could see it. He moved his head and thought he felt resistance, a palpable, intense, oppressive presence. His lungs struggled to breathe.

He could not last long in here.

He was tied up like a rotisserie pig, on his haunches, hands at his side. He could barely move and there didn't appear to be far to go. He tried to squirm—

He felt something. A person. Someone else, not moving.

He rocked from side to side. He felt someone on the other side as well.

He was not alone. But he was apparently the only one conscious.

Dark, hot, many people, unable to escape. This was a death trap.

"Helllllp! Help meeeee!"

His words echoed, but not for a moment did he imagine anyone had heard him. There was a metallic tone to the echo. This was a small enclosed space with little clearance. When he shouted, it sounded thunderous.

He was inside something. Metallic. He felt the wall behind him. Iron, or so he thought.

A cascade of memories flooded back. They had entered a bakery. She had a key. That should have made him suspicious, but he was hot and he wanted her and that blacked everything else out of his brain—

A bakery.

He felt a tightening in his already tense chest.

Was he in the oven?

His pulse raced. He pulled at the ropes binding him, his hands so wet with sweat he could barely maintain a grip. He knew some of these artisanal bakeries had large ovens. If you removed the trays, you could easily fit a person inside. You could fit several people inside.

Is that why he felt others all around him? This was like a concentration camp oven. This was a weapon of mass destruction.

He'd been put here to die.

"Helllllp! Please help me!"

If he was inside the bakery, then they were on Central Avenue, not far from the arcade. Not far from one of the busiest pedestrian areas in the city. Surely someone would hear him. Surely.

He leaned forward because the wall behind him was so

hot it burned. The atmosphere was oppressive. The miasma was so thick he could barely breath. He sensed he was breathing the same air, over and over again, and he knew that could not continue for long.

"Helllllp me! Helllllp!"

"Oh, be quiet already."

He would recognize that voice anywhere. The voice was faint, but nearby.

"Let me out. Please. Let me out of here."

"That is not what I have planned."

"I don't deserve this."

"I disagree. Obviously."

"No one deserves this." The panic was so intense his voice trembled. He could barely focus. "Look—I'm sorry."

"Are you? Or just terrified?"

"I—I know I didn't— -I should've—I was a fool. I see that now. I was only thinking of myself. I—I care about you. Truly. I always have, I just —I don't know. I get confused. I do what I think I'm supposed to do when I should listen to my heart. I'm genuinely sorry."

"Wow. Concern—for someone other than yourself. This is new."

"You're not a bad person. You don't want to do this."

"Pretty sure I do."

"You'll regret it. Over and over. For the rest of your life."

"Or maybe it will fill me with unbridled joy every time I think of it."

"You'll never have peace."

"Peace is overrated." A long pause, then, "I prefer justice. Justice is paramount."

"Let me out of here. I can't stand this."

"You can and you will. Since you have no choice."

"How long do you think I can last?"

"Only a few minutes. Slowly roasting. Before you explode and die."

"That's inhuman."

"You let me suffer far longer."

"Not like this!'

"You're the one who's inhuman. You're the one who thought he could get away with anything. While you're in there, I want you to think about what you've done."

"I can feel my skin melting! I can smell my flesh cooking! Do you *hate* me?"

He heard a creaking as an outside door swung shut. "No, Nick. I love you. I always have. You're my eternal flame."

CHAPTER FIVE

DAN CAREFULLY PLACED THE PASTA BOWL ON THE KITCHEN island. When he first joined this firm and learned they'd converted a Snell Isle mansion into their office, he thought it a bit odd. But when he saw the magnificent kitchen, he decided he could live with it.

"Here it is, ladies and gentlemen. Daniel Pike's super-special deluxe and delicious spaghetti aglio e olio."

Jimmy beamed. He looked hungry. Stout. Sweater vest. African-American. "That looks scrumptious." He grabbed a plate.

Garrett looked up from the keyboards. He was playing something jazzy. Tall. Rays t-shirt. Fingers moving faster than the eye could follow. Eyes gazing skeptically at the serving dish. "Is there...going to be a sauce, Dan?"

He placed his arms akimbo. "Seriously? You want to bury this masterpiece in pasta, made from dough I kneaded with my own two hands, under a red sauce?"

Garrett shrugged. "And maybe some shredded mozzarella."

He shuddered. "Barbarian. You won't even be able to taste the pasta."

"Pasta doesn't taste like anything anyway."

"Not if you eat crap out of a box. I use a blend of durum semolina flour and—"

"Yeah, yeah. Have we got some Prego in the fridge?"

Maria stared at her phone. Slender. Long rich dark hair. Tight jeans. Pursed lips. "Did you put kale in it?"

"No, Millennial Child. And I never will."

"Did you sauté it in butter or oil?"

He frowned. He was getting tired of this insufficiently appreciative interrogation. Or perhaps he should he expect a group of lawyers to cross-examine the cook? "Oil."

"EVOO?"

"EVOO is a finishing oil, not a sautéing oil. Why do you care?"

"I have to enter the right oil into my Fitbit app."

Well, you don't *have* to. "Why?"

"It keeps track of my diet. Let's me know when I've hit my calorie limit. I gotta tell you, it's not happy about all this starchy food."

"Carbohydrates are good for you."

"That's your story." She raised her voice slightly. "Alexa, how many calories are in spaghetti aglio e olio?"

A blue ring circled around the top of a black cylindrical device, Maria's new Amazon Echo. A perky female voice emerged. "Two cups of spaghetti aglio e olio has 779 calories."

"Tattletale," he mumbled.

Maria halved her serving. "Sorry, Dan. Just bought new jeans. I have to fit into them."

"Gucci Genius?" He was familiar with Maria's fondness for designer clothing, which was some sort of loving tribute to her deceased father. "A.P.O.?"

"D&G. Dolce & Gabbana."

"Better than Gucci?"

"I don't know. Honestly, I just like saying it aloud." She

affected a rich Italian accent. "Dooooolchey and Gabbaaaaaaana."

He scooped his pasta. This team had its eccentricities, which definitely complicated cooking, but he had learned to appreciate them for their unique talents, not to mention their unique personalities. The youngest, Maria, was the master strategist, teasing out the theme and theory to best sell a case to a jury. The eldest and most conservative, Garrett, was in charge of investigations and legal research. Jimmy took point on all the briefing, and perhaps even more importantly, had the social connections to unlock doors and persuade the unpersuadable. And he was the courtroom miracle worker, although in truth, most of those so-called miracles were the product of a ton of preparatory work.

Garrett finished the riff he'd been playing. "Stole that last bit from Chick Corea. What a genius that man is. You listen to his work, Dan?"

In truth, he'd never had much affection for jazz, which always sounded to him like exactly what you'd expect when musicians are making it up as they go along. "If that's what you were playing, then I like it."

"Why are you people talking when you could be eating?" Jimmy hovered over the bowl. "I'm going back for seconds. Possibly thirds."

"Please do. The cook always appreciates enthusiastic eaters."

Maria pursed her lips. "Then use more kale."

"Or chocolate," Jimmy suggested.

"What a bunch of smart alecks. Uh, do you think K—"

The perky female voice returned. "I didn't catch that. 'K' is the eleventh letter of the alphabet."

"What? Why—?" He thought a moment. "Oh, I get it. 'Alecks—uh' sounds like 'Alexa.'"

"Did that answer your question?" the black box asked.

"No. But there was no—"

"Would you like to continue listening to your audiobook, *Passion in the Prairie?* You were in chapter—"

"No thank you, Alexa," Maria said hastily. "Damned spy…"

He raised an eyebrow. "Your voice-activated drone reads you erotica?"

"Oh, grow up. It's women's fiction."

"Okay…"

"Just something to pass the time while I'm putting on my face. I forget the damned robot remembers every word I say."

He heard a beeping sound. "Is that what I think it is?"

Garrett ran to his open laptop and punched a few buttons. "Mr. K. He's ready to begin. Grab a plate and let's move to the living room."

They gathered on the circular sofa facing a large-screen television. Garrett used Airplay to put the call up on the screen. Not that they could see anything. All they got was a voice.

"Hello, team. How's everyone doing?"

Enthusiastic responses.

"Much better now that we've eaten," Jimmy said. "Dan's cooking is fantastic."

"Says the man whose favorite food is churros," Maria murmured.

"Yes," Mr. K said. "I was aware of Dan's prowess in the kitchen. That's the real reason I drafted you for this team, Dan."

He sat up. "What?"

"Just kidding. I wanted your courtroom skills."

He folded his arms across his chest. "That's what I thought."

As he had learned, Mr. K ran the firm, but he never appeared in person. He met with them by Skype, but only by voice, never video. They had no idea where he was or how he chose the cases he assigned, but they always turned out to be worthy endeavors. He only gave them one case at a time, which left them free to take pro bono cases if they wished. And they didn't have to worry about keeping time sheets or billing clients. Mr. K handled all the administrative duties and paid them a regular—and extremely generous—salary. "What have you got for us this time?"

"Something completely different. But you like a challenge, don't you, Dan?"

"Sometimes. Criminal matter?"

"Not yet. But it could become one. I've emailed Garrett all the relevant documents."

Garrett glanced at his laptop. "Got 'em."

K continued. "Your client will be Camila Pérez."

His eyes widened. "The mayor?"

"The one and only."

"I thought we represented underdogs."

"Underdogs come in many different shapes and sizes. Think you can work with her?"

"If I must." Mayor Pérez had been an important witness in a murder case he handled several months before. He'd gotten his client off and exposed the true murderer—but only after suggesting the mayor might be a suspect. He hoped she wasn't the type to bear a grudge. "Has she gotten herself in some kind of trouble?"

"Yes. Campaign finance problems. An investigatory committee believes she may have violated state regulations."

"Because she took contributions from known gangland figures?" Another tidbit he learned during the previous case.

"No, apparently that has nothing to do with this. It's all very technical and she's the best one to tell you about it. I've made an appointment for her to talk with you this afternoon."

"And...she's okay with me as her lawyer?"

"She's a smart woman. That's why she's achieved as much as she has. She knows you're the best in town."

He remembered Jazlyn mentioning that something big

was in the offing. This must be what she was talking about. The DA filing charges against the mayor, technically his boss, would be a controversial big hot mess. "So what do we do?"

"Ideally, prevent them from filing criminal charges. Talk them out of it. Show them the error of their ways. And if that doesn't work—win the case."

"Got it. How did this happen?"

On the other side of the Skype line, he heard a big intake of air. "The charges were filed by a woman named Prudence Hancock."

"Never heard of her."

"She heads a non-profit organization called Citizens for Responsible Democracy. The acronym is CRED. Though some people call it CRUD."

Jimmy jumped in. "I've heard Hank talk about them." Hank was his husband, a physician at Flagler Hospital. "They were trying to get the hospital to adopt regulations requiring potential patients to show proof of citizenship."

"Okay. I hate them already," Maria said. Not surprising. He knew her father had immigrated from Mexico. "How do people like that get funding?"

"In this case," Mr. K said, "CRED's primary contributor is a man named Conrad Sweeney, who by the way, is Prudence Hancock's boss. Heard of him, Dan?"

He had not.

"I have," Jimmy answered. Of course. He knew everyone. "Lex Luthor."

"Not a bad comparison," Mr. K replied. Apparently Jimmy's encyclopedic knowledge of DC Comics lore had some use. "He's believed to be the richest man in St. Petersburg, and he wants everyone to know it. Made his fortune in tech, cloud computing, and systems integration. Control freak. Craves power. Probably involved in a host of illegal schemes, but he works through underlings who always take the rap. Nothing ever traces back to him."

Maria's lips pursed. "Is he trying to take down the mayor so he can fill the vacancy?"

"I don't know if he wants the job himself. He simply prefers people he can control. Mayor Pérez has been extremely resistant to control."

"Especially by a sexist pig. I gather he's uber-conservative?"

"Hey now." Garrett sat up straight. "Let's not be trash-talking conservatives."

"I'm not sure if Sweeney is a Democrat or a Republican," Mr. K said. "I'm not sure partisan politics matter to him. He just wants power. He wants to be the top dog. In some ways, he's the most dangerous kind of operator. Completely amoral, so you're not going to appeal to his conscience. Only cares about himself, so you're not going to get to him through friends or family. And completely ruthless. But you're probably going to have to talk to him, Dan."

"Okay by me. I'll bring my kryptonite."

Jimmy rolled his eyes. "That works on Kryptonians. Not villains."

"My bad. This Sweeney sounds like exactly the kind of guy you formed this firm to fight, K."

The prolonged silence from the television was revealing. "I'm glad to see we understand each other. Let me ask you a question, Dan. When you dealt with Mayor Pérez before—what did you think of her?"

He shrugged. "Quick. Whip-smart. Hard-working. Dedicated. Believes what she says. I liked her."

Maria made a snorting sound. "You liked her because she's cute."

"Why do people keep accusing me of only caring about women's appearances?"

"I'm not saying it's the only thing you care about. But it's definitely the first thing you notice."

"I don't think you know me that well."

"I think I know you better than you know yourself."

"I'm being wrongfully accused."

Maria grinned. "You know what you need? A good lawyer."

Mr. K cut in. "I believe we're facing a leadership crisis in this country. The land is only as strong as its leaders, and right now, too many of our leaders are jokes, in politics for all the wrong reasons. Too often the genuinely good people get beaten down and crushed because they're too nice, or because they've lived real lives that occasionally involved making mistakes. But Camila Pérez has real potential. A lot of people in the world of politics have their eyes on her, even at the national level. She could become a major force for good. She could be exactly what this country needs."

"Unless someone destroys her barely launched career over some campaign finance triviality."

"Exactly. She's a lodestone for those who want a better tomorrow—and as a result, she's a target for those who oppose change."

He nodded. "I think I understand the mission. We'll talk to the mayor. And we'll get this thing disposed of as soon as possible."

"I know I can count on you, Dan. I just want you to understand that…even though this isn't a case where someone's life is on the line, that doesn't mean it isn't important. If we want a better future for this nation—we have to stand up to the bullies."

He pushed himself off the sofa. "As it happens, Mr. K, standing up to bullies is what I do best."

CHAPTER SIX

By now, Dan had learned to walk to the passenger side of the Jaguar F-Pace SVR (the "company car"), when Maria accompanied him. She liked to drive. Being relegated to shotgun had been a bit jarring at first, but he'd adapted. The only real problem was that the universal law these days seemed to be that the driver programmed the radio, and Maria's musical tastes—largely FM pop—were difficult to bear. How long could a grown adult listen to those thumping bass beats and sappy lyrics? He preferred opera—you could appreciate great vocalists without being distracted by the foreign-language lyrics he didn't understand.

"Do we have time to get food?" Maria asked.

"You just ate. And complained about fitting into your jeans."

"Just something light. My tummy's rumbling. Maybe a takeout sushi burrito?"

"Drive. You can snack later."

She grudgingly complied. "Looking forward to seeing the mayor again?" She hung a left toward downtown.

"I'm hoping she doesn't bear a grudge."

"Because you accused her of being a murderer?"

"I didn't exactly accuse her…"

"Just made a highly aggressive suggestion?" Maria laughed. "I'm sure she's forgotten all about it. By the way, for the record, I like her."

"I do too."

"Yeah, but you like her because she's a snack."

"Would you stop that?"

"I'm impressed that a petite Latinx woman with no connections can turn herself into the most prominent woman in the city. I really admire what she's accomplished. She's a spitfire."

"You're right about that."

"She's like a political Disney princess."

"Let's not go overboard, Maria."

"I thought about going to work for her. Back when she ran the first time."

"Seriously?" He gave her a quick once-over. She had never struck him as the political type. "What stopped you?"

"Mr. K made me an offer I couldn't refuse."

He understood. "You want to take the lead on this?"

"Don't be ridiculous. You're lead counsel. Just don't ask her out while I'm standing there. Totes awk."

"Would you stop? I can't ask out a client. And she's not my type."

"Why not?"

"Too high-profile. High-society. Probably high-mainte-nance. I'm just a regular guy."

Maria stopped at a red light and gave him a long look. "Is this a joke?"

"Not at all."

"Dan, you live on a boat. You're a gourmet chef. You go in for extreme sports."

"Lots of guys—"

"*You drive a Bentley!*"

He shrugged. "Mr. K told me to do something special with

my signing bonus."

She pulled into the parking lot, grinning. "Yup. You're just a regular joe. Salt-of-the-earth. Now let's go find the mayor."

INSIDE THE MAYOR'S OFFICE, DAN WAS GREETED BY A SLENDER woman in a two-piece suit. Toni blonde. Too much eye makeup. Cat-eye glasses. Clipboard. "Good afternoon. I'm Benji Ringgold."

"Pleased to meet you." He and Maria shook her hand. "Benji?"

She adjusted her glasses. "Long story. When I was little I had a lot of hair, and my nana thought I looked like this dog from the movies."

Of course. "We're here to see the mayor."

"I know. I'm her Chief of Staff. I manage her appointment schedule."

"She's expecting us."

"Yes, but that doesn't guarantee you an audience." Benji glanced at her clipboard. "Mayor Pérez is extremely outgoing and has a tendency to schedule more meetings than she can manage."

"She'll want to see us."

Benji had a professional, no-nonsense attitude. Not unfriendly, but efficient. He could see where she might be useful to someone who tended to be friendlier and more accessible than a mayor could afford to be. "You're lawyers, right?"

"Why?" He wasn't sure if he should be offended. "Do we not look like lawyers?"

"You're tan, ripped, and you use hair mousse. No, you don't look like a lawyer. More like a Chippendale's dancer."

Observant, and a smartass sense of humor. He liked this woman already. "Nonetheless, we are attorneys, and the mayor is expecting us."

"We need someone to solve problems, not exacerbate them."

"That's our specialty."

"Which one?"

"The solving one."

"I hope you can solve this little problem we're having. The mayor doesn't need the distraction. This is the worst possible time."

"It always is. Is she in her office?" He was prepared to do an end run around this gatekeeper, if necessary.

"No. She's on the beach. I'll have someone show you the way."

Of course. He'd walked the beach with her before. "No need."

He turned toward the door, but Benji stopped him. "A word, if I may."

"Okay."

"Do you understand how important the mayor is to this city?"

"We do," Maria answered.

"And I probably don't need to tell you that some people can't stand the thought of a strong woman in a position of power. That's true of men and women both. Sexism runs wide."

"That's what you think these charges are about?" Maria asked.

"I know that's what they're about. And I don't want them to go any further than they already have."

"We will do whatever—"

"I love Camila Pérez," Benji said, with an unrestrained enthusiasm that impressed him. "I would lie down on the tracks and die for her. If it weren't for Camila, I'd be a lonely woman sitting at home with her cats. Camila gave me a life. She's the best thing that ever happened to this city, maybe this country. The thought that her career could be curtailed by a sexist dirty-tricks campaign makes me physically ill."

"We will make every effort——"

"Do more. Do everything and then some. Bury this old-school BS. *Please!*"

An employer who inspired this level of devotion must be someone special. "We will do our best."

"We talked to other lawyers. Didn't hear anything helpful."

He looked her square in the eyes. "That explains why our boss sent us. He calls us the Last-Chance Lawyers. Believe me, if there's anything that can possibly be done here, we will do it."

DAN THREADED A PATH THROUGH THE BACK ALLEYS AND eventually made his way to the beach. Fortunately, he'd followed this path before and had an excellent memory. It only took him about ten minutes to find the beach. Maria trailed close behind.

He loved the St. Petersburg beach. Best in the world, as far as he was concerned. Main reason he'd stayed here, even though he technically didn't have anything tying him to Florida anymore. Not even a home, at least not in the conventional sense. But he loved to feel the salty spray bathing his sinuses. He loved the reassuring heat of the sun on his face and the cry of pelicans diving across the horizon. In the distance, he could see children playing, running, building sand castles. Not a better place on earth.

He spotted his quarry sitting on a sand dune, a small raised hill that gave her a relatively discreet vantage point. So far as he could tell, there was no security detail, no entourage, no press secretary. And she didn't seem to be doing anything in particular. Just gazing out at the water.

"Mind if I share your dune?"

Mayor Camila Pérez looked up. Petite. Windswept hair. Dragonfly brooch. Red eyes.

She rose and greeted him. Her smile was as strong as her grip. "We meet again."

"So it seems. You remember Maria?"

"Of course. Join me? The office swirls with endless emergencies. This campaign finance business. A former employee who has disappeared. I came out here for some peace. I need quiet time to gather my thoughts and plan for the future."

"I think our boss already reached out to you. You're looking for someone to represent you on charges of campaign malfeasance, right?"

"I'm looking for someone to crush the bastards who are trying to destroy my political existence."

"Same difference. More or less." He was glad to see she wasn't letting this sap her spirit. "You think this is politically motivated?"

"I know it is. It always is."

He held up his hand to block the sun. "Who wants you out of office that badly?"

"Many people. Bigots. Sexist swine. If I'm removed, I'll be replaced by the deputy mayor—a Caucasian male. And many people in this town will be much happier."

"I would hate to see that happen."

"I would hate it even more. So I need to lawyer up. Some people already see my administration as a sinking ship. We will show them they are wrong, yes?"

"Yes," Maria said firmly.

"I haven't worked this hard and come this far to let these penny-ante charges lay me low. Sit with me."

He took the invite and sat beside her on the dune. Maria appeared to hesitate.

The mayor noticed. "I will share my blanket." She pulled

it out from under herself and unfolded it to accommodate three people.

"I don't mean to be trouble," Maria murmured.

"You are not. If I was wearing those jeans, I'd take care of them too."

"You're a fan of D&G?"

"I cannot afford such things."

"Oh, they aren't *that* expensive."

"That is not what I mean. I can't afford to be seen in such things."

Ah. "I feel like we should clear the air," he said. "We have some history. If this is going to be awkward, Maria can take the lead. You may not be comfortable having me involved at all."

The mayor waved a hand in the air. "Don't be silly. You were only doing your job."

"That's very understanding of you, mayor."

"And please call me Camila, at least when we're not on camera. All my friends do."

"If you wish—Camila. Glad there are no hard feelings."

"Listen to me. In my world, there is so much backbiting, scheming, controversy. I have learned to sense when someone cannot be trusted. You put me on the witness stand and did your job, but there was no malice in it. I much prefer that to the people who come into my office offering smiles and gifts—but in truth, bear only hate."

He thought he understood what she was saying. "I don't think I'd care for the world of politics."

"You would survive. You're tough, I can see that. And you have good instincts. A gift for seeing beneath the veneer. Piercing the facades people erect to conceal reality."

"Connecting the dots," Maria added. "That's what he calls it. Careful observation, putting info into deep storage, then using it to make connections most people miss."

He objected. "You're making me sound like some kind of

weird computer. The HAL 2000."

Camila laughed. "You like classic movies."

"The good ones."

"I'd much rather watch a classic with real characters and clever dialogue than watch CGI superheroes fight every six minutes. Favorite movie?"

"*City Lights.*"

She clutched her chest. "My heart aches every time I see it."

"And yours?"

"*Mr. Smith Goes to Washington.* Naturally."

The more time he spent with her, the harder she was to dislike. "What can you tell me about these alleged campaign finance improprieties?"

Camila sighed. "Back to business so soon?"

"If I'm going to talk the DA out of pressing charges, I need to understand the issues."

"Fair enough." She drew in the sand. "There are two problems, though more than one instance of each. The first relates to a loan I took to finance my last campaign."

"From a bank?"

"Unfortunately, no. I had already taken as much from banks as they were willing to lend. This came from two friends. About a hundred and fifty thousand, total. I needed it to pay for the final surge of advertising."

"Apparently it worked," Maria said. "You won by a large margin."

"Yes, it worked. But now my opponents want me to pay for it dearly. As you likely know, Florida limits the amount you can receive from individuals. Basically, it's $2700 per cycle, per donor. If this loan is reclassified as a donation, it will vastly exceed the limit."

"Did you paper the loan?" he asked.

"Of course. We drew up a note and executed it. I have copies of all the papers for you."

"Good. I think we can deal with that."

"You think we can win?"

"Ultimately, it doesn't matter if we win. If you have to pay a fine, so be it. I just have to convince the DA there was no criminal intent. The prosecutor who I think has been assigned to this case is a reasonable human being. What's the other problem?"

Camila drew in her breath. "That is more complicated. Most of the television advertising run during my campaign was paid for by a PAC—a political action committee. They have the freedom to do much that I would not be allowed to do personally, including raising large quantities of money."

"Every candidate uses PACs. So what?"

"The PAC supporting my campaign— the St. Petersburg Committee for Change—was headed by Dr. Albert Kazan."

"The architect? The one who designed and organized The Meeting Place?" A previous case—the one that put Camila on the witness stand—left Dan extremely familiar with Kazan, and everything he did to make St. Pete's premiere public park a reality. "You worked with him on that project, right? Eminent domain. Tax breaks."

"Yes, and that is the problem. By law, candidates and their campaigns are not allowed to have direct contact with PACs. It must be independent. No coordination."

"Which is unrealistic and pointless, since the money is all going the same place. But those are the rules. Otherwise, PAC money is subject to the usual campaign finance regulations."

"And if that happens to the huge sums Kazan collected, I will never be able to make it right."

"Is there evidence of coordination?"

"According to the district attorney's office, my campaign manager, Frank Esposito, met with Kazan on two occasions during the last week of the campaign. Frank says they only talked about the park. The DA suspects they talked about the campaign."

"Were any third parties present?"

"I do not know."

"I can't see Kazan turning against you. Much less your own campaign manager."

Her eyes turned downward. "I would hope not."

He had the strong sense there was something she was not telling him. "I need to talk to my friend in the DA's office. Find out what they have. This may be all smoke and mirrors. I want to nip it in the bud before it gets a lot of media play."

"Too late."

"Ok, before it gets any more. Some people never remember how a story came out. They only remember that accusations were made. I don't want this messing up your reelection campaign."

She sighed. "I had such ambition for this city. Build the future by reclaiming the past. Bring in new business. Expand tourism. Renovate downtown with bright colors and modern enterprises. Mass transit."

"You'll do all that. We just need to make these accusations disappear."

She spoke slowly. "I...have been contacted by the National Democratic Committee."

Maria leaned in. "You're on their radar? That's fantastic! Isn't it?"

"There's a Senate seat that may become vacant soon. They were exploring the possibility of me running for it."

"The US Senate! That's incredible! Our mayor!"

"And it needn't stop with the Senate. There's been talk of me addressing the next national nominating convention. Many expect the next Democratic presidential candidate to be female, possibly a woman of color. I would fit right in."

He knew a convention address was widely seen as a testing ground for someone perceived to have major political possibilities. Possibly even presidential possibilities. Mr. K had it right. She had enormous potential—which was no doubt what turned her into a target. "We'll prepare a report addressing each allegation and explaining that your actions did not violate the rules. Garrett's researching this as we speak, and Jimmy is pulling all your campaign filings. Who knows— maybe this stems from a bookkeeping or accounting discrepancy. At any rate, I'm sure I can convince them there's no basis for criminal charges."

"I thought attorneys never made predictions about outcomes."

That was the smarter approach. But he thought Jazlyn was too smart to be dragged into anyone's political agenda. He could bring her around. "We'll do everything possible. We won't let you go down without a major fight. You're kinda Maria's hero, you know."

Camila pressed a hand against her chest. "Me?"

Maria looked as if she wanted to crawl under a rock. "I didn't say that...exactly."

"She compared you to a Disney princess."

Camila laughed. "I am nothing like a Disney princess!"

"She even told me she'd thought about working for your campaign."

Camila pivoted. "Do you dislike working with this man?"

Maria's face was a bright crimson. "Only when he acts like this."

"My staff is almost entirely female. I could use a smart cookie like you in my reelection campaign. If I still have one."

"And you will," he insisted. "But stop trying to poach our talent. We'll do everything possible to help you."

"Good." She thought for a moment. "Seriously? A Disney princess?"

"I'm sorry." Maria looked completely flustered. "I didn't intend to trivialize you. I meant no offense."

"None taken." She paused. "Wait, which Disney princess?"

CHAPTER SEVEN

OFFICER DIETRICH STARED AT THE BAKERY, WONDERING WHAT bizarre assignment he'd drawn this time. He was accustomed to expecting the unexpected. He'd become the designated hitter for downtown oddities—and there tended to be a lot of them. When someone had to tell the churro-cart guy he couldn't run a three-card monte game as a side hustle, he got the job. No, Mr. Miranda, that is not covered by your food permit. And when someone had to tell the panicking caricature artist in Safety Harbor to stop telling children there were alligators in the sewers, he drew the short straw. And the antiques dealer who thought shedding his clothes on a sunny day was a Fourth Amendment right—well, you guessed it.

Today was going to be a first. He'd been sent to investigate —not an activity, not a criminal act, not a fight or a fraud— but an odor.

Yes, today he was on smell patrol. Not the first time that had ever occurred in this part of the city. Anything that drew so much traffic, from both tourists and residents, was bound to acquire a few foul fumes. The sanitation department cleaned almost twice as often as they once had, thanks to the current mayor prioritizing tourism. She arduously defended the rights of St Pete businesses to sell their merch in a non-odoriferous environment. But the odd skunk, possum, or dead squirrel did occasionally turn up. (And in truth, alligators did get into the sewers—but don't tell the kids.)

He could see why this temporarily abandoned bakery had drawn so many complaints. He suspected a dead skunk, possibly a nuclear family of dead skunks. He'd jumped through the usual hoops. He tried to find the owner. The deed was held in the name of a corporation, but when he called the number on the corporate documents, no one answered. He left a message and could undoubtedly track down the owner in time, but he wasn't sure the people in this area could stand it that long. The odor was strong enough to constitute a health hazard, and that was sufficient to get him an entry permit. Similar to a warrant, except he wasn't searching for anything other than the cause of the potential health hazard—in this case, the foulest stench this side of Hades.

The bakery hadn't been closed for that long. And it hadn't been completely out of operation. On more than one occasion, he'd noticed smoke billowing from the rooftop stacks. The oven appeared to be in use. The word on the street was that they were closed for repairs, maybe a little renovation. If there were imminent plans to reopen, they probably wouldn't mind having this noxious stink eliminated.

Dietrich used wire cutters to snap the relatively flimsy padlock on the front door. Sorry, mysterious owner, but you can get a replacement at Walmart for five bucks. He pulled the front door slowly open. It creaked like something out of an old Universal horror film.

The fetid air hit him with such impact it almost knocked him to the floor. No exaggeration—he felt as if he'd encountered a wall of putridity, something mere mortals were not meant to experience, much less inhale. He pulled a handkerchief out of his uniform pocket and pressed it over his nose and mouth. Didn't help that much, but with something this foul, even a minor assist was welcome.

Did he say a family of skunks? More like a nation of skunks.

He took a tentative step inside. The lights were off, but large overhead windows admitted some light into the gloom. It was warm in here. In fact, it was hot. Too hot, given the mild temperature outside. And there could only be one explanation for that.

The oven had been on. Recently.

He shone a flashlight into the gloom. A counter where the baked goods were sold, and lots of tables where the patrons could sit while they consumed. One of the tables was overturned. Someone got rowdy? Hard to imagine anyone being able to stay in here for long with that smell. And eating? Impossible. They did still have a problem with street drugs in this town. Crystal meth was on the rise, and he supposed if the kids were sufficiently hopped up on Ecstasy or MDMA, they might be oblivious to odors.

He could use some good sense-numbing drugs right now. He pushed past the counter and located a door that led to the kitchen. In the rear, he found what had to be the oven. The iron door was huge, almost as high as he was. He supposed it needed to be. An operation like this could do a brisk weekend business, producing doughnuts and cragels to compliment the coffee.

As he approached the oven, the smell became vastly more intense.

Had the skunks gotten into the oven? That could be a disgusting mess. Maybe he needed to call animal control. But first he should lay eyes on the critters, whatever they were.

He placed a gloved hand on the door handle. It was warm but not so hot he couldn't touch it. He suddenly felt woozy. He could feel himself tottering. Maybe Marjorie was right. Maybe it was time for him to get into another line of work. He still hoped to get his pension, but right now, a cozy security job sounded pretty good.

Better get it over with. He drew in his breath, held it, and pulled open the oven door.

The air gushed from his lungs like someone had tackled him. Waves of nausea cascaded across his entire body. His lips trembled.

Oh no. Oh dear God, no!

CHAPTER EIGHT

DAN PARKED HIS BENTLEY IN FRONT OF THE SNELL ISLE office/mansion with a dramatic screech. He felt seriously pumped. Great morning. He'd risen with the sun and hit the water early. Kitesurfing was fantastic—he managed two 360 loops and a new, personal-best speed. Thought he might get in a little paragliding later, but he wanted to check in with Garrett first and see how he was coming with the campaign finance investigation. His early take was that they could beat the charges, but ultimately, cases like this always came down to the details. He hoped to meet with Jazlyn before the end of the week and put this problem to rest before it did Camila any great harm.

He stepped through the front door wearing a tank top and swimsuit. "Hey, beach buddies. Today is a great day to be—"

He stopped short. Three faces stared back at him. Maria, Jimmy, Garrett. They did not appear to be high on life.

He didn't blink. "Something has gone horribly wrong."

Maria nodded. "Cops are at the mayor's office. They say they're arresting Camila."

"Called it." They were moving much faster than he expected. He did an about-face. "Tell the client I'm *en route*."

Maria looked appalled. "You're going dressed like that?"

"No time to waste. I've got four suits in my office upstairs. Jimmy, would you mind bringing one over?"

He didn't. "Superman always helps those in need. So shall I."

"I'm coming with." Maria ran to the door.

"Garrett," he shouted as they exited, "send your report to my phone. Whatever you've got."

Garrett nodded. "Already underway."

He slid behind the wheel of his car. He wasn't sure what disturbed him most—that the DA was rushing ahead with charges without conferring with counsel, or that his peaceful at-one-with-the-universe mood had been shattered.

He shifted into first. "Apologies, Maria. You're probably embarrassed to be seen with someone who's dressed like this."

She shook her head. "I'm glad to be with someone who knows how to respond to an emergency. Camila needs us. Drive."

DAN FOUND NO PARKING OUTSIDE CITY HALL, OR FOR THAT matter, anywhere nearby. News media trucks not only took most of the prime spaces but also prevented access to the front door. He had to park almost a block away, and even then, he wasn't sure the spot was legal. If his Bentley got towed, he would blame the press. Why not? All the best people did it.

He and Maria jogged to City Hall. A uniformed officer held everyone at bay. He wondered how long that would last. Technically, this was a public building, a government office.

"I'm sorry, you have to stay out until the police finish their business." The officer looked seriously stressed. Probably hadn't expected to be fending off a pack of reporters this morning.

Reporters shouted questions the cop couldn't begin to

answer. He felt sorry for the man, though that didn't stop him from creating more problems for him.

He pushed his way to the top of the stairs. "Daniel Pike, attorney-at-law. I represent the mayor."

A flurry of photos followed his announcement.

"I'm sorry," the officer said, "we're not admitting—"

"I represent the accused and she has a right to have her lawyer present." Probably. "You cannot prevent me from representing my client. That's a constitutional violation that could taint the entire prosecution or even lead to a dismissal."

"You're a lawyer?"

"Yeah." Why, was he thrown by the sweaty tank top? "Wanna see my bar card?" Which he didn't have on him, but it sounded like something a lawyer would say.

"I don't know..."

"Do you want to be the reason they have to dismiss the charges? I'm sure Internal Affairs will love that."

The creases across the officer's forehead intensified. "Ok, you can go. But only you."

"And my trusty co-counsel." He and Maria surged ahead without further discussion. The officer blocked access behind them, creating another flurry of complaints.

He raced up the stairs, making his way to the mayor's office. The first person he spotted was Camila's Chief of Staff, Benji.

"Thank goodness you're here. I was—"

He cut her off. "Brief me."

"They showed up about twenty minutes ago, no appointment, no advance warning. The mayor was outside and it took a while to track her down. They say they're arresting her. Why didn't they make an appointment? I don't function well when people don't have appointments."

"They hope if they catch people off guard, someone will do something stupid."

"I tried to get the mayor to duck out the back door, but she refused."

"Thank goodness." He pushed past her into the office. A uniformed cop moved to stop him. He cut the man off before he spoke. "Daniel Pike. I represent the mayor. All discussions stop now. All questions go through me."

About three feet away, in the middle of the office, he spotted Camila—in handcuffs. She was talking, fast, loud, and forcefully. Three plainclothes officers surrounded her. He knew one of them—Jake Kakazu. "Seriously, Jake? Handcuffs?"

Kakazu shrugged. White undershirt. Ill-fitting suit—he'd lost weight. Missed a spot shaving. "Standard procedure."

"Good thinking. She might overpower you. Did you hear the part about no conversations?"

"Loud and clear. But of course, the mayor can still talk if she wishes."

Camila almost snarled. "The mayor wishes to speak to someone in charge. Whoever sent the flunkies out to smear me."

Getting angry wasn't going to help anything—especially if the press saw it. "And that's the last word you say. No discussions with anyone about anything. Not the case. Not the weather. Not with the cops, and not with the other people in lockup. Assume they're all snitches. Because they probably are. Understood?"

Camila was holding up better than most people in this situation. But he could still see the stress lines. Her eyes were redder than they had been the day before. She looked as if she hadn't slept. "Understood."

He addressed Jake. They had history, even if most of it was as opponents. If they both treated each another like professionals with a role to perform, he was much more likely to receive reasonable behavior. "This is unnecessary, Jake. Do you think she's a flight risk? Let her come in voluntarily."

"Sorry. No can do."

"Because someone is yanking your chain?"

"Nobody yanks my chain, Pike. Including you."

"Are you trying to create a show? Hoping to get on the evening news?"

"I don't want to be on the news. My good suit is at the cleaners."

"You have a good suit?"

"Hey, watch it." He put a thumb under his lapel. "My wife bought me this."

Maria frowned. "Does she hate you?"

"No."

"Do all her influencers work for J.C. Penney's?"

"Says the woman working with the guy in shorts and a tank top. You look more like a homeless person than a lawyer, Pike."

"That's how I stay under the radar. Look, there's a legion of reporters outside. Can we take her out a back exit?"

"Too risky. She might make a run for it."

"You're joking, I assume."

"I'm not. Desperate people do desperate things."

"And once she's busted loose, you'd never find her again. Because who would recognize the mayor of the city."

"Look, Pike, just stay out of the way. Once we have her booked and processed, you can meet her in lockup and make all the smartass remarks you want."

"Isn't this a little over-the-top for a white-collar charge? You're not dealing with El Chapo here. She's the duly elected mayor of St. Petersburg."

Kakazu's eyes narrowed. "Now...what?"

"I said—" He stopped, recalculated. His brain was trying to tell him something, but he'd been talking too much to hear it.

All these cops. Media already present. Handcuffs. Jake Kakazu, top detective on the squad.

The homicide squad.

"Let me clear the air, Pike. These charges have nothing to do with campaign money. Your client is being charged with murder. The cold-blooded torture-murder of her former employee and lover, a man named Nick Mansfield. And three other men, as yet unidentified. Cooked to death in an oven. In a bakery she owns. We're talking about murder in the first degree. And then some."

CHAPTER NINE

"Murder?" Dan felt a hollow clutching at the base of his stomach. "The mayor?"

"Yes, I am aware of who I'm arresting, thank you very much."

"When was this…Mansfield murdered?"

"Yesterday, apparently. Baked alive."

"Why would you accuse the mayor?"

"Because they had some kinda thing goin'. Plus she fired him. And oh yeah—the victim fingered her."

"How?"

"By writing her name—in blood."

He and Maria exchanged a glance. Their little accounting matter was worsening by the second.

Kakazu motioned toward his officers. "Let's get the suspect downtown. The sooner we get this show on the road the better."

He spoke directly to Camila. "I'll see you as soon as I can."

She seemed dazed, almost as if she had disconnected from reality. Perhaps her way of coping was to disassociate, to act as if she were an observer rather than a participant.

Maria leaned in. "No one is going to believe these charges, Camila. They're trying to destroy your reputation, but it won't work."

He heard Kakazu chuckle. "Lady, you better read the report before you go talking about what people will believe."

He was probably right about that. Some people always chose to believe the worst.

"No one downtown has any doubt about what happened here," Kakazu continued. "And once the facts are made public —neither will anyone else."

The officers led Camila out the door. He followed close behind, even though he knew there was nothing he could do.

He nudged Maria, who already had her phone out. "Text Jimmy. Find out what's been filed. Then call Garrett. We want to know everything there is to know about a former employee of the mayor's office named Nick Mansfield."

"Already on it. Anything else?"

"Yeah. Find me a damn suit. They'll never let me into the holding cells dressed like this."

AS IT TURNED OUT, THE QUICKEST SOLUTION WAS TO STOP IN at Sartorial Inc. and buy a new suit. Make the best use of the time Camila spent in Processing and Booking. He'd been wanting something in pinstripe anyway. They had his measurements and a charge card on file, so he didn't have to try anything on and the fact that he lacked a wallet wasn't a problem. Didn't mind having Maria there to help choose, either. The woman did know her clothes. He'd come back for alterations later.

Jimmy had been the first to introduce him to Frank, the elderly man who oversaw the holding cells and apparently had done so since the dawn of time. He hoped that some of the positivity Jimmy incurred wherever he went rubbed off. He wanted to get in as quickly as possible.

As it turned out, he didn't even have to identify himself. "You're here to see the mayor, aren't you?"

"You've heard I'm on the case."

"I've heard she's in jail. Only other person who's arrived in the last four was an indecent exposure, and I doubt you're repping him."

"You think I attract a classier clientele."

"That guy could never afford you."

Defense lawyers always took crap from law enforcement— and more or less everyone else. "Would it surprise you to learn that I don't charge my clients at all?"

"Would it surprise you to learn that I can fly like a bird?"

He smiled. He kind of liked the old guy, even if he probably shouldn't. "How soon can I see my client?"

"I believe she's entertaining gentlemen callers now."

About ten minutes later, an armed and uniformed officer escorted Maria and him into the interview room. They put the inmates on the opposite side of a Plexiglas screen and allowed them to speak through old-style telephone receivers. The whole setup seemed at least forty years out of date, but he supposed renovating the visitation room for arrested felons wasn't a municipal priority. Maybe that was something the mayor could put on the agenda at her next city council meeting. If she had one.

About five minutes later, a female officer led Camila into the room. She sat on the other side of the screen and took the receiver. Her face was almost entirely expressionless. She looked like a pale revenant of the firecracker who had previously inhabited that body. She wore ill-fitting coveralls and her hair was disarranged.

Her first question took him by surprise, though it shouldn't have. "Are there reporters outside?"

He nodded. "They can't get in here."

"Those vultures would love a photo of me in prison garb."

"Not gonna happen."

"It will. They took lots of mug shots in here. Someone will leak one. The money will be irresistible."

Sadly, there was probably some truth to her paranoia. "How are they treating you so far?"

"As you would expect. Sniggering, patronizing, superior attitudes. My, how the mighty have fallen. All those who feel insecure about their own accomplishments, or lack of accomplishments, can comfort themselves, thinking, 'At least I'm not behind bars.'"

In his experience, most jailhouse personnel stayed cool and unemotional. But having the mayor around might make it hard to act as if this were business as usual. "They printed you?"

"And took a DNA sample. Blood. Hair."

"I didn't authorize that."

"Guess they don't think you need to. Forced me to change clothes. To strip in front of two female officers. Who did not look away, not for one second. And then searched me. Made sure I wasn't carrying contraband into the jail."

He closed his eyes. "Because that was likely."

"They did not do this because it was likely. They did this because they enjoyed it."

"They have to be careful. You'd be amazed what people have tried."

"I am the mayor of this city, not a common criminal. And I have been humiliated. Threatened. I am not safe in here." She paused, fighting back her anger. "And perhaps that is the point. Someone sent me here, where it will be so much easier to eliminate me. How quickly can you get me out?"

He drew up his shoulders. Here's where the conversation got unpleasant. "I'll ask for bail at your arraignment. But I can't make any guarantees."

"I am the mayor!"

"But you have been charged with first-degree murder. That's as serious as it gets. The DA could ask for the death penalty."

"For the mayor?"

"And that's another problem. I got a text from your Chief of Staff, Benji. Given your current...inability to perform your duties, the Deputy Mayor has announced that he will serve as Interim Mayor."

"That man has wanted my job since before my term began. This is his golden opportunity."

"Yes, frankly, it is. Some are already calling for you to resign."

"That will never happen."

"I think it's premature, in any case. But no one will argue that a mayor behind bars can perform her usual duties."

"Then get me out!"

"I will try. But bail in capital murder cases is rare."

"Where could I go? Everyone knows who I am."

"Which I will argue. But I can't promise results. So much depends upon the judge we draw. I know some who would not even consider bail under these circumstances."

He could tell this was not the answer she wanted. "I am a strong woman. Always have been. But I will not last long in here. I'm a target."

He didn't doubt it. "Jimmy knows a lot of people. I'll ask him to see if there's anything we can do to increase security."

"This has been engineered to dispose of me, one way or the other. Finally, my enemies have me where they want me. I know how this will end." She drew in her breath. "If the publicity doesn't kill me, a shiv in the showers will."

"Camila, is there anything...you need to tell me?"

"Like what? Whether I killed those men in the oven? I did not. I barely knew Nick, and I have no idea who the others are. I am one hundred percent not guilty."

"Anything else I should know? Believe me, the prosecution

will leave no stone unturned. Better that I know everything up front than get blindsided with it later."

She paused a long time, as if running a thousand possibilities through her mind. "I have a record."

His heart sank. "Criminal record?"

"Arrest record. Juvenile. When I was young. Sixteen."

"What happened?"

She shrugged. "Got in a fight with...another girl. Embarrassingly enough, we were fighting over a boy. He was playing us both and not worth the trouble. But I was young and stupid. We struggled. She fell backwards and broke her arm."

"Did she blame you?"

"Not really. But...her mother did. The police came and arrested me. I spent a night in jail. They let me go the next day. They didn't press charges."

"How has this not come out before? During the campaign."

"Because I was a juvenile, my record was expunged."

"This happened a long time ago. It shouldn't matter." But he knew it would, if the prosecutor found out. It was evidence of a strong temper. Perhaps an irrational, uncontrolled rage. And whoever committed this ghastly crime had serious anger issues. Or was completely psychotic. Either way, this incident did not help. "I'll bring a motion when we get closer to trial. See if I can keep it out."

"Do you think you will succeed?"

"Again, depends on the judge. No one likes to exclude evidence. But if judges let in something prejudicial, they risk getting reversed on appeal. I'll give it my best shot."

"Thank you, Daniel. I..." Their eyes met. "I trust you. And..." She swallowed. "And I know you will fight these people who are determined to bring me down."

"I will."

"I do not wish to spend the rest of my life in prison. Or be executed. But what is more important is the future of the country. We cannot allow secret forces to control everything and everyone from behind closed doors. The selfish might of the rich and powerful is killing this country, preventing the changes we so desperately need. I will fight this to the bitter end."

She looked out and pressed her hand against the Plexiglas. "And I will be stronger for having you at my side."

CHAPTER TEN

"TELL US WHAT HAPPENED. START AT THE BEGINNING," DAN said to Camila. "Give us everything you know about this Nick Mansfield."

"He worked in my office briefly. He was an accountant and a former banker. Handled financial matters, mostly."

"Like campaign contributions?"

"Of course."

"But you let him go?"

"Yes. He had been brought on as a temp to handle a specific job. When it was finished, I terminated his employment."

"Couldn't you find something else for him to do?"

"He had a drug problem. Heroin. He showed up at the office completely strung out. Benji reported it to me."

"I get the impression she runs a tight ship."

"She is invaluable. She makes it possible for me to do my job while she manages the minutia."

"I wouldn't mind having a Benji myself." He looked up abruptly. "Was that inappropriate?"

Maria scowled. "Ish."

"You know what I mean."

"True."

He cleared his throat and pressed ahead. "You fired Mansfield. Did he take it well?"

"No. He argued and asked for another chance. Said he recognized that he made a mistake and he would do better in the future. I told him he needed help and found him a rehab. He was there three weeks."

"I sense…there's more to this…."

She sighed heavily. "We…dated. Briefly. Sort of."

"You dated an employee?"

"No. After he was terminated. After the rehab. And we only went out once. Dinner."

"And after that?"

"He became…obsessive. Wanted to see me again. I declined."

"Good."

"But he wouldn't let it go. Started sending me…photos by text. Photos of his…endowments."

He blinked. "This clown sent the city mayor…"

Maria cut in. "Nick-pics?"

Camila smiled. "Exactly."

"We could pull those off your phone," he said, thinking aloud. "Although in some people's minds, that might give you a motive for murder."

"It certainly gave me a motive to never see him again. Didn't even respond to his texts. Totally ghosted him."

"Did he know anything that could be used against you?"

"No such thing exists."

"He must have thought there was something serious brewing between the two of you."

"I gave him no reason to believe that."

He and Maria exchanged glances. "We need a better story."

"I am not telling stories!"

Maria took the receiver. "Camila, let me explain what Dan means. He's not talking about lying. But presenting a case at trial is all about storytelling. Some people have gone so far as to say the jury votes for the side that tells the best story. Jurors have a hard time following all the testimony and evidence, and they typically aren't that great at determining which witnesses are lying and which aren't. They end up believing the story that makes the most sense to them. Likeable protagonists, convincing motivations, plausible actions."

"You make it sound as if I should hire a novelist instead of an attorney."

"We do have one advantage—we get to hear the prosecution's story first. Then we present ours. They have to give us all their evidence up front, whether it helps them or us. We don't have to give them anything."

"You can plan a story that explains away their story."

"Exactly. Trust me, Dan is already searching for a story he can sell."

"And so far," he added, "I haven't heard one. Why would you go out with this loser? Given what you knew about him?"

Her face reddened. "He was a handsome man. Single. I stay very busy but...I have perhaps not paid sufficient attention to my personal life." Her eyes turned downward. "Sometimes even a mayor gets lonely."

"But you didn't want a second date. Even before he started sending porn. Why?"

"Many reasons. I thought he needed more time clean and sober. Plus he was on the rebound from a previous relationship, and I think he was not yet over it. Talked about his ex all through dinner."

"Who was the ex?"

"He never said. I did not ask."

"Did you have drinks before dinner?"

"I do not drink."

"And it was just dinner?"

"Just dinner. Chez Guitano."

"Best place in town. Expensive. Exclusive."

"I could get us in."

"No doubt. Who paid for dinner?"

"I did. He was having financial problems. Kept talking about needing to 'scrape together some Georgies.' Was that a mistake? Should I have made him pay?"

He drew in his breath. "I'm not even sure. It would've been better if you'd gone Dutch. Did you pay by credit card?"

"Of course."

"Then the prosecution likely already has a copy of the receipt."

"I cannot believe this. A man has been murdered and we're talking about a dinner date."

He pulled a few documents out of his backpack. "At this time, we know next-to-nothing about the murder itself. Jimmy got the filings, but they don't reveal much. Except that someone apparently went to a hell of a lot of trouble to make death painful. Not only for Nick but for three other men."

"Who were they?"

"No one knows. There have been no matching missing-persons reports. And they are all seriously burned. The coroner's office is running tests, prints, DNA, dental records, to identify the bodies, but so far they have nothing. They've warned us that a positive ID may take a while. That's why you've only been charged with one murder. So far."

"You believe there will be more charges?"

He spread wide his hands. "Whoever killed Nick also killed the other three. Someone dragged all the corpses to the oven. And someone turned the heat up, gradually. So they would suffer."

Camila winced. "That is…unbelievable."

"It indicates more than a mere desire to kill."

"Revenge?"

"Retribution. Punishment. Serious hate-on. Or maybe just a cruel streak. Sadism."

"Such people do exist," Camila said, her eyes distant.

"It's possible this is the work of a twisted serial killer. But the cops don't think so. They think it was you."

"Because I fired Nick?"

"And because you own the bakery. Through a shell corporation."

"I bought it to set an example. I have encouraged the business people in this town to acquire old storefronts. To invest in the city. Create attractions for residents and tourists."

"The police think the killer had a key."

"Many people know how to pick a lock."

He shuffled through the rest of his notes. So far, he had not heard a single fact he considered encouraging. This was the most hideous murder he'd ever heard about. And all the evidence seemed stacked against their client. "The police also believe he was trying to identify you by writing your name in blood. I haven't seen it, though I will. And they admit that the job was never finished. They say he scratched out the letter 'C.'"

"That could mean a thousand different things."

"They also say there are eyewitnesses who can put you in the general area at the time the oven was turned on."

"I was downtown that day. I frequently am. That means nothing."

"Your prints are on the premises. In the kitchen."

"I own the building!"

He closed his backpack and folded his hands. "I admire your fighting spirit, Camila, but the prosecution has a serious case. Believe me, they wouldn't have arrested a public official if they didn't think they could make it stick. I want you to give me a list of everyone who might have any relevant information."

She spent the next ten minutes thinking hard, compiling a

list of names. Maria took them down on her phone and forwarded the list to Garrett and Jimmy.

"As we speak, I'll bet the police are getting warrants to search your home and office. What will they find?"

"Nothing incriminating."

"You're certain?"

"There is nothing to find."

"Think harder."

Her jaw tightened. "There is nothing to find."

"They'll mirror the hard drives on your computers. Laptops, tablets, phones. Is that a problem?"

"What do you think they will find? Child pornography?"

"I don't know what they will find. And I don't want to learn for the first time from the prosecuting attorney. I will do everything in my power to fight these charges. But they are not going away. Unless you cop a plea—"

"I would never."

Exactly as he thought. "Then this is going to trial. And this will likely be the hardest, meanest, ugliest fight any of us has ever seen. And by the way—no press conferences."

"The prosecution will speak to the press."

"But we will not."

"That will make some people assume I am guilty."

"Some people already assume you're guilty and they probably always will. Sorry, I can't help that. But a press release won't change anything. The less said, the better. And don't talk in jail. Don't talk at all. Here's the truth—you don't know who your friends are. Anyone can be subpoenaed or bribed, and any testimony can be twisted around by a skilled questioner. Do your friends a favor. Don't turn them into potential witnesses."

"Anything else?"

He allowed a small smile. "You've been fighting like a tiger for years. Now it's time to let us be the tigers. And we will be. We will leave no stone unturned, take every risk. We care about you. I can't guarantee a good result. But I can guarantee I will never stop trying."

Maybe he imagined it, but he thought her mood improved slightly. "I thank you for that."

He shook his head. "Thank me when you address the Democratic Convention."

CHAPTER ELEVEN

NEXT MORNING, DAN WAS AT THE OFFICE AT SIX SHARP. HE did a little surfing, though not with the kite. That would take too long and he had a busy day ahead. Still, a little time in the gulf cleared his head and helped him face the day to come. Everyone had their routine, right? Some people liked coffee. He liked sea spray. This time, however, he made a point of changing before he came to the office.

He entered, scanning the newspaper. Maria was staring at her phone. That part wasn't surprising. The expression on her face was.

"I know," he said, cutting her off. "Camila's mugshots are all over the internet."

"There's more. Photos of her being printed and searched."

"Tell me it wasn't a strip search."

"So far, she's fully clothed. But they aren't pretty. They make her look like a criminal."

Which was exactly the point. "Where did they come from?"

"I don't know. Garrett's working on it. Someone inside

must've had a phone and discreetly took a few photos. Sold them to an online news service. If that's the correct term."

A digital version of the *National Enquirer*. Hadn't Camila predicted this? She said she was a target—and less than twenty-four hours later, the world proved her right.

She also said jail would be the perfect place to eliminate her.

He had to get her out of there.

Jimmy wandered in. "Brace yourself. More bad news incoming."

Maria lowered her phone. "Seriously? Ugh. I haven't even been to Starbucks yet. I need a caramel brulée latte, Dan."

"Skinny. No cream. Almond milk. Venti."

Maria blinked. "How—?"

"I've been to Starbucks with you before."

She smiled. "And you remember what I like?"

He nodded. "Coffee that tastes nothing like coffee."

Jimmy looked up from his laptop. "Camila's case has been assigned to Judge Hayes."

A communal keening filled the room. Hayes was a notorious hardliner, the modern-day equivalent of a hanging judge. A defense attorney's worst nightmare. "Isn't there anything you can do about that? Pull some strings maybe?"

"Unless you're suggesting I hire a hit man, no, we're stuck with Hayes. Camila's making her initial appearance before the judge later this morning."

That much he knew. He'd received an alert on his phone. "Anything else?"

"Yeah, but this is on the QT. You know Hank is an ER doc down at the hospital, right?"

"And?"

"He got a look at one of the corpses. Nick Mansfield. Apparently, the cop on the scene thought there was a remote chance he might still be alive. Skin was so hot and charred taking a pulse was difficult. Anyway, anyone want to guess the actual cause of death?"

This was a grisly version of Twenty Questions. "Heat stroke?"

Jimmy shook his head.

Maria entered the game. "Asphyxiation?"

"Strike two."

Garrett came down the stairs from his private office. "Suicide."

"I'll bet Mansfield wished he could kill himself. But how? No, according to Hank, the guy's internal organs boiled. Got so hot they failed to function. Total shutdown. So basically, his entire body stopped working. Then erupted."

Maria pressed a hand against her forehead. "I so do not need this first thing in the morning."

"And as you can imagine, you don't live long after your entire body stops working. But Hank thought he saw signs that the guy was taking drugs. And guess what? On the inventory sheet of items found at the crime scene?" He waved a piece of paper in the air. "The police found a glass vial."

Maria frowned. "Containing what?"

"Very good question. Someone needs to get out to the scene of the crime and take a look before it's been completely dismantled. You hearing this, Dan?"

He was. And making mental notes. Ghoulish as it seemed, anything that could assign culpability to the victim helped their case. Of course, Mansfield probably didn't tie himself up or turn on the oven. But it was a start. He turned to Garrett. "You have anything for me?"

"A little. I spent all night searching online databases."

"Because you don't sleep." They'd covered this ground before.

"True. Here's what I found. Camila Pérez did indeed own the bakery. Bought it about six months ago. In fact, she owns three different downtown properties, and that fact was widely known, because she'd bragged about it in press conferences. This was part of her campaign to refurbish downtown with bright colors and yuppie stores that would attract tourists and people with shopping addictions."

"Hey!" Maria said. "I resent that."

"Resent, or resemble?"

Dan jumped between them. "Ok, kids, let's not squabble."

"They don't mean it," Jimmy explained. "It's like Spock and McCoy, not Anakin and Obi-Wan."

Ok, that made it perfectly clear.

Garrett continued. "Our client initiated refurbishment on all three properties, including the bakery."

"Can she afford that?"

"A good question." Garrett made a note. "Which I will look into. But here's a point of interest. The work crew supposedly turned the power off. Disconnected it."

"The oven shouldn't have worked?"

"It would've required more than turning a dial, at any rate. Someone had to reconnect the power. So we're not looking for a random homeless person here. We're looking for someone who knew what they were doing. Someone who planned this well in advance."

He understood the legal ramifications of that statement. This was an intent crime. Planned. Premeditated. Any chance of getting manslaughter or some other lesser offense was out the window. "Anything else?"

"Still searching. I'll text you if I find anything important."

"Jimmy, can you come with me to the courtroom this morning?"

He was obviously surprised. "Don't you want Maria there?"

"Always. But maybe you could join me for the first appearance."

Jimmy's eyes narrowed. "Is this because Judge Hayes is black? Are you using me as your token diversity lawyer?"

"It's more than that." But yes. "Don't you know Hayes? A little?"

"We're both on the Disciplinary Complaints committee of the Bar Association. Hardly best friends."

"But he knows you. And I assume he respects you."

"He's supported my work on the committee."

"Good." Jimmy stayed involved in the community, made the right contacts, and that usually paid off for them. "How is he on LGBTQ issues?"

"Hard to say. He is an arch-conservative. But he's performed gay marriages."

"Excellent. Then you're coming with me. But as soon as the appearance is over, get down the clerk's office and find out what you can."

"I've read everything that's been filed."

"Talk to people. Get the scuttlebutt."

"That I can do."

"Any other suggestions?" No one spoke. "All right then. Let's get to the courthouse."

CHAPTER TWELVE

DAN EXITED THE CAR AT THE CURB. WHILE MARIA PARKED, HE and Jimmy made their way to Judge Hayes' courtroom on the second floor.

The courthouse was almost a hundred years old and needed attention. The courtrooms were small and the hallways were narrow. The slow-moving elevators had caused more than one attorney to show up for court late. And the vending machines offered nothing remotely healthy. He'd suggested they stock granola bars in the coffee shop, but oddly enough, they had yet to replace the doughnuts.

He spotted Jazlyn outside the courtroom. He was not surprised.

"Jimmy, take my stuff and go inside. I'll meet you in a minute."

"Roger that."

Jazlyn looked terrific, but then, she always did. Unlike some female attorneys, she let her hair fall naturally, and she wasn't afraid to wear colors other than brown and black.

"Morning, Jazlyn. You're looking pretty fly this morning."

"Only fly? I was hoping for dope."

"Least I didn't say you looked lit."

She suppressed a smile. "Maybe you should leave the hip slang to Maria. Is that a new suit?"

"Emergency purchase. Long story. You're handling the Mayor Pérez case?"

"I am indeed."

"I figured the DA would want his best prosecutor on this."

She batted her hand against her chest. "You flatter me. But I'm not sure I was chosen for my courtroom prowess."

"Then why?"

"I was chosen because I have experience dealing with you. This case is too important, and far too high profile, to be stolen from us by the St. Pete miracle worker and his bottomless bag of tricks."

"I've never stolen anything from anyone. I have prevented the DA from putting away innocent people on more than one occasion, though."

"That's your story. I gather the mayor is going to fight this?"

"Damn straight. She's got way too much at stake to allow herself to be railroaded by…whoever is ultimately behind this."

"Oh my. Do I hear the nascent seeds of a conspiracy theory?"

"Someone started this ball rolling. Someone who wanted the mayor gone."

"Dan, all the evidence points to her."

"Because she bought a bakery? Your case is flimsy and you know it."

"I don't know that at all."

"It's more like someone cherry-picked the facts because they don't really care who did it. They just want the mayor gone."

"Chill, Dan. You're sounding a little cray-cray, even by your tenuous standards of normalcy."

"Whoever committed this crime is a serious whack job. Not a functioning member of society."

"Most serial killers have day jobs."

"How many have been the duly elected mayor of a major metropolitan city?"

She granted him that point. "Any chance you'll throw in the towel? I'll make you a good deal."

"I'm going to expose this case for the political rat-screwing it is."

"Okay then. Good talk." She turned toward the door.

"By the way," he said, a little more quietly, "you look great in blue. Matches your eyes."

She shook her head and entered the courtroom.

A FEW MOMENTS AFTER HE AND JIMMY TOOK THEIR SEATS AT the defendant's table, the marshals brought Camila into the courtroom. She was still wearing the orange coveralls. Since no jury would be present, the powers-that-be saw no need to allow her to change into street clothes. Of course, like most law enforcement policies, it was completely wrong and favored the prosecution. The judge was the most important player in a criminal trial, and he couldn't help but be influenced by seeing someone in prison garb, looking as everyone did who lived under prison conditions. Moreover, it would be almost impossible to bring her over from lockup without giving some ardent paparazzi a chance to snap a page-one photo.

Normally, the marshals marched close and surrounded the defendant, but he noticed that on this occasion they kept a discreet distance. Perhaps they were aware that this woman had been their boss and could be again. Or maybe it was the fierce don't-mess-with-me look in her eye. At any rate, it was working.

"How are you?" he asked, once she was seated.

"Mad as hell, mostly." He noted the dark circles around her eyes, but she did not appear as impaired as most.

"People treating you ok?"

"In jail? What do you expect? At least they are keeping me in isolation."

"That might be lonely. But I think it's for the best."

"They could still get to me."

"They?"

"My enemies. The people behind this."

Jimmy leaned in between them. "You mean Lex Luthor?"

She blinked. "Excuse me?"

"Sorry. Conrad Sweeney."

Her eyelids lowered. "You know about him?"

"Yeah. Garrett's checking him out. And I'm trying to set up a meeting."

"He wanted to buy me. When that didn't work, he swore to take me down. He fancies himself the big cheese in this town and doesn't like competition. For that matter, he doesn't like women, he doesn't like Hispanics, and most of all, he doesn't like people he can't control."

"You're saying you think he barbecued those men?"

"No. He would never take that kind of risk. He's a puppet master. But one way or another, he gets what he wants. And what he wants now is me gone, preferably dead. If this hearing doesn't go his way, he'll send someone after me inside."

He would like to dismiss this as errant paranoia—but he couldn't. "Better if I can get you out of there."

The bailiff appeared in the rear doorway that led to the judge's chambers. "All rise."

He noticed a few people in the gallery who appeared to be reporters. Not many, but then, this was only a preliminary hearing. He needed to get used to it. This case involved a local celebrity, so it would attract media attention—and the demeanor of most judges changed when they were performing for an audience. With luck, this might restrain Judge Hayes from some of his more outrageous pro-prosecution shenanigans.

Judge Hayes entered, his black robe flowing behind him. Medium-height. Well-fed. Wedding ring. Jagged hairline. Rubber-soled shoes.

The judge took his seat and called the style of the case. "Are the parties present and represented by counsel?"

He and Jazlyn rose. "The defendant is present, your honor. Waive the reading of the preliminary charges. Waive the reading of the rights, though of course not the underlying rights themselves."

The judge nodded. "How does the defendant plead?"

Camila didn't need nudging. "Not guilty. To all charges."

Jazlyn spoke. "Your honor, given the gravity of the crimes, we're assembling a grand jury. We expect to present our case to them by the end of the week."

"Thank you, Miss Prentice."

Out the corner of his eye, he saw Jazlyn's neck stiffen. Like most single women these days, she preferred to be addressed as Ms. Prentice.

He knew there were only two good reasons for prosecutors to go through the hassle of calling a grand jury. First, because the defendant was a high-profile politician and to whatever degree possible they wanted to eliminate the inference that the charges were political in-fighting. And second—because a grand jury indictment was required in Florida if you seek the death penalty.

Not surprising, really. The killer had taken four lives in the cruelest manner imaginable. He wasn't an advocate of executions, but if this wasn't a death penalty crime, nothing was.

"Are there any motions we can take up at this time?" He noted that the judge seemed a little stiffer, more formal, than usual.

"Yes, your honor." He would return the favor by being equally formal. "I would ask the court to consider bail."

"Out of the question," Jazlyn replied, not that anyone asked her. "This is a murder case, potentially a capital murder case. We will likely recommend the death penalty. There have been four murders already, and they were…horrifying. Let's not give the defendant an opportunity to commit more."

"Just as a reminder," he said, "the accused is only that. Accused. She hasn't been convicted of anything yet, and given how flimsy the prosecution case is, she probably never will be."

Judge Hayes gave him a stern look. "Counsel."

Yeah, yeah, don't argue the merits of the case during a motion hearing. But everyone did. If you had a chance to bend the judge's ear, you took it. "The question with respect to bail, your honor, is whether there's a danger to the community or a flight risk. In this case, neither exists. As the court undoubtedly knows, the defendant is the duly elected mayor of the city. She's a public figure and possesses a readily recognized face. There is nowhere she could go without being identified."

"Didn't stop her at the bakery," Jazlyn muttered.

"Furthermore," he continued, "there is no chance she could leave town without being spotted."

"Again," Jazlyn said, "just not true. She does have a driver's license."

"She has no motivation to go anywhere. To the contrary, she wants to have her day in court to defend herself against these politically motivated charges and hopes for the earliest possible trial setting."

The judge's head bobbed back and forth as if he were watching a table tennis match.

"If I may correct opposing counsel's misstatements," Jazlyn said. "This case is not motivated by politics. I don't care anything about politics. I just want to get murderers off the street."

"I'm not talking about her, your honor. I'm talking about the people who pull her strings."

Jazlyn appeared incensed. "You're crossing the line, counsel. No one pulls—"

He held up his hands. "I meant no disrespect. But Ms. Prentice does not run the DA's office. Even the DA himself has people he must answer to."

Judge Hayes cut off the debate. "We're not going to discuss politics in this courtroom. As for the rest, I agree that the danger to society is probably minimal. But I am concerned that releasing a defendant on trial for first-degree murder might set a dangerous precedent."

"That's a slippery-slope argument," he said, trying to correct the judge in the gentlest manner possible. "And as we all remember from law school, that's a logical fallacy, not a valid justification for a decision. It's a way of avoiding arguing about the matter at hand by conjecturing about where it might lead in the future. None of us is Nostradamus. We should focus on the here and now."

"As I was saying," the judge continued, looking increasingly irritable, "it sets a dangerous precedent." Note to self: Don't interrupt the judge. "And I don't agree with you with respect to the possibility of flight. It is entirely possible that a prominent citizen could flee. It has happened before."

Thinking about Roman Polanski? That was the name that typically arose when judges denied well-known defendants bail for no apparent reason. "Your honor, the defendant will agree to surrender her passport." He hoped. He hadn't actually thought to discuss it with her.

Judge Hayes shook his head. "Lots of places to hide in the continental United States."

"Then the defendant will agree to wear a collar. That should put the court completely at ease." By a collar, he meant an electronic tracking device. The most common was an ankle band that would tell where the wearer was and, to some extent, what she was doing. The best ones, for instance, could detect stress or alcohol and drug consumption.

He saw Camila looking at him. She probably didn't like the idea, but if that's what it took to get her out of the jailhouse, she wasn't going to complain.

The judge appeared torn. "I might be able to live with this if we can monitor her movements. Perhaps place her under house arrest."

Jazlyn cut in. "Your honor, the state objects. That's just not enough. Would a collar have told us that four people were about to be rotisseried at a bakery? We'd know where she was —so what? She's cool enough to avoid elevated stress signs. We have to keep the public safe."

"The best way to do that would be to find the fiend who actually committed the crime." He knew that would irritate Jazlyn, but hoped the reporters would splash it across the headlines. "Your honor, we have an extraordinary case with extraordinary circumstances. This calls for individualized attention from the court."

The judge pursed his lips. "We haven't even discussed the matter of money. A bail of this nature, on these charges, will be expensive."

Yes, he knew they'd get to this eventually. He thought cash-based bail was distasteful, unjust, unconstitutional, and an inexcusable means of raising money and increasing overcrowding in jail. Many defendants endured long jail stays on minor charges just because they couldn't raise the cash to purchase their freedom or pay a non-refundable fee to a for-profit bail bondsman. Those jail stays could cost jobs, leave children unattended, and destroy lives. Some people pled guilty to lesser charges just to get out of jail. Many organizations, including the Civil Rights Corps, thought this was unjust and served no purpose in a world with electronic monitoring, pretrial risk assessment, and court reminders that could be delivered to the defendant's phone. But sadly, it was a fundraising device still frequently used, even in jurisdictions where the jails were so rough that a twenty-four-hour stay could be deadly.

Camila, of course, was not poor. But that didn't mean jail couldn't be hazardous to her health. "Name an amount, your honor." A dangerous challenge, but necessary. "Any reasonable amount. We'll raise it."

"I don't want campaign funds used here. Only the defendant's personal resources."

"Of course. How much?" His question assumed the judge had already decided to grant bail, which was probably not the case, but it couldn't hurt to act as if he had. "If she can't finance this personally, I believe the defendant will have little trouble obtaining a loan."

The judge appeared to recognize the truth of this argument. "I suppose the state opposes?"

"Darn right," Jazlyn said. "At the very least, wait until we've heard from the grand jury."

"That could take weeks."

"I will pledge to have it done before the end of this week."

"I appreciate that." The judge hesitated. "But I don't honestly think this defendant poses much flight risk. I will agree to bail for the present, subject to review after the grand jury speaks, on the condition that the defendant agrees to wear an electronic monitoring device. Bail is set in the amount of twenty-five thousand dollars."

"Your honor!" Jazlyn said. "This is a murder charge!"

"I'm aware of the charges, counsel," the judge replied sternly. "Don't get your papers in a twist."

He and Jimmy exchanged a look.

The judge continued. "The defendant will be restricted to her home, her attorney's office, and limited shopping for necessities approved in advance by her surveillance officer.

The defendant may also visit her workplace...if that's necessary."

The judge apparently knew the deputy mayor had already seized the reins. "The defendant agrees to all those conditions, your honor. And we thank the court."

Jazlyn was not amused. "The state strongly voices its objection."

"I've already ruled, Madame Prosecutor," the judge said.

Many people would be outraged by this decision, and Jazlyn undoubtedly wanted to make it clear this was not her idea. He was surprised, if not astonished, himself. Maybe Judge Hayes was not so adamantly right-wing as everyone thought. Or maybe he wanted to seem reasonable and impartial now—so he could lower the boom later, when it mattered.

"Is there anything else?"

He pondered. He had a victory, and he didn't want to mess it up. "We're going to have to discuss venue at some point, your honor."

"Later. We'll let the grand jury speak, see how the pretrial publicity plays out. Then we can decide whether anything needs to be done."

That was imminently reasonable, even if they both knew the publicity would be enormous. "Then I have nothing more, your honor."

"Very well." The judge looked out toward the gallery. "I see there are some members of the fourth estate in my courtroom today. We're all aware that this cute gal at the defendant's table is our mayor. I know you'll feel compelled to report on these proceedings, but I will urge you to avoid any statements that might prejudice the jury pool. We all want a fair trial."

He could see Camila's jaw tighten, but to her credit, she kept her mouth shut. The "cute gal" had a lot of self-control.

The judge banged the gavel and left.

"Did you follow all that?" he asked his client.

Camila nodded. "Not that complicated. I get out of jail. And the judge is a sexist pig."

He didn't argue. "The marshals will take you to the surveillance office. There's a lot of rigmarole and paperwork, but you should be free by this afternoon. We'll meet up later and compare notes."

"Am I really going to have to ask permission before I go to Whole Foods?"

"I'm afraid so."

"Drug store? Doctor's office?"

"Definitely."

She sighed. "Better than having my meals brought on a tin tray, I suppose." She rose and the marshals led her away. Unless it was his imagination, they were showing even more deference now.

He loaded his backpack and started out of the courtroom. He was glad he got Camila out of jail, but this hearing had given him a strong taste of just how hard this case was going to be to win. One fact was certain—he might have seen some success today, but the battle was far from over.

CHAPTER THIRTEEN

DAN FOUND JAZLYN WAITING FOR HIM OUTSIDE THE courtroom. "I can't believe you put a first-degree murderer back on the street."

"I'm a little surprised myself." He raised a finger. "You meant *accused* murderer, right?"

"No, you did. I know she's guilty. I can see it in her eyes. And don't use that as a segue to some sexist remark about my beautiful baby blues."

"I would never." Pause. "Though your eyes are gorgeous. But I don't want to be inappropriate."

"No, I know what a straight-shooter you are. How am I going to explain this to my boss?"

"Sucks to be you."

"He will not be happy."

"You have nothing to fear. He knows how good you are. He depends upon you. But there are other people involved in this, aren't there?"

"Is this more of your conspiracy nonsense? Some diabolical plot to put the deputy mayor in power so he can undermine democracy?"

"I doubt if the schemers are the throttlebottoms at city

hall. But I am getting the impression that some seriously powerful people are trying to influence the outcome of this drama. Maybe throwing some big money around."

"I can guarantee none of it has come my way. I can't even afford new shoes."

"You don't need them. You're rocking those heels. Can you get me into the crime scene?"

Her face puckered up. "Do you really want that?"

"I don't think it sounds fun. But I've got to check off all the boxes on this one."

She understood. "I'll tell them you're coming. Anything else I could do for you?"

He grinned. "Oh yeah. Lots. But let's wait till this case is over."

DAN STRONGLY SUSPECTED THIS WAS A TITANIC MISTAKE. At least he'd had the sense to tell Jimmy and Maria to stay home. Promised to take pictures—and he did. But these wouldn't make it into the file.

This was the worst, most horrifying scene he'd observed in his entire life.

The police had removed the bodies from the oven. But they hadn't removed the smell. Probably couldn't, not without completely scrubbing and sanitizing it. Or demolishing it, which might be better. None of that could happen until the intense evidence collection was completed. He knew a hair and fiber team had already scoured the premises, and he observed CSIs working with luminol and other chemical compounds, while a videographer took detailed records. He did not envy them this job. Though everyone wore masks, rubber gloves, and footies, including him, it was not nearly enough to diminish the horror.

One side of the oven was almost completely splattered

with blood. Unless he missed his guess, that was the remnant of a corpse that had exploded due to the intense heat. The floor of the oven was covered with a black char, and he couldn't rule out the possibility that some of that was crispified flesh.

He took several fast gulps of air, trying to steady himself. It would completely ruin his tough-guy image if he hurled at the crime scene. And knowing how unpopular he was with the DA, he might end up charged with evidence tampering.

He heard a voice behind him. "Like something out of a demented Jackson Pollock painting, right?"

He grunted. "If Pollock was a serial-killing sadist."

"Some of Dante's circles of hell look like this. But I've never seen a crime scene that did."

Detective Kakazu stood behind him. Cut beneath his left ear. Smudged fingernails. Same jacket as before. Was it his only one?

"Well, I give you props for coming." Kakazu was a Japanese name but he spoke with a British accent. He'd been raised in Hong Kong. Stood out from the rest of the Floridians. This was a complete stereotype and possibly misleading, but he had to admit it—an upper-class British accent made everyone sound smarter. "Most mouthpieces wouldn't have the guts."

"Thank you for making my life complete."

"I'm not following."

"I've heard cops call lawyers 'mouthpieces' on television, but never in real life. Now I can die happy."

"Always the smartass, aren't you, Pike?"

"Nah. Just when I'm with you."

He shook his head. "The D.A. is right. You're an acquired taste."

"Yeah?"

"And I haven't acquired it."

He knew Kakazu had to put on a show of hostility toward

defense lawyers, but he didn't sense any real animus. For his part, he liked the man. He was by far the most capable homicide investigator, and probably the best-educated. He'd apparently acquired degrees in both art and religion before somehow settling down to police work.

Kakazu showed him inside. "Mayor must be paying you a bundle to handle this mess."

Why did people always make assumptions about his paychecks? "Actually, she's not paying me at all."

"She's a charity case?"

"I get paid a salary by my boss. I don't get anything from the client."

"That's whacked."

"Works fine for me. I noticed the heel marks on the linoleum. Somebody dragged the bodies to the oven."

"Did you think they climbed in there voluntarily?"

"And I suspect I'm not the first to notice that the mayor is an extremely petite woman."

"She could've managed."

"Unconscious bodies are like big heavy potato sacks." Sadly, he knew this from experience. "Mayor Perez weighs, what? 105?"

"But she's highly determined."

"If you say so. Are you sure the blood scratch was intended to be a 'C'? I thought it was unclear at best."

"Men baking to death often don't have the best penmanship."

"You know how many words in the dictionary start with 'C'?"

"I'll bet you do."

"4609."

"But only one of them is the name of the leading suspect."

"You're assuming he was writing a name, like some cornball 'dying clue' in an old Ellery Queen mystery. But it could've been anything."

"Given all the other evidence, I feel our theory is sound."

"The man was dying. Burning. So he twitched, and his finger twitched with him."

"And made a 'C?'"

"You only see a 'C' because you want to see a 'C.'"

"I see what's there. And I know what it means."

He cast his eyes toward the lobby. "Any theories on why one table was cleared?"

Kakazu shrugged. "Probably banged into it while dragging corpses around."

He shook his head. "It's not in the path to the kitchen. Off to one side." He looked back at the door. "Where someone would go if they didn't want any chance of detection from the outside."

"Or maybe it was cleared by a random construction worker. Or a strong wind."

"Or two people having sex."

Kakazu ran his fingers through his thinning hair. "How the hell did you get to that?"

"Lugging unconscious bodies around is hard, so you don't want to have to do it any longer than necessary. Better to lure the victims in here—then knock them out."

"And in your mind, that means sex?"

"That's when men are typically at their stupidest."

"You think the killer is some femme fatale."

"Why are you assuming the killer is female?"

"You said—"

"Evolve, detective. Not every killer is heterosexual. And the person who lured them in is not necessarily the killer."

"Are you saying—"

"We need to explore all possibilities. And you need to have this table tested for the telltale signs sex leaves behind. Semen.

Vaginal secretions. DNA. Any sign of someone using a seda-
tive or anesthetic."

"We did find a broken vial on the floor."

"I heard. Have it tested for drugs."

"We will." Kakazu somewhat reluctantly pulled out a pad
and scribbled a few notes. "Any reason you're helping us?"

"I'm certain that whatever you find won't incriminate my
client. And might lead to the true killer."

"What if we find your client's DNA?"

"Since we know she was here on several occasions, that
wouldn't be shocking. But I bet you won't find any indication
she had sex on that table. She's way too smart for that."
Unless she was fooling everyone, including him.

"I'll run the tests."

"And let me know what you find?"

He shrugged. "The DA makes those decisions."

"The DA has to produce all exculpatory evidence."

He grinned. "Like I said, the DA makes all those decisions.
Anything else I can do for you?"

"Yeah. Get a new jacket."

Kakazu's eyes widened. "Would you stop with the clothes
insults? My nana got me this jacket."

Once again, he found himself liking the detective. "I was
kidding. It's a great jacket. Just needs to be cleaned."

"I had it cleaned last week."

"Did you have lasagna for lunch?"

"Yeah. How—?"

He saluted with two fingers. "Better get the jacket cleaned
again."

———

DAN STEPPED OUT OF THE BAKERY—AND BLINKED. ON THE
other side of the street, near the corner, he thought he
someone suddenly duck out of sight.

He blinked again. Had he imagined it?

He thought about running that way, but he knew he wouldn't get there in time. Why would anyone be watching this bakery? Or him? Had they staked the place out—or followed him here?

The temperature was in the 80s, but he still felt a cold chill as he made his way to his car.

CHAPTER FOURTEEN

DAN WONDERED IF HE WAS WASTING HIS TIME. BUT THERE WAS something to be said for tradition, he told himself, and his tradition was that whenever a grand jury was called to decide his client's fate, he attended. The prosecutors wouldn't let him inside. But he watched the jurors file in and he watched them file out. He knew they would return an indictment—grand juries almost always did—but he wanted to read their expressions.

It didn't require Sherlock Holmes to deduce that the evidence they would hear would be disturbing. But was the evidence strong enough to make them believe the mayor of the city committed this heinous crime? Would they feel enough revulsion to put the death penalty on the table?

He was surprised to see Camila's Chief of Staff, Benji, approach bearing two coffee cups, but they were Starbucks, not the sludge they sold downstairs, so he was forced to be friendly.

"For *moi*?" he asked.

"Thought I'd join you on the stakeout, if you don't mind."

"Glad to have the company." He took a sip. "White chocolate mocha?"

"You have a discerning tongue."

"A chef must. Though I've never ventured into the world of exotic coffee drinks. I normally drink it black. But this is good. Thanks."

Benji hesitated a few moments before speaking. "You think there's any chance they won't indict?"

He took another swig of the coffee. "Not the slightest. This is the prosecutor's show. They present their case and no one disputes it. Given how bad this crime is, most jurors would feel like they were obstructing justice if they didn't give the DA what he wants. Really, it's a waste of time. They should rewrite the Constitution and get rid of grand juries. Just let the DA indict like they do in most cases."

"So…you think this case is going to trial?"

"Yup."

"And at trial…?"

"Way too soon for me to know anything. Got a lot of people to talk to first." He gave her another look. This chitchat was fine, but it wasn't what brought Benji here. "Was there…something else you wanted to ask?"

She shrugged. "Is there anything I can do to help?"

That wasn't what brought her here either, but he'd go with that. "Can you suggest anyone I should interview?"

"I saw the list Camila gave you. I think that about covers it."

He tried again. "I don't want to talk out of school, but… Camila confided that she dated Nick Mansfield."

"Yes, I knew about that." She looked away. "I was against it, but I knew about it."

"Why were you against it?"

"I thought he was trouble. And I was right."

"You supported her decision to fire him?"

"One hundred and ten percent."

"Did he get another job after he was fired?"

"Don't know. Don't care. Heard nothing about him. Till he turned up dead."

"I think someone lured him to that bakery. Drugged him. Then killed him."

Benji shuddered. "Will you be able to help her? Don't let the scumbags bring her down. She's much too special for that."

"You seem very…attached to Camila."

She smiled awkwardly. "I told you I love that woman. I've known her for years. Since college. I knew she had big ambitions. I was interested in politics, but I never got anywhere on my own. Every time I tried to knock down a door, some man pushed me back. Only Camila had the strength and perseverance to break the ceiling—not because men permitted it, or liked it, but because she ignored them and created her own path. She empowered me." The admiration was apparent in her eyes. "I knew there was nothing brilliant about me, but I thought if I hitched my wagon to her star, I could bask in a little reflected glory."

"You shouldn't sell yourself short. Camila told me you were a terrific Chief of Staff. She's lucky to have a friend like you."

"She's a brilliant woman. With so much promise. The luck is all mine." She stood. "Make sure you take good care of her."

THREE HOURS LATER, THE GRAND JURY FINISHED ITS BUSINESS. Jazlyn announced the result, though he already knew what it was. "We'll file the indictment and send a copy to your office."

"Cool. I'm starting a collection."

A few minutes later, he watched the jurors file out of the gallery. He didn't expect them to grin or act as if they'd been to a party. They'd just heard about a mass execution.

But he wasn't expecting this, either.

The first juror out the door had an expression that almost seemed familiar, though it took him a moment to place it.

It was the same expression he had at the crime scene, just after he stuck his head into the oven.

This was going to be even harder than he'd realized.

They felt more than just an obligation to indict. They *wanted* to indict. The horrible nature of this crime so rent their souls that they needed to do something to ease their consciences. There would be a gaping injustice in the world until someone paid for this crime. The quicker they could make that happen, the better.

That kind of attitude, of course, would be disastrous for the defense at trial.

He needed to do more than simply undermine the prosecution's case. One way or another, he must supply a satisfying resolution, to give the jury the feeling that they now understood what happened, what truly lay behind this cruelty. And it didn't have anything to do with Camila.

If he didn't, the jury was certain to convict. What else could they do? If that was the only way to clear their heads, their consciences, they would convict the mayor or, for that matter, the mayor's dog, whatever the prosecution wanted. They would do anything to get the image of that bloodsoaked oven out of their heads.

He understood this so well—because he felt the same way.

CHAPTER FIFTEEN

NEXT MORNING, DAN WENT TO THE COURTHOUSE WITH Camila for another perfunctory arraignment, this time in response to the grand jury's report.

Judge Hayes spoke with pronounced volume and clarity. "The grand jury has indicted you on a charge of first-degree murder. How do you plead?"

"Not guilty." Was he imagining it, or was there a slight tremor in her voice that had not been present earlier? Criminal charges were never fun, but to have the death penalty dangling over you—that was something else again.

DAN RODE SHOTGUN WHILE MARIA DROVE THE JAG TO VISIT Camila's campaign manager, Frank Esposito.

"How is Camila holding up?" she asked, eyes on the road.

"She'll be ok. This is hard for her. She's put so much effort into crafting her public image. But she has a strong motivation to survive."

"Even if we can get these charges dropped—won't it

impact her future? The Democratic National Committee can't embrace an accused murderer."

"I think that depends." The neighborhood she steered into was one of several that still needed some of the mayor's urban renewal. But everything was better when he could smell the gulf in the distance. "If we prove she's being framed for political reasons, and she beats the rap, she could become a modern-day folk hero."

"Then let's do that."

"Working on it. How are you holding up?"

"Me?" Maria hung a sharp right. "I'm fine. Why?"

"I know Camila is kind of your hero. Or Disney princess, whatever. No one wants to see their hero under attack."

"It just reminds me how modern-day politics systematically eliminates people who might have the ability to make real change."

"Keep a strong upper lip, partner. Later I'll take you for a freakshake."

"Are you being patronizing?"

"I was trying to be supportive."

"Oh." She parked in the closest spot to the door. "Well, that does sound kinda good, actually."

FRANK ESPOSITO SAT BEHIND A DESK CLUTTERED WITH ENOUGH files to fill the Library of Congress. If all those files represented clients, Dan thought, this man would be the wealthiest accountant in Florida. But he suspected the files all pertained to one client, in which case they didn't indicate wealth so much as massive disorganization.

Esposito did not rise when they entered his office. Midsixties. Suspenders, no jacket. Cigar smoke. Unkempt thinning hair. Trace of Brooklyn accent. "You Pike?"

"I am." He hadn't expected to receive the same warmth

he felt from Camila, but still. "We're the mayor's lawyers. And you're her campaign manager?"

"An increasingly dated job description, I suspect. Have a seat." Esposito sort of growled when he talked. "I was freelance. Never actually a member of her staff."

He and Maria took the proffered seats. "Did you want to be?"

Esposito shrugged. "I wanted to be paid, which I've haven't been, for more than a month. Other than that, I didn't care. Pérez wanted a female staff. Thought she was making a statement. Breaking the glass ceiling, who knows? I didn't care. I wasn't interested in politics. I'm a numbers man. Numbers don't lie."

"But people do?"

"Like I have to tell this to a lawyer? You know what I'm talking about. Liars permeate politics. You wanna be in politics and never get your hands dirty? Fuhgedaboudit."

"Do you think Mayor Pérez lied to you?"

"She's one of the better ones, actually. But nobody stays squeaky clean in politics for long. Just doesn't work that way. I had a report for you." He leaned forward, grunting a bit. He appeared to be about thirty pounds over his recommended BMI. Possibly because he spent too much time at this desk. He fumbled through tall stacks of paper but didn't seem to be able to lay his hands on what he wanted. "You two were handling the finance irregularity charges? And now you're handling the murder?"

"We're ambidextrous."

"I guess. I made a report explaining what I think went wrong. Ah! Eureka!" He pulled a blue folder out of the middle of a stack, like a magician withdrawing a rabbit from a hat. "Here it is. Use it."

He took the file. "Can you give me a summary?"

"I could, but you'll need the details, and it's all in there. I think the charges about the PAC are bogus. Albert Kazan said there was no collusion. And there was nothing wrong with the loan—though maybe the funds weren't disbursed perfectly. The DA found some columns that didn't add up. Made it look like we were trying to hide something. I don't know how that happened. Wasn't my fault, I can tell you that. I love numbers and numbers love me. I don't make mistakes."

Maria cut in. "Everyone makes mistakes."

"Not me, missy. At least not with numbers. Now if you want to talk about my marriages…"

"We don't. If you didn't make the mistake, who did?"

"I never said there was a mistake."

Maria looked flummoxed. "You said—"

"I said the numbers didn't add up. That's not because I can't add. It's because someone changed the numbers."

"You're saying there was fraud?"

"Absolutely. You handle fraud, too, Pike?"

"I do." He thumbed through the report. He'd let Garrett scrutinize this later. He hated spreadsheets. "If money was supposedly hidden…where did it go?"

"That's the sixty-four-thousand-dollar question. Answer that and you'll crack the case."

"Will that help Mayor Pérez—or hurt her?"

"Depends on the answer. If you find out she sidelined money to pay off a porn star, she's toast. Oh wait—that's ok now."

"Only for men," Maria murmured.

"But I seriously doubt Pérez had her fingers in the cookie jar."

"Then who did?"

"No idea."

"Who had access to the documents before they were filed?"

"Probably everyone in that office."

"Would that include Nick Mansfield?"

Esposito leaned back in his chair. "I figured we'd get to

him. Sure, he probably had access. But remember, he wasn't a full-time member of the mayor's staff any more than I was. He suffered from the terminal disqualification of being male."

"But he was in the office frequently."

"Constantly." A smarmy grin spread across his face. "And from what I hear, he saw the mayor quite a bit after hours, too, if you know what I mean."

"The mayor isn't denying that there was a personal relationship at some point."

"That's one way of putting it. She had the hots for him, big time. Practically drooled the first day he entered the office. I didn't see what the big deal was myself, but boy, she did. She wanted what he had, and she wanted it fast and often."

He could see Maria's lips purse. He thought he'd better speak before she did. "She terminated his employment. The personal relationship began after."

"Is that what she told you?" More grinning. "I heard she caught him screwing around with someone else and went all Tasmanian Devil on his ass."

"You're saying she caught him with another woman?"

"I never specified woman. I don't know, I wasn't there. But I know that relationship ended. And then he turned up dead. In her oven." He whistled. "Hell hath no fury."

"Did you like Mansfield?"

"Like him? He was a junkie. Little better than a gigolo."

"He did drugs?"

"Been to rehab, I heard. Lost his banking job. Something really messed him up."

"Did you see any of this?"

"No."

"Who's your source?"

He waved a hand in the air. "I promised I'd keep my lips shut."

"If you keep secrets from Camila's lawyers, you're crippling her defense."

"Believe me, none of this could help her. Quite the contrary."

He paused for a moment. Badgering Esposito would never work. He needed to come at this from a different direction. Maybe get the man to say something that would allow him to suss out the source. "I'm getting the impression you're not crazy about the mayor."

Esposito shrugged. "She's a client."

"That doesn't mean you like her. Sounds more like you resented her. Is that because she's a highly successful woman?"

"No. Some of my best friends are women."

He tried to suppress his laughter.

"I don't care what women do," Esposito continued. "I just don't like the attitude. The arrogance. The strident tone."

Which only bothered you because she's a woman. "Have you had any contact with Conrad Sweeney?"

Esposito seemed startled by the sudden change of topic. "He's a client. Why?"

"Ever talk with him about Camila?"

"Once or twice. Only natural. She is the mayor."

"Is he a fan?"

Esposito drew in his breath slowly, then exhaled. "I'm not the only one who's put off by arrogant attitude."

"So Sweeney doesn't like her?"

Esposito chuckled. "He calls her 'La Cucaracha.'"

He'd take that as a yes. "I'm guessing he didn't support her campaign."

"To the contrary—he offered her a lot of money. Even offered to form a PAC for her benefit. She turned it down. Bizarre. As you know, she's taken money from dubious people. Kazan. Gangs. But she wouldn't take a cent from Sweeney, the one guy who could transform her life big time."

"Is Sweeney behind the campaign finance charges brought by the DA?"

"I have no idea." Esposito glanced at his watch. "Anything else, Pike?"

He had the distinct feeling they'd gotten all they were getting out of this man. He cast a meaningful glance toward Maria, asking nonverbally if she had anything more to ask. She didn't.

He rose. "If there's nothing else—"

"Let me give you some advice. Watch your back."

His jaw lowered. "Are you...threatening me?"

"Of course not. I don't give a damn what you do. I don't give a damn what any of these people do. I'm from New York. Believe me, the politics back home makes these people look like kids playing in the sandbox. I'm just saying—you're treading into dangerous waters."

"Still sounds like a threat."

"Not from me. I wouldn't harm a flea. But the mayor dove into the deep end—and look what happened to her. You ruffle too many feathers in this world, you get hurt. That's the way it's always been. And if you think you're immune because you're some hotshot lawyer— you are sadly mistaken."

CHAPTER SIXTEEN

DAN LOVED THE HISTORIC OLD NORTHEAST PART OF ST. Petersburg. He didn't get out here often enough. He stayed reasonably busy and when he did have spare time, he tended to gravitate toward the water, but this neighborhood had some of the nicest homes in the city, plus restaurants, hotels, and great attractions like the world-famous Dali Museum and the Sunken Gardens. Later, they might cross the cable Sunshine Skyway Bridge, which connected St. Petersburg to Terra Ceia Island. The bridge collapsed in 1980 but was rebuilt in 1990s and had since become a Florida icon—and sadly, a popular spot for suicide jumps.

"We're going to a spa?" Garrett asked, as if he hadn't quite heard the first time.

"That's where she wanted to meet. Said she had an appointment and didn't want to break it."

"And you went along with that?"

"Jimmy made the arrangements. I was grateful we could get in to see her. I'd like to know as much about this case as possible before we're back in court."

"And you wanted me to come with you because...?"

"I find your insight invaluable."

"But seriously."

"I am serious. Maria is at the mayor's office, interviewing everyone in sight. I thought that since she's such a fan, and since the staff is virtually all female, she'd be the best one to do that. Jimmy is busy setting up more interviews."

"So I was the only person available?"

"I could've come alone. But I'd rather hear your…thoughts."

"I get it now. This woman's a super-feminist, probably a liberal, so you brought your token conservative friend along to argue with her. Maybe get her stirred up so she says more than she should."

"I value your opinion."

"And you're not denying anything I just said. I'm not an extremist, you know. I believe all people should have equal rights under the law, regardless of their gender or anything else." He paused. "I also think that historically, some family structures have worked better than others."

"Tell me that doesn't mean you think women should stay in the kitchen."

"It doesn't. I think you should stay in the kitchen. You're a much better chef than—" He stopped short.

"Than lawyer?"

"I didn't say that." Garrett turned and peered out the window. "But you know, good cooks are hard to find…"

GLORIA CULPEPPER WAS ALREADY IN A MASSAGE CHAIR WHEN they arrived. Long brown hair with streaks of gray. Weathered skin. Patched jeans. Open-toe sandals.

"Hope you don't mind. I already started." She didn't rise, but she did extend her hand for shaking. "You must be Pike."

He took it. "I am. Call me Dan. This is Garrett."

She gestured to her side. "I saved spots. The staff is

waiting for you. I signed you up for oatmeal pedicures. Hope you don't mind."

He glanced at his companion. Garrett did not appear excited at the prospect of oatmeal between his toes. But they both took their seats. Maddie, the woman in charge, pulled a plastic cover around them, then placed a bowl of warm water at their feet.

"Oatmeal, huh?"

Culpepper laughed. "It's the best, trust me. Feels wonderful. And it's completely natural. Everything here is. That's why the place doesn't smell like some spas do. No chemicals."

The water felt warm. It did have a somewhat soothing effect. He hoped the oatmeal didn't spoil it. "I have to tell you, I was surprised when I heard this was where you wanted to meet."

"Because I'm a notorious feminazi?"

"Those weren't my exact words…"

She laughed, loud and hearty. "Hey, if you can't beat 'em…own it." She laughed again. "I know, women rights activists aren't supposed to go in for girly stuff like mani-pedis and massages. We're supposed to wear flannel, sport butch haircuts, and grow our own hemp."

"Well, I don't know about the hemp part…"

"Get with the program, dude. I'm a real human being, not a '70s cliché. I like sensual experiences—doesn't everyone?"

Maddie poured the oatmeal into his bowl. "Some more than others."

"Look, I hike. A lot. Twenty, twenty-five miles a week. My feet require attention." Maddie started pouring in her bowl. "Oh my. Doesn't that feel good? Like when you're a kid and you squish mud between your toes. Sometimes when we get older we forget what feels good in life."

He had to admit, the sensation was rather calming. He felt guilty now for not having brought Maria. She would've gone for this in a big way. "Nothing wrong with a little pleasure in life."

"Or a lot of pleasure. Which is what these babies are about." She raised her hands and cupped her breasts. "Just got a brand-new pair."

"Um…excuse me?"

"Don't pretend you didn't notice. I saw where your eyes went the moment you walked into the room."

"I don't think—"

"I had my first pair for about twenty years, but they needed to be replaced. So I got myself a new set."

"Isn't that…unusual?"

"That a feminist wants to look hot?"

"Some would say you're playing into male objectification based upon artificial body images."

"I didn't do this for men. I did it for me. And unlike most women, I'm not reluctant to talk about it, because I have nothing to be embarrassed about. Breast augmentation is commonplace. It's the most requested surgical cosmetic procedure in the US. To me, it's no different from being in this spa or going back to school—I wanted to improve myself. Frankly, I was always flat-chested and it embarrassed me to death when I was young. I envied the girls with fuller figures. They looked happier. Like it or not, breasts are a defining feature of womanhood and I felt I was being held back. I wanted to be bold and brassy, bodacious. I am woman, hear me roar, you know? And I roared much louder once I got a little work done."

"I'm happy for you…I guess."

"I'm in my 50s now, and I'm more active than ever, enjoying my life much more fully than I did when I was a kid. These girls are just part of the package."

Maybe it was time to discuss the case? "Thank you for agreeing to talk to us. Camila thought you might be able to help."

"I doubt that." Culpepper closed her eyes and leaned back into her chair. "That lady has gotten herself into some serious trouble."

"Agreed. She thinks it's all politically motivated."

"I wouldn't be surprised. Politics is a dirty business. And women in positions of power always attract enemies."

"Did you know the victim they've identified? Nick Mansfield?"

"Oh boy did I know him. Dated him for a while."

His eyes widened. He recalled hearing that Camila dated Nick when he was "on the rebound." "Was it serious?"

"Oh, who knows? At my age, I'm not really looking to settle down in the suburbs and have a passel of kids. I just like companionship now and again, if you know what I mean."

"How long did you two date?"

"Maybe a month. We weren't terribly compatible. He was a former banker, you know. Worked for Chase. Talked about money all the time. Big plans to make 100K per annie, as he put it. I may not have been looking for marriage, but I don't think that boy was looking for anything but a pair of breasts with a pocketbook. Like being with a grubworm. I cut him loose."

"How long ago was that?"

"Maybe six months."

"Did you know when he started dating Camila?"

"I knew. And I warned her that he might not be looking for a long-term relationship. But she didn't listen. She was lonely, and I think, smitten. She was bitter when it ended."

"Bitter enough to…?"

"Fire him? Definitely."

"That's not what I was asking."

"Murder him? I don't know. I can't believe she'd kill anyone. And even if she had a motive to off Nick—what about the other three guys?"

Garrett cut into the conversation. "How did you come to know the mayor?"

"I was one of her earliest supporters. I knew she had the goods the moment I met her. I've always been politically active, but never for one minute did I consider running for public office. I don't have the charisma. The camera appeal. But Camila had it in a big way. I thought she could make a real difference, and not just in Florida. I backed her every way I could."

"Were you a financial supporter?" Garrett appeared puzzled. "I've reviewed the campaign finance documents, and I don't recall seeing your name."

"I helped raise funds. I didn't contribute myself. I'm not a wealthy woman. Most of my resources have gone to the cause. I never sought personal gain—which is good, because it certainly never sought me."

Garrett smiled. "Do you know anything about the campaign finance investigation by the DA's office?"

"Not much. I was never involved with the PAC, and I certainly never gave Camila a loan. All that accounting stuff is way over my head. Another good reason for me to stay out of politics. I'd get into so much trouble even Dan here couldn't get me out."

He took that as a cue to jump back into the convo. "Do you know Frank Esposito?"

She made a loud snorting noise. "That pig? Hate the man."

"You and one of my partners share similar views. Do you think he created the reporting problems?"

"No idea. But it wouldn't surprise me. I don't think he's big on female equality. I told Camila she needed to find someone else, but she always made excuses for him."

"Did you see signs that Esposito disliked her?"

"Little things. A glance here. A remark there. Nothing

concrete. I'm sure he wouldn't jeopardize his career. But someone like that might be smart enough to leave a Trojan."

Was she referring to Greek mythology or condoms? "I'm not sure what you mean."

"Trojan horse. A virus. A ticking time bomb. Something that would explode, or be detected, much later, and couldn't be traced back to him."

Was that possible? He needed to know more about the finance problems. "When did you and Camila work together?"

"During the first two years after she was elected. Two peas in a pod, you might say. I wasn't actually on her staff, but I worked with her about as much as the people getting paid."

"Tell me about your work."

"The thing I'm proudest about is the women's shelters." He knew what she meant. Mayor Pérez had renovated old buildings in danger of being condemned, used eminent domain powers to seize them, and converted them to shelters. "Women need a safe place. There are still too many females who are basically economic slaves. We may have abolished one kind of slavery, but there are still women afraid to leave an abusive man because they don't know how to take care of themselves or their children. You wouldn't believe how hard it is sometimes to get women to press charges against their oppressors."

In fact, he would. He'd handled cases where fear kept women from helping themselves. Incredibly frustrating.

"If we can get the women and kids into a safe place," Culpepper continued, "where the abuser can't get to them, take care of their fundamental needs, we're far more likely to get them to testify. Get the man behind bars, or get a protective order—or at the very least, a divorce."

Garrett appeared uncomfortable. "Those shelters end a lot of marriages."

"Some marriages need to be ended," Culpepper said. "Don't you agree?"

Garrett spoke slowly and carefully. "I think marriage is a sacrament. A lifelong commitment. Not something you ditch just because you hit a rough patch."

"Surely you're not saying a woman should stick with a guy who's beating her."

"I think both parties should explore every possible avenue for keeping the marriage together."

"You're in favor of spousal abuse."

"I'm in favor of the nuclear family. It's the bedrock of our way of life."

"And let me guess. You dislike having women in the workplace."

"Not true. We have a female partner, and she's terrific. Invaluable. But she doesn't have children, either. The more mothers in the workplace, the weaker the family unit. The weaker the family unit, the more crime, and that's a statistical fact. The weaker the family, the more kids who fail to launch. The next generation is impaired, and soon the whole country is on the decline."

"That's the voice of the male hegemony. The voice that has kept women down for centuries. Stand by your man, even when he's beating the hell out of you."

"I didn't say that."

"Sounded like it. Let me tell you, if you'd spent ten minutes with some of those women, blackened eyes and bleeding, in fear for their lives and their children's lives, you'd feel differently."

He thought it was time to change the subject, if he didn't want to see the conversation come to a premature end. "I gather you and Camila have parted company."

"Classic blowout. Jane Fonda and Joan Baez all over again. I felt strongly that she should initiate a movement to get the Equal Rights amendment passed. Florida never ratified it, you know."

"The mayor is not a state legislator."

"All the better. She has some distance. She could inspire people without being accused of deal-making. As you may know, back in the 70s, thirty-five states ratified the amendment, but it needed thirty-eight, so it never became part of the US Constitution. But two more states have passed it since, so Florida could cast a deciding, historic vote."

Maddie wiped the oatmeal from his feet and scoured his heel with some kind of scrubbing pad. "Didn't the original amendment have a ten-year time limit?"

"Good memory. Yes, Congress gave it a bizarre ten-year fuse, but Congress could waive that easily enough with a piggyback bill. Thirty-eight states adopting the amendment would be a good reason. Polls show 94% of all Americans favor a constitutional amendment guaranteeing gender equality."

"Many people think that's already the law."

"I know. But it isn't, at least not on a national basis. So here was Camila's chance to do something important. There's still a need. The disparity in women's pay is shocking."

"To be fair, women do not always have entire families dependent upon their income," Garrett said. "And the pay gap has narrowed significantly in recent years."

"But we are still far from equal. Why should fifty percent of the population be required to settle for *some* of their rights?"

"The two sexes are different. It's unrealistic to pretend otherwise."

"They may be biologically different, but they should not be treated differently by the law."

He could tell Garrett was becoming agitated and finding it increasingly difficult to contain himself. He had brought the man in to be confrontational, but the strategy was not working the way he intended. Everyone was just getting mad.

"You're not being realistic," Garrett added. "There's a reason why men have dominated all societies since the dawn of time."

"That's not even historically true. We have archeological evidence of many early matriarchal societies. That doesn't change until men realize they play some role—however small —in producing children."

Garrett pushed out from under the plastic cover. "We are different for a reason. That's the way the design works."

"The so-called design was created by men to benefit men." Her voice rose. "It doesn't need to be enshrined. It needs to be replaced by something less medieval."

Dan held up his hands. "Can we talk about my client? I gather Camila wouldn't support your ERA initiative."

Culpepper settled back into her chair, still plainly agitated. "Maddie, please start on my nails." She turned back to face him. "You're correct. She thought it would stir up too much trouble but gain too little. She said she didn't want to sacrifice her career to achieve a so-called pyrrhic victory."

"She focused on programs that directly benefitted people. Like the shelters. And the downtown renovations. And The Meeting Place."

"I think she made a big mistake. She gave up her moment in history for…what? A playground? The world is changing, whether your pal here likes it or not. The #MeToo movement grows in power each day. #Time'sUp means something to an entire generation of women. I think Camila was afraid of alienating the elderly retired people that make up a large chunk of her constituency."

"You parted ways?"

"Not before we exchanged some harsh words. That woman has a temper, as you may have heard."

"You fought?"

"I'm a doer, not a fighter. But that lady has a mouth on her, and she's not afraid to throw a punch or two if necessary, either. I was starting to worry about what she might do if I didn't get out of her way."

"Surely you're not suggesting you thought she might be...murderous."

"I don't know if she killed those men in the oven. But if you're asking me if she could, if it's theoretically possible that she might do something like that given a good reason—I can't eliminate the possibility."

CHAPTER SEVENTEEN

DAN PARKED TWO BLOCKS FROM CAMILA'S HOME—BECAUSE that was as close as he could get. From a distance, her house looked like a mound in an ant farm. Reporters swarmed around it. News trucks were parked up and down the street and around the corners on both sides. As he approached, he saw journalists of all stripes blanketing her front lawn. He hoped Camila didn't care much about her grass, because there wouldn't be much left when they were done.

Camila's house itself was a modest one-story affair, pueblo pink, maybe 2500 square feet, in a normal middle-class neighborhood. He admired her restraint. She hadn't bought this because she wanted to impress anyone—at least not in the usual way. Perhaps she wanted to remind her constituency that she was a regular person, just like them. Today wouldn't be a good time to make that argument. Most citizens didn't have the fourth estate crawling over their property, thank goodness. He could imagine what might happen if these hordes descended on his boat. They might sink the marina.

"Attorney of record. Make way." He barreled through the crowd, not waiting to see if anyone was listening, parting the bodies like Moses at the Red Sea.

One of the reporters, a woman he vaguely recognized from television, spoke to him. "Mr. Pike! Can you comment on the grand jury indictment?"

He answered without stopping. "Grand juries do what prosecutors tell them to do. It doesn't mean anything." He reached the front steps.

Someone in the rear shouted. "Did she bake her boyfriend?"

He pivoted on one foot and glared. "She did not. You need to go back to journalism school. This time, don't sleep through class."

The first woman replied. "We're just doing our job. Covering the news."

"By camping out on my client's porch? You're not covering the news. You're creating the news. And harassing the innocent. Making a nuisance of yourself in the hope of snagging pointless footage of someone fighting to get their mail." He knew he should keep his mouth shut, but he couldn't. He understood the value of a free press but didn't feel that gave reporters greater rights than anyone else, or overrode privacy rights. Camila couldn't speak out against them, of course. But he could.

"Is she worried about the death penalty?"

He laid his hand on the doorknob. Camila texted him to let himself in. Just go inside, a voice whispered.

But he didn't.

"She's not worried because she didn't commit the crime. This is a plot to stifle a promising political career. And you're all pawns in the scheme."

"That's what crooks always say."

His jaw tightened. "I would lecture you on the meaning of 'presumed innocent' and 'reasonable doubt,' but I know it wouldn't matter to you. You're the reason the quality of our leadership is so low. Good people with actual experiences don't want your scrutiny of their personal lives, digging for dirt, reporting on irrelevancies and calling it a character issue. When a great leader like Camila Pérez finally comes along, you act like jackals picking at carrion rather than affording her the respect she deserves."

That quieted them. For about two seconds. He walked inside, pushing the door firmly shut on a host of shouted replies.

Camila sat on the sofa in the living room. Business casual. Light makeup. Broken fingernail on her left hand. "I see you've met my new friends."

"If that's what you want to call them."

"Is it wise to provoke them?"

"Better me than you." He set his backpack on the coffee table. "We have a lot to review. I've picked up some interesting information. And I have pretrial motions this afternoon."

"Do I need to be there?"

"No, it's actually better if you're not. Judges prefer to handle purely legal matters without distractions. And given that this entourage would follow, you would be a major distraction."

She stood and took a few steps closer. "I'm going to give a press conference."

"No." He put on his sternest dad face. "Absolutely not."

"I've already decided."

Now he understood why she wasn't wearing sweatpants and a t-shirt. "As your legal counsel, I'm advising you not to do it. It will backfire. You won't get the satisfaction you seek. And it may alienate the judge."

"You said the judge might issue a gag order."

"At the very least, he'll strongly advise us not to speak to the press. I expect that to happen this afternoon."

The corner of her lips tugged upward. "Then I'd better do it now, hadn't I?"

This was a lawyer's worst nightmare—the client who wouldn't listen. "What do you think it will accomplish? Some people have already decided you're guilty, and nothing will change their minds—not even a not-guilty verdict. What can you say that will change anything?"

She thought a moment before answering. "It's not so much what I say. It's the fact that I won't be silenced. I will be right there in their faces, strong, resolute, making it clear I won't let the bastards get me down."

He shook his head. "You're going to be severely disappointed. The media will spin it and create the story they want, not the story you want."

She took another step toward him. "Here's something I don't think you get yet, Mr. Miracle Worker. I'm not your usual client. I have big plans, and even though this is a major disruption, I'm not going to let it derail me. Once this mess is cleared up, I'm moving forward." Her chin rose. "That's what I need to tell everyone."

He could see this was important to her. Still a massively bad idea, and one that could very well bite her in the back later. But she was right about one thing—if she was determined to do it, now was the time.

"Here are the ground rules. You don't talk about the facts of the case. At all. Understand? You can say you didn't do it, but nothing more."

"Got it."

"Don't mention Nick Mansfield. Don't discuss your relationship with him."

"I don't plan to."

"And no questions. Make your statement and shut the door."

"I will discuss my work as mayor—and assure everyone it will continue."

He frowned. "I guess I can live with that. When are you going to do this?"

"No time like the present." She winked. "I'm ready for my close-up."

She opened the door. Despite the fact that the sun was shining, a flurry of electric flashes erupted. He heard the subdued whir of minicams. Microphones on selfie sticks pressed into her face. He stood just inside the door and watched.

"Ladies and gentlemen of the press. I'd like to make a brief statement. As you know, false and politically motivated criminal charges have been alleged against me. I will respect the wishes of the court and the judicial system and will not attempt to influence the process or the potential jury pool. But let me make one thing absolutely clear. I did not do this. I did not commit this crime. I didn't commit any crime. And once these charges against me are dropped, we will leave no stone unturned until we discover who did commit these depraved acts." She took a deep breath, surveying the crowd. "Once I am back in the mayor's office—and make no mistake, I will be back in the mayor's office—I will continue with our agenda, rebuilding St. Petersburg's business district, strengthening our families, and improving our way of life."

Another flurry of photography. The female reporter he had spoken to earlier asked, "Mayor Pérez, will you take questions?"

Camila unfurled a big irresistible charismatic smile. "Of course. What would you like to know?"

CHAPTER EIGHTEEN

DURING THE DRIVE TO THE COURTHOUSE, DAN NOTICED A painful gnawing in his stomach that even the memory of his breakfast—homemade bread topped with ghee, grass-fed, with Himalayan sea salt—couldn't fix. What was going on with him? This was the kind of anxiety he associated with the first day of trial, not pretrial motions. Was all this talk about Camila's leadership potential getting to him? He had always fought for justice, fought to prevent government agencies from ruining people's lives. But he couldn't shake the feeling that there was more at play this time. Every time he thought about it. Every time he looked into Camila's eyes.

"OMG." Maria had one eye on the cell phone in the in-dash cradle as she drove. "Our client is really trending."

"I assume this is a reference to Facebook?"

"All social media. The video of Camila's press conference got posted to YouTube. Over seventeen thousand views in twenty-four hours."

"And that's good?"

"For a politician? It's like striking oil. People are posting about how strong and determined she is. Says that's why the white-male patriarchy is trying to bring her down. They're turning her into a resistance symbol."

"All those people like her and approve of her?"

"Most." She hung a sharp left toward downtown. "She's big on Instagram too."

"Isn't that mostly pictures?"

"Yup. Instagamistas are commenting on her clothes, her house, the way she does her hair."

"Glad they're taking her seriously."

"She's becoming an influencer without even trying." While paused at a street light, she flicked a few screens with her thumb. "Incredible! That video has accumulated a thousand more views while we've been talking. This thing is going viral." She made a left turn toward the courthouse. "This bogus murder charge could be the best thing that ever happened to her. If she survives."

"And that's where we come in. Will this social media surge help our case or hurt it?"

"It will make selecting a jury trickier. Judges tell jurors to avoid media stories about the case. Will that include Instagram coverage of her blunt cut?"

"Sounds like all this social media stuff has little to do with the case."

"Oh, there are dozens of online bulletin boards and subReddits devoted to the case. Lots of uninformed losers opining about her guilt or innocence."

"Based upon——?"

"Their own personalities, mostly. But they're obsessing over that 'C' scratched in blood."

"Would you please tell them it's not a 'C?' More like a random twitch. The man was dying."

"Stop being a spoilsport. The case is so much sexier if the victim left behind a mysterious clue. Someone says the young banker had a fondness for puzzles."

"Why are they calling him a young banker? More like a

professional gigolo running through a series of older woman and trying to wheedle money out of them."

"Ouch. I sense major hostility."

"I'm not impressed with Nick's resume."

"And that explains why you're getting all aggro? You know what I think?"

"I'm about to."

"I think you have feelings for Camila."

"Any feelings in particular?"

"You like her and that's why you dislike her ex."

"You are welcome to think whatever you like."

"I notice you're not denying it." She parked the Jag. "That would also explain why you're so edgy this morning."

"I don't recall saying I was edgy."

"You think you're the only one with powers of observation?"

"Mine are fueled by facts. Yours are fueled by avocado toast."

She adopted a sing-song tone. "Danny's got a cru——ush."

"You don't know what you're talking about."

"And yet, I notice you still haven't denied it."

He pushed the car door open. "Let's not be late for the hearing, ok?"

"Okay." But she kept grinning. And singing. "Danny and Cammy up in a tree…"

———

DAN HAD TO FIGHT HIS WAY THROUGH THE THRONG IN FRONT of the courthouse, even thicker than the throng outside Camila's house. He was beginning to understand how powerful social media had become. That viral video, coupled with all the other online activity, skyrocketed the visibility of the case. The press once led public opinion, but today, it was social media.

Inside the courtroom, the gallery was almost full, and unless he missed his guess, the crowd was mostly reporters. He rarely saw a full courtroom for a trial, much less pretrial motions.

Maria leapt past him, springing like a gazelle up and down the short expanse of the courtroom nave.

When she passed near again, he asked the obvious. "What are you doing?"

"Getting in my steps," she replied breathlessly.

"And…why?"

She stopped, jogging in place. "Fitbit quota. I'm under my weekly steps goal."

"Maybe this isn't the time and place?"

"Why not? I'm not doing anything. I'll stop when the judge emerges, promise."

"You are controlled by your wearable electronics."

"I thought you said I was controlled by my cell phone."

"They're not mutually exclusive."

He found Jazlyn at the prosecution table. She appeared to be handling this hearing alone, though he was confident she would have more help at trial. "Are you ready to offer a deal?"

Jazlyn gave him a long look. "Why? Because your client is winning Instagram?"

"Because she didn't do it. And your case is paper-thin."

"I'm afraid my boss doesn't see it that way."

"Truly? Or does he just feel like he has to act like he's solved the case to avoid criticism?"

"I am not privy to the DA's private thoughts. I am privy to his orders, however."

"Which were?"

"Win."

"Drop the charges, and we won't sue for wrongful prosecution."

"Now you're joking."

"No. I think this prosecution was politically motivated. I

think your boss's strings are being pulled by wealthy, powerful forces that want to destroy my client's political viability."

"If that was the goal, I'd have to say they failed. Your client is more popular than ever."

"That will end if she goes to prison."

"True dat. But it's too early to make deals. Anything else?"

"Well...yeah." He adjusted the lie of his necktie. "You put my last invitation on hold. Care to get dinner tonight?"

"Seriously? Give it up, Pike. I'm a mother now. It would ruin your carefree playboy image."

"I never had a carefree playboy image."

"You do."

"Lobster Thermidor is good for the soul."

A door loudly closed back in chambers. "Look, it's show time. Let's continue this conversation later."

CHAPTER NINETEEN

JUDGE HAYES DID NOT APPEAR TO BE IN A GOOD MOOD. DAN knew most judges liked having an audience, even if they pretended otherwise. But Hayes spent several minutes shuffling papers, as if this case were an annoying ordeal he had to work himself up to tackling.

"What is this judge's problem?" Maria whispered.

"I don't know."

"I think he doesn't like women."

"Then this case is going to be hell for him, since there are women on all sides of it, including half the potential witnesses."

Hayes made a growling noise deep in his throat, which was apparently his unique way of calling the court to order. "We have some pretrial motions we should address at this time. Mr. Pike, I believe this is your venue motion."

He stood. "Yes, your honor. We respectfully request that the case be transferred to another venue. Preferably outside the state of Florida."

"You don't feel your client can get a fair trial in my courtroom?"

Great. The judge had decided to take this personally. "We mean no disrespect to this court or—"

"Sure sounds that way."

He glanced at the gallery. "This case has garnered an extraordinary amount of publicity."

"From what I understand," the judge said, "that's mostly your client's doing."

He paused and tried to stay calm. "It's not relevant who caused it, your honor. I could argue that the prosecution caused it because they brought these charges. My client is a public figure, and some feel that's the main reason she's been targeted. We all have roles to play in this drama and we're playing them. But the fact is, it would be virtually impossible for local citizens to avoid being influenced by the enormous coverage."

The judge pursed his lips, as if he had an unpleasant taste in his mouth. "Do you agree, Madame Prosecutor?"

Jazlyn blinked. Usually judges addressed the prosecutor by name, but once again, he was using a gender-based job title. "No, your honor. We see no need for a change of venue, which would dramatically increase the cost of prosecuting this case. We are confident the defendant can receive a fair trial right here at home. And we see no reason to believe the trial would be any fairer anywhere else. Based on what I saw this morning, the online coverage of the case and…Mayor Pérez herself…is all over the internet, and thus all over the world. And as the court has noted, that is largely her own doing. There is no place we could go where people couldn't access the Internet and potentially be influenced by it. I would simply suggest that the court screen potential jurors and give strong instructions to avoid all coverage, online or elsewhere, pertaining to the case or the parties in it."

"Seems reasonable to me," the judge said. He shifted his weight, adjusting his considerable girth from one direction to the other. "We do have procedures in place. This isn't the first case that ignited a little attention in the outside world."

"If I may." He was certain the judge wouldn't welcome continued argument. But he was also certain he was going down in flames if he didn't speak. "And let me emphasize that I still intend no disrespect. But I'm sure the court is aware that jurors are not always completely obedient when it comes to the judge's instructions." He recalled that several members of the jury that convicted El Chapo said they had followed media coverage, including Twitter feeds, and shared that information with others in the deliberation room.

"We have procedures in place to deal with that as well."

"Still, at the end of the day, no one can compel compliance, unless the court sequesters the jury, and maybe not even then. It is the nature of human beings to be curious. It is the nature of jurors to want to do the best job they possibly can, which means trying to get the whole story, even the parts that are withheld from them in court. In another town, where my client is not the mayor, the temptation to break the rules might not be as great."

"Doubtful," Jazlyn said. "Ms. Pérez is clearly trying to reach a national audience. We can all speculate as to her motives there."

"Nonetheless," he continued, "if there is even the slightest chance the trial might be fairer elsewhere, that the jury might be less tainted, in the name of complete fairness the court should remove the trial to another jurisdiction."

"No trial is ever completely fair," Judge Hayes said. "And no appellate court has ever required that. Human beings are not perfect, and as a result, the institutions of human beings are not perfect."

"Your honor, I think we have to consider the possibility that…our decisions are subject to the influence of prejudice. Prejudice is an invasive thing. Even when we are not consciously aware of it, it can permeate our thoughts and burrow into our decision-making processes.

Intense frown lines etched across the judge's forehead. "What exactly are you saying, counsel?"

"I'm saying that even when jurors are trying to do the best job possible, they are readily influenced by outside forces." That was not at all what he was saying, of course, but it would suffice for an answer. "Let's not turn this into an Iron Man Challenge. Let the case be tried in a calm environment where every prospective juror doesn't already know the mayor, much less already have opinions about her based upon politics, gender, or which newspaper they read."

He felt certain the judge had received the subtext. Whether that would be helpful, or a tragic error, remained to be seen.

The judge spoke, his eyes locked on the defense table. "The court will deny this motion. Traditionally, venue motions are designed to deflect the influence of pretrial publicity. But today we live in a global community, an increasingly connected digital community, and the idea that we can make a trial fairer by moving it a few miles down the road seems truly dated. Better for the court to stick with its tried-and-true procedures for eliminating juror misconduct, and that is what we will do. I will allow extensive questioning of the panel of venirepersons by counsel, and I will quiz the jurors individually and periodically to ensure they have not been compromised by outside influences. Do you understand me, Mr. Pike?"

"If the trial isn't going to be moved," he said quickly, "then I respectfully request that that the jury be sequestered."

"This is completely premature," Jazlyn interjected. "We don't have to make this decision now. Let's see where things are when the trial starts."

"Why delay? There are many reporters in the courtroom. Let's assure them that the court is sensitive to the special circumstances of this case and intends to take all measures, even extraordinary ones, so that justice is served." Appealing to the vanity of the judge, especially an egotistical one, in front of a large audience, could only help. "Let's tell everyone up front the jury will be sequestered."

The judge waved his hand dismissively. "No. Feel free to raise the motion again when it's actually relevant, but sequestering juries is expensive and I've yet to see any studies that suggest it made for a fairer trial. The OJ jury was sequestered for months, and they still proved to be one of the most agenda-ridden juries in the history of the world."

There it was again, the dreaded specter of the OJ trial. Seemed like any time a court needed an excuse to deny something to the defense, they hauled out OJ. "Your honor, surely we won't put a price tag on fairness."

"And I'm not. I'm saying I won't spend a lot of money and not get anything for it."

"Surely it's better to be safe than sorry."

The judge's volume rose. "The only thing I'm sorry about at the moment is that I allowed oral argument. I should have ruled on the briefs."

Maria made a quick slashing motion across her throat. He got the message. He wasn't going to change the judge's mind, and there was no point in making the man mad.

"Very well, your honor. Thank you for your consideration. As you suggest, I'll consider raising this again when we reconvene for trial."

Judge Hayes didn't appear particularly excited about that prospect, but he was placated by the show of deference. "Is there anything else we can address at this time?"

He cleared his throat, weighing all the possibilities in his head at lightning speed. Not the best way to make a decision, but that was what trial practice came down to, most of the time.

He saw Camila looking up at him pointedly, but he didn't

get the impression she wanted him to back down. So he didn't. "Your honor, I'd like to continue exploring the problems inherent in any case attracting this much attention. If we aren't going to move the trial, and we aren't going to sequester the jury, could we at least have a gag order?"

The judge's bushy eyebrows knitted. "You don't want your client giving any more press conferences?"

"I don't want anyone in this case giving press conferences. In fairness, the prosecution has also made statements to the press."

"Not on YouTube."

"They could. And that's my point. Why don't we take this possibility off the table?"

"Are you suggesting that I try to prevent the press from reporting on the case?"

"No." Some courts had tried that in the past, but it usually ended up overturned on constitutional grounds as a prior restraint on speech. "But no public statements by the parties. No leaks about the defendant's private life."

"You can't stop the press from doing what they do."

"No. But bear in mind, the government has now spent days snooping around in my client's home and office. They seized her personal belongings. They mirrored the hard drive on her computers. They confiscated her cell phone. I'm sure they've acquired information that, while not relevant to the murder charge, my client would still not like broadcast to the public. We all have secrets. Doesn't make us criminals. It just, to quote your honor, means we're all human beings and as such not perfect."

The judge hesitated. At least he appeared to be considering the possibility this time. "I don't know. Would Madame Prosecutor like to be heard?"

Jazlyn rose. "Yes, your honor. We see no need for this motion either. Just to be clear, we have no intention of polluting the waters with defamatory leaks. The Code of

Professional Conduct specifically precludes that kind of behavior. But we don't wish to be handcuffed either, or put in a situation where we need opposing counsel's permission to make a statement—especially since I know from experience we would never get it."

The judge nodded. "I tend to agree with the little lady."

Jazlyn's lips parted.

"We're all professionals here," the judge continued, "and I expect you to behave professionally. If I get information indicating otherwise, I will take strong and immediate action. Do you understand what I'm saying, Mr. Pike?"

"Of course."

"If this were a situation where there was a danger of trade secrets being revealed, or security issues were involved, I might consider a motion like this. But that's not what we have here. At best, we have the remote possibility of an invasion of the mayor's privacy. But the truth is, she gave that up long ago. She decided to become a public figure, and that decision automatically comes with a loss of privacy. She chose this bed. Now she'll have to—I mean, you know—I think she understands."

He stared at the judge. *What?*

"Is there anything else?" the judge said, as if daring them to speak.

Both he and Jazlyn gave a slightly stunned shake of the head. The judge's clerk established deadlines for other pretrial matters and set a trial date. He was glad Maria was there to take it all down. Because his brain wasn't working quite right yet.

"Very well." The judge raised his gavel. "Let me say one last thing." He looked directly at Camila. "I may not have forbidden pretrial statements. But if any are made, you may rest assured that I will be listening. And I'd better not hear anything I dislike." He banged the gavel. "Court dismissed."

CHAPTER TWENTY

THE MAN IN THE PENTHOUSE SAT BEHIND HIS HUGE REDWOOD desk with hands calmly folded in his lap. There were no other chairs. The woman on the other side of the desk was forced to stand. Because he wanted it that way.

"Thank you for coming to see me today, Shawna. Is it all right if I call you Shawna?"

She smiled a bit, but it didn't take psychic powers to see the smile was nervous. "Sure. I mean, that's my name, isn't it?"

He glanced at the dossier on his laptop, complete with photos, spreadsheets, and records going back to her grade-school years. "That's your given name. Shawna Marie, correct?"

She said nothing.

"Do you like working at the courthouse?"

Her weight shifted from one foot to the other. "It's a job."

"It is that." He smiled, but in a way he knew was more unsettling than reassuring. Like the smile of a cobra.

"Pays the bills."

"And feeds your...what is it?" Clickety-click. "Three children. And that nephew you're putting through school."

"He's great boy. Smartness off the charts."

"I'm sure." Clickety-click-clack. "B-average student."

"Well...yes."

"And you hope to send him to college."

"Yes."

"Community college?"

"Well...maybe at first."

He looked at her for a long time. He could do a piercing glare without even trying. "You've lasted at the court clerk's office longer than most."

"I run a tight ship." She laughed, but he did not join in. The laughter sounded forced. It faded awkwardly. "I like to think I do a good job."

"You have your hands on the tiller?"

"I like to think so."

"Know what's what?"

"That's part of the job."

"What are your thoughts about this murder trial that's getting so much attention?"

He could see that the mention of the case made her supremely uncomfortable. "You mean with the mayor?"

His eyes turned patronizing. "You know that I do."

"I don't know much about it."

"Now you're being disingenuous."

Her reaction was slow, and her discomfort increased. Possibly, he speculated, because she didn't know what the word meant. Which was exactly what he had intended. "I don't think so..."

"Do you believe she's guilty?"

Shawna looked as if she wanted to scream and run, but of course, she wouldn't. She knew who he was. Every word he spoke was intended to remind her how powerful he was. That's why he orchestrated this meeting in his penthouse suite. To convince her that he was not someone she wanted to trifle with.

"I don't know." Another awkward laugh. "To tell you the truth, I've never liked that woman. Kind of uppity, if you ask me. Thinks she's so all that."

"Do you think Judge Hayes likes her?"

She shrugged. "I don't know."

He stared at her and waited. A long time.

"I have heard him say some things about her that... weren't great. I mean, not now. Before the case began."

"He doesn't care for the mayor?"

"He's a little...old school when it comes to women. Prefers seeing them in...traditional roles."

"Did he mind you running the court clerk's office?"

"Oh no. I don't think so. But in his mind, that's basically a better-than-average secretarial position. Lawyers, that's different. Politicians, that's different."

"Hayes doesn't like women in positions of authority?"

"Like I said. Old school."

He smiled and leaned forward. The cobra was ready to lunge. "See, you've already told me something I didn't know. You understate your value, Shawna. I think you could be valuable to me. If you wish to be."

"What...um, what is it you might want?"

"Information. The most valuable of commodities."

"Like...?"

"I want to know what's going on behind closed doors. In chambers. In conference rooms."

"How would I know—"

"You'll make it your business to know. Ask the judge's clerk. The bailiff. The judge's wife, if necessary."

"That would be awkward."

"Who knows, we might have an opportunity to...influence the judge's decision."

She looked at him incredulously. "Judge Hayes cannot be bought or swayed."

He laughed, so loudly he surprised himself. "Naïve girl.

Everyone can be bought. Everyone has something they'd do anything for. It's simply a matter of knowing the price. And making sure you can offer it."

"I have no way of knowing what's happening in private meetings."

"Use electronic eavesdropping devices."

"Oh, I could never—"

"You've done it before."

The expression drained from her face. "I—don't know what you're talking about."

"Oh, but you do. I'm referring to one of your past transgressions. One of many." He pushed to his feet and leaned closer to her. "I'm talking about Gabriella Valdez. And what you did for a certain someone. Who was in fact working with me at the time. We had big plans that fell apart."

"You—You were behind—"

"That doesn't matter now. I never dwell on the past. I focus on the future. I need to make sure this trial goes the way I want it to go, and I'm concerned about this lawyer the mayor has working for her. He has an annoying history of winning, successes that undercut my plans." He felt his fists clenching. He willed himself to relax. "You will bring me information, whenever you can. I will expect daily reports. I want to know everything there is to know and then some."

"I—I can't do that." Her voice trembled. "I'd lose my job."

"Only if you're clumsy. Or stupid."

"Still—I can't—"

"Would you rather lose your job or your life?"

Her knees wobbled. "Are you—Are you—"

"All I need to do is make one phone call. The DA will learn that you were in league with a certain person currently residing in the penitentiary. That you bugged the consultation room on the third floor. You will be fired. And then you will be tried on criminal charges. And what will happen to you in prison?" He patted his hand against his chest. "It's such an ugly place, prison. Ugly and violent. Almost anything could occur. And so often does."

"I was just trying to get money for my nephew."

"And you succeeded. But actions have consequences."

"I can't spy on a judge."

"You can. Or you can suffer the consequences. It's entirely your choice."

"Please." Her voice choked. She couldn't speak for several seconds. "I wouldn't survive prison."

"You're right. You wouldn't." He eased back into his chair. "Do we have an understanding?"

"Yes. Of course. Anything you want."

"That's what I like to hear." He suddenly reached across the desk and grabbed her arm. "And just to be clear, you will send me a daily report on every development in the case. But you will also report on the activities of that defense lawyer. Watch him like a hawk. If you see anything that might make him vulnerable—a misdeed, a questionable choice, an infelicitous turn of phrase—you will tell me immediately. Any chance to have him fired, removed, disbarred, or eradicated from the face of the earth—I want to hear about it."

He settled into his chair, eyes fluttering, hands once again calmly folded in his lap. "I don't like to lose. And I do not intend to let it happen again."

CHAPTER TWENTY-ONE

DAN WALKED TO THE STREET NEAREST THE MARINA. HE DIDN'T feel like spending the night alone on his boat, and since Jazlyn had already given him the get-lost speech and he wasn't dating anyone, he called Maria. He said they needed to confer on their trial strategy, but she didn't need his help to devise a trial plan.

He just didn't want to be alone.

Maria said she'd pick him up. About three minutes later, he saw a shiny Jag SUV zoom onto the street. Even in the darkness, it was an impressive automobile.

The car pulled up beside him. He opened the door and slid into the passenger seat. "Thanks for coming. I thought we might discuss—"

He glanced at the driver.

It was not Maria.

Dark glasses, beard, and a low-slung hat obscured most of his face.

Before he could open the door again, the driver floored it. In seconds, they were doing sixty down a straight stretch of city road. If the driver made it to the highway, he could maintain that speed for a long time.

Jumping out of a speeding car in the dark seemed like a poor idea, so he tried conversation instead. "Who the hell are you?"

The driver smiled. "I'm your personal chauffeur. Where can I take you?"

"Home."

"To your boat? *The Defender?* Registration #FV67392?"

He felt a chill in his bones. The man was showing off, making a point. Effectively. "Yeah. That one. Take me there."

"In time. Perhaps."

"What do you want?"

"I'm just here to deliver a message." He careened around a curve, hitting it so hard wheels lifted off the pavement. "From my boss."

"And who would that be?"

"Names aren't important."

"Useful, though."

"My boss is concerned about this case you're handling."

His teeth clenched. "Your boss wants me to quit?"

"Nah. That would attract too much suspicion. You can keep the case. Just make damn sure you lose."

He scanned the car, searching for something he might be able to turn into a weapon. He didn't see any contenders. Could he somehow signal? Get someone's attention? Seemed unlikely. Grab the wheel? Too dangerous. Punch the driver? Equally risky. "You realize I'll probably lose even if I try to win. The prosecution has a strong case and the press has already convicted her."

The driver jerked the wheel one way then the other, throwing him wildly back and forth across the Jag. He braced his arms against the top and side of the car, trying to avoid bashing into the dashboard. Was this some bizarre suicide mission? If the driver crashed at this speed, they were both dead.

He pulled out his cell phone. "I've put up with enough of this. Take me home or I'm calling the cops."

"Put that thing away."

He held his finger over the screen. "Last chance. Take me home."

"Put it away, Pike."

"Dialing." He touched the screen.

"Put it away or you're dead." A glint of reflected light told him the driver held a gun.

He weighed the chances he might be able to wrestle the gun away. It was not impossible. The driver had to keep one hand on the wheel, and for matter, had to keep his eyes on the road. Or should.

But could he get the gun before the man pulled the trigger?

Doubtful.

He eased the phone back into his pocket.

"That's a good boy. Now listen. We're watching you, understand? We're watching you every second of every day. Inside the courtroom and outside. We have eyes everywhere."

He remembered earlier, when he thought he saw someone outside the bakery. Was that this goon? Or someone else working for the same boss?

"Go ahead, try the damn case. But you make sure you lose. Botch a cross-examination. Give a lame closing. We don't care how you do it. All we care is that the bitch ends up behind bars where she belongs. For a good long time. Until she's no longer a contender. For anything."

"Are you that afraid of her?"

"It ain't about bein' afraid. It's about being smart."

This seemed like an extreme way to eliminate an opponent, even given today's toxic political environment. There had to something more to it. "Do whatever you like. You don't scare me."

The driver grinned. "We won't just be watching you, of course. We'll be watching Maria Morales. You like her, right?"

He did not respond.

"We'll be watching Jimmy Armstrong. We'll be watching Garrett Wainwright. We'll be watching Jazlyn Prentice. And what's that cute little girl of hers called? Esperanza? We'll be watching her too."

His eyes turned cold. "Representing clients literally *is* my business."

"Well, do a crappy job of it, or everyone you know in the world is dead. Got it, Pike?"

He realized he was breathing hard and fast. His pulse raced, almost as fast as the death car he was riding in. "I noticed you didn't threaten my client."

"Boss don't wanna do that. Says it might turn her into a martyr. He wants to destroy her a different way."

By turning her into a convicted murderer. "Are you waiting to hear me agree? Do you want me to sign a contract in blood?"

"You're a smart boy. We're confident you'll use common sense." All at once, much too suddenly, the driver slammed on the brakes. Dan's head crashed into the dash. The driver must've laid a mile of tread on the pavement. "We've arrived."

He looked out the window. They'd done a complete loop. He was back where the man had picked him up. And if he wasn't mistaken, that was Maria's car a few feet in front of them.

Before he knew what was happening, the passenger side door popped open and a strong pair of hands shoved him out of the car. He toppled face-first onto the pavement. The car peeled off into the darkness. He didn't have time to get a license number.

Slowly, he pushed himself off the pavement. He sat upright, then touched his face. His chin was bleeding, and his head felt like it had been cut open.

He heard a car door open. Maria ran toward him. "Dan! What happened?"

He shook his head. "I'm not sure."

She helped him to his feet. "Are you okay to walk?"

"I'm fine. Just a little…shaken."

"Who was that?"

He limped toward her car. His left ankle felt twisted, maybe sprained. "Someone who does not want us to win Camila's case."

Maria pulled out her phone. "I'll call the police. Then Jazlyn."

"No." He clamped his hand over her phone. "They can't do anything. I have no ID to offer. And it might be perceived as a stunt to garner sympathy."

He braced himself against her car and eventually opened the passenger door. "Our priority is Camila. Doing what's best for her and her case. Even though someone very much doesn't want us to." He slowly lowered himself into the seat. "And they are…watching."

CHAPTER TWENTY-TWO

DAN COULD TELL MARIA WAS UNHAPPY WHEN SHE PICKED HIM up the next morning, even before she spoke. The morning was crisp and bright, typical St. Pete paradise sunrise. But the atmosphere inside the car was entirely different. He could feel the fog.

"You're still angry." He believed in being direct rather than letting things fester.

Maria, however, might be more in the festering camp. "I don't know what you mean."

"Because I didn't go to the police. About last night." He'd cleaned and bandaged the wounds on his face, but he knew they were still impossible to miss.

Her neck twisted at an unnatural angle. "You're...a grown adult. You can make decisions for yourself."

"But you don't approve."

"I'm not your mother."

"But you don't approve."

Her head whipped around with such suddenness it took him by surprise. "No, I don't approve! You could've been killed! You're being a blithering idiot! A stupid blithering nincompoop."

"Wow. Harsh, bro." He tried to smile. "Look, if he'd wanted to kill me, he would've killed me. He just wanted to scare me."

"Or maybe you got lucky."

"I read him as soon as I saw him—best I could, given his disguise. He was under orders to put a chill on our defense. But another murder would've attracted too much attention. And it would've made it clear there was a murderer in town who wasn't wearing an electronic ankle bracelet."

"You're an officer of the court. You have an ethical obligation to report misconduct."

"I hardly think—"

"You have a team that depends on you! You have friends! You have—You—" Her voice choked off. She turned away, presumably so he wouldn't see the tears.

He fell silent for a moment. "I'm sorry."

She wiped a hand across her eyes. "I'm sorry, too." She drew in her breath. "But what if he comes back?"

"He won't."

"You don't know that."

"He's already accomplished his mission."

She put the car in Park and leaned toward him, invading his space. "And what happens when they see you aren't backing off? What will they try then?"

That thought had occurred to him of course. And he didn't have an answer. "I don't know."

"You should carry a gun."

"No way. No one does that."

"Dan, this is Florida. Teachers can wear guns in the classroom."

"Well, I won't. I couldn't get it past the metal detectors in the courthouse. I think you're overreacting because you feel—"

"Don't mansplain this to me, you jerk. *I'm worried about you!*"

He took a deep breath and fell silent. She pressed her hand against her forehead.

A moment later, she reached out and ever so gently touched his hand. "Your friends care about you, Dan. I love this firm and I believe in what Mr. K is doing. But no case is worth dying for."

He straightened awkwardly. "I appreciate what you're saying. But going to the police won't accomplish anything. I didn't get any info that would enable them to track the driver down. And the press would turn it into some nefarious scheme to invent a conspiracy. The judge might, too."

"I'm beginning to think there *is* a conspiracy." She pulled the car out into the street. "Someone seriously wants to terminate Camila's political career." She paused. "And I don't think they're too crazy about you, either."

DAN WAS A HUGE FAN OF PASS-A-GRILLE BEACH, ONE OF THE most historic parts of St. Pete. Even though shopping wasn't typically his idea of a good time, he loved to stroll down to Eighth Avenue and check out the activity. In truth, it was only a short stretch, just a couple of blocks from bay to beach, but those blocks were jam-packed with quirky shops, galleries, and restaurants. It was also the best place to catch a shuttle to Shell Key—and the only way to get there, since there was no bridge.

Maria pointed. "This way."

"You know your way around?"

"Are you kidding? Best art jewelry in the city. They know me by name."

"Of course. Been to the new restaurant yet?"

"No, but I hear it's delicious."

"Good word of mouth?"

"Good Yelp."

They saw Deputy Mayor Denton in front of the restaurant, glad-handing and posing for photos with citizens. He seemed like a natural politician. A sincere smile. A gift for making people feel as if they were the center of his attention.

"What do you think?"

Maria grimaced. "I don't trust him."

"Something in his eyes?"

"Something on his legs. He's wearing corduroy."

"You're going to hang him for fashion crimes?"

"Probably wears Crocs on the beach. Ick."

He spotted Benji outside the new seafood restaurant. She looked prim and professional, as always. "How goes the dedication?"

"About as you would expect. Ceremonial nonsense. A chance for the Deputy Mayor to get on the news, and a chance for the new crab shack to get some free publicity."

"How are you holding up?"

Just the tiniest twitch in the eye. "I'm fine." She flashed a fake smile. "Holding up. Best as possible, given the circumstances. I will be very glad when this is over and Camila is my mayor again."

"You and me both."

"Thank you for getting her out of lockup."

"Just doing my job."

"I hate to think about what might have happened if she'd been behind bars much longer."

"While we're doing the mutual-admiration-society thing, thank you for sticking with the job. I know how you feel about the deputy mayor. Learned anything interesting?"

Benji looked both ways, as if checking to make sure no one else was within earshot. "Denton had a visitor last night," she whispered. "Very late last night."

"At the office?"

She nodded. "I was burning the midnight oil, putting the final touches on this PR dog-and-pony show. I thought I was the only one still in the office. When I heard someone creeping in, I thought it was a burglar. I was halfway to dialing 9-1-1 when I heard Denton's voice. He brought the visitor into his office and they spoke for about ten minutes. Very hushed tones. I couldn't pick up a word of it. But I feel confident they weren't discussing zoning issues."

"Can you describe the visitor?"

"Not well. Pretty sure it was a man, though. Face was obscured. Big beard. Hat pulled down low."

Like the driver in the car that grabbed him. "How long was he there?"

"About ten minutes. As he left, I heard Denton say, 'Keep me informed.' Then he grinned a bit and added, 'And drive carefully.'"

He felt the hairs on the back of his neck stand on end. Was this a reference to the Jag abduction? Or was he working too hard to make puzzle pieces fit together based upon superficial coincidences? "If that man shows up again, try to find out who he is. This might relate to the case."

"I thought the same thing. And I also—"

"Benji, is this my ten o'clock?"

He turned and saw Deputy Mayor—now Acting Mayor—Alex Denton. Crease across the bridge of his nose. Deep-etched forehead lines. Biceps detectible through his Oxford shirt.

"You must be Mr. Pike."

He extended his hand. "Pleased to meet you, sir."

"The pleasure is mine. I've heard a lot about you." He pivoted. "I assume this is Ms. Morales."

Maria took his hand. "Thank you for meeting with us, Mr. Mayor."

"Acting Mayor, please. I'm happy to help. Camila and I may have had our differences, but I find it inconceivable that she was involved in anything as ugly as that bakery business."

Benji excused herself. He watched Denton carefully as he

spoke, trying to discern how much of this was politician BS and how much of it evidenced genuine feelings, if any, for Camila. "I can't believe it myself. Though I haven't known her nearly as long as you."

"Why don't we go for a stroll? People like to see their mayor on the street, acting something vaguely like a regular person." He grinned a little. "And I'm afraid that's as close as we're going to get to anything resembling privacy today."

He couldn't object to staying outside, since it was a gorgeous day and he loved the neighborhood. "Do you know anything about the bakery incid—"

The mayor interrupted. "Ms. Morales, have you seen the new line of Silpada jewelry at Bamboozle's?" He pointed toward a shop with a shell mosaic mermaid outside. "It's extraordinary."

Maria's eyes brightened. "No, I haven't."

"It's just out. My wife can't get enough of that stuff."

Maria laughed. "That sounds like a dangerous addiction."

"Tell me about it. Designer jewelry doesn't fit into a deputy mayor's budget."

He smiled, but the report Garrett gave him earlier said that Denton had been a banker and that he was independently wealthy. Politics was basically his retirement job.

"I have a little Silpada lapel pin," Maria said, "a star shape. My daddy gave it to me. He couldn't afford much. But he wanted me to have that. Because he said I was his superstar."

"Sounds like a fine man."

He thought it was time to try to steer this chitchat back to the main topic. "Sir, do you know anything about Nick Mansfield? Or what happened to him?"

"Sorry. I already talked to the police, but the bottom line is, I don't got bupkis. I didn't know the man well, and frankly, I didn't care for the man at all."

That caught his attention. "You didn't like having Mansfield around?"

'I didn't think he belonged in the mayor's office. I didn't think he belonged in any government office. I thought the only reason he was there was because he was bonking the mayor." He caught himself. "Oh—I'm sorry, Ms. Morales. That was crude."

"No worries. I've heard cruder. And call me Maria."

"Thank you. I will. And again, sorry. But you know what I'm saying."

He knew, and he didn't want to let it go that easily. "Camila told me she only went out with the man once, and that was after his employment was terminated."

Denton raised an eyebrow. "Really. Only once."

"You don't think that's correct?"

"I didn't follow the two around. What do I know?" He took a few quiet steps. "But more than once I caught them in the breakroom or the hallway and they seemed..." He tossed his head back and forth. "You know."

"I don't. Can you tell me?"

He shrugged. "Flirty. Handsy."

"Like what specifically?"

"She couldn't keep away from him. Like she'd never had sex before in her life. I mean, yes, he was younger and vaguely handsome, in an underwear model sort of way. But come on. She was the mayor. She should know how to behave herself, at least in public, if not in private."

He watched Denton's face carefully, but the man played it close to the vest. Not many tells. Should he believe this? Or write it off as slut-shaming by a politician who did not want her to return to her previous office?

"What about the campaign finance problems? Know anything about that?"

"It's all part of the same thing, isn't it? Corruption in one arena is often indicative of corruption in another."

"That assessment seems severe."

"Call it what you like. That business with the loans? That's just skeezy. My background is in finance, and I'm here to tell you, that's a mistake no one could make by accident. That's the sign of an administration that doesn't care about the rules."

"Does this have anything to do with Mansfield?"

"He comes from the banking world too. And what a coincidence—just about the time he comes on board, doing no-one-knows-what, she gets involved in these dubious campaign finance schemes."

"Are you the one who turned Camila in to the DA?"

He stopped walking. He seemed taken aback. "Are you joking? Reporting on my boss? That would be grossly disloyal."

"Or an ethical obligation, depending on how you look at it."

"I didn't feel that was my role. I tried to rise above the darkness, if you know what I mean. I waited quietly for my opportunity to do better."

"And now that opportunity has arisen, hasn't it?"

Denton's eyes narrowed. "I'm not sure what you mean."

"You're mayor now, for all intents and purposes."

"And," Maria added, "the word is you're planning to run for mayor in the next election."

Denton paused thoughtfully. "I think we need continuity. I'm in charge, but I don't have the authority of a duly elected mayor. I think it's in everyone's best interest to eliminate that problem. Get the political capital I need to do the job right."

Denton was slipping into campaign rhetoric, no doubt his comfort zone. "Forgive me for saying so, but you seem rather…judgmental."

"Why shouldn't I be? I have the same right as any other citizen to call people out when they don't live up to their promises. I worked hard to get where I am today. I put in my ten- thousand hours. I rose to the top of the banking world. Once I was financially secure, I wanted to see if I could contribute to society in a bigger way, to give back. I'm a patriot, and I believe we all have a duty to serve our country. This is how I serve."

"By trashing Camila behind her back?"

"By rooting out corruption, yes, and by fighting for what is right. Do you care about the future of this country? Because I believe we're at a crossroads, and if we take only a few more steps in the wrong direction, it will be too late for anyone to save us. That woman may have you caught in her web, but I've seen her behind closed doors, and let me tell you, that hot tamale is little better than a whore, swinging her ass for money and anything else she wants."

His lips parted wordlessly.

Maria cut in. "Forgive me, Mayor, but there are rumors that you've had an affair or two yourself. Isn't this a double standard? Women can't do what men do every day?"

"I never put my hands on someone in the office kitchen, that's for damn sure. Even when I wasn't at my best, I kept it out of sight."

"I think you don't like the idea of a woman in power. I think you resent her. Maybe you're even a little scared of her."

"Balderdash. FYI, I've hired more women than Camila ever did. I think the gender balance should be fifty-fifty in all arenas, and that's not just a theory, that's what I put into prac-tice in my bank. Why didn't Camila do the same? The only male she ever hired was her personal boy toy. Do you think she cares about women's issues? The only person she cares about is herself. She's really more like a man than a woman."

"What does that mean?"

"Look at her! Listen to her! Thinks she has the biggest dick in every room she enters. More than once I've wondered if she was secretly trans or a hermaphrodite or something."

He drew in his breath. "Not that there's anything wrong with that. But you know what I'm saying."

"You want to destroy her. And if that's your goal...there's no telling what you might do."

Denton stepped closer. "Let me give you a heads-up, lawyer. I don't have to destroy her. She's already destroyed herself. I don't care if she's convicted. Her career is over. No one could bounce back from this. She couldn't get elected dogcatcher. No matter what, most people will always think of her as the chick who baked her boyfriend in an oven. She wanted him dead *bad*."

He shook his head. "Everything about this case suggests that murder was only one goal. The frame was just as important. Someone wanted to bring Camila down." He paused. "Someone who didn't like her at all."

"Are you planning to turn me into your straw man? Your SODDIT? That's what lawyers say, isn't it? Tell the jury Some Other Dude Did It." He stepped in closer, practically nose to nose. "Don't screw with me, Pike. I have lots of money. And friends."

"Like the one you met last night in your office?"

Denton pulled back. That one caught him by surprise.

"Who was that, anyway? He neglected to give me his name last night in the car."

Denton took another step back, glaring. "You mess with me and you will be very sorry, Pike."

"Is that a threat?"

"I don't threaten. But I will protect myself. I didn't get this far by being weak. I know how to cover my back. Find another SODDIT. I'm no one's victim. Not now, not ever."

CHAPTER TWENTY-THREE

JIMMY APPROACHED THE FRONT DESK OF THE COURT CLERK'S office. He had deliberately chosen to come at this time, just before closing. He knew Shawna would be out front, and probably not all that busy. Shawna was the big boss of the office, but she took the front desk during the last hour, just to keep her hand in. He'd known her for years and could usually get what he wanted.

"Shawna!" He stretched his arms across the dividing counter. "You look marvelous."

"I look like I've been working in the clerk's office for far too long."

"You rise above your environment. How's that nephew of yours? Got him through college yet?"

"Well, I got him in. That's a start."

"A big start. Tuition at USF? That's not chump change. You must've had to move heaven and earth."

"That would be one way of putting it. He's going to community college for a year, then he'll transfer. How's Hank?"

"Still the love of my life. Being married to a doctor is so

much cheaper than health insurance. Are you getting some kind of treatment, Shawna? Your skin is positively glowing."

"Just something I got at Sephora. Had a little more money than usual this month, so I splurged."

"Have you tried a hydro-facial?"

"Can't say that I have."

"It is the absolute best. You'll be amazed. There's a little place in Safety Harbor that does them, and it's not as expensive as you might think. The treatment cleanses your skin of impurities, while the technician removes dead skin and hydrates you with their secret serums. They have this wand thingy that gets up close and personal with your pores, making sure you get just the right amount of whatever you need. Nutrients in, toxins out. Seriously, it'll take ten years off you. When you're done, you'll look nineteen."

She gave him a dubious look. "What is it you want, Jimmy?"

"You wound me. My words come from deep-seated devotion."

"I know. But seriously, what do you want? And let me say up front—no special favors, no bending the rules."

"Perish the thought."

"And I won't change my mind for strawberry cream pies."

Just as well. Dan was the one who actually made those inducements. "I just need to file a motion."

"You don't need me for that. Any fool can do it."

He decided not to take offense. "It's a motion *in limine*. But we want it filed *in camera*. Judge's eyes only."

"I need a judge's order before I can do that."

"But I'd have to file for that. And we're talking about some seriously confidential information. You know how famous our client is."

"You mean the mayor? Yeah, I've heard of her."

"And like it or not, we have to discuss some personal

matters. Ironically, we have to reveal the nature of the personal matters to get the judge to exclude them at trial. But if the press has already splashed everything across Page One, it becomes a Pyrrhic gesture. You see the dilemma."

"No one ever said being a lawyer was easy."

"Actually, Hank says it all the time. You know how doctors are about lawyers. So insecure."

"And you live with this man?"

"He just can't quit me."

She grinned. "This is highly irregular."

He pushed a sealed envelope across the counter. "Just take this to the judge. Let him decide. He can call the prosecutor in for a closed hearing, if necessary."

"He won't like this."

"He will appreciate the need for secrecy. The general public does not need to know. Just us, the DA, and the judge." He winked. "And you, of course."

Her head rose slowly. "This envelope contains information...no one else knows?"

"Definitely not part of the public record."

"But it might be harmful to the mayor's case if it got out?"

"That's about the size of it. Hence the motion."

"I understand." She nodded, then quickly tugged the envelope across the counter. "I'll take care of it."

"I knew I could count on you."

"I'll take it to the judge. I won't actually file it yet."

"Can you do that?"

"It is irregular." Pause. "But this is a special case. And a need-to-know situation."

"Shawna, you're an angel."

"Yeah, yeah. Just don't tell anyone about this."

"I won't breathe a word. Ever. And next time you're in a spa—first facial is on me."

"I might take you up on that."

"I'm counting on it. You've helped me more than you can possibly imagine."

"No problem," she replied, as if lost in thought. "I'll do what I need to do."

CHAPTER TWENTY-FOUR

Dan was pleased to be in the driver's seat. He liked the Jag, though it was no substitute for his Bentley. But mostly he liked the feeling of being in control. He didn't have to wait for a ride and hope it was someone who wasn't trying to kill him.

Maria decided to stay in and work on her trial plan. She had an archive of jury-pool stats she wanted to review. Garrett was buried under research. He said he had serious questions about some of the forensic reports and the conclusions the prosecution drew from them. He didn't quite say it, but he seemed to think the DA's office was being pushed to reach conclusions they couldn't support. And one piece of evidence—the flask found at the scene of the crime—had disappeared.

Since Maria was busy, Jimmy rode with him. He always preferred to have a "wingman" when he did these interviews. His powers of observation were excellent, but that didn't preclude the possibility that someone else might see something he did not. He just wished Jimmy would stop referring to the man they were meeting as "Lex Luthor."

"Or the Kingpin," Jimmy said, in an ominous tone that made it sound as if he were describing Jack the Ripper.

"Wheels within wheels. He's the primary mover and shaker in the city. But he does it all quietly and through minions."

He arched an eyebrow. "Minions?"

"Hoods. Henchmen. Goons. Call them what you like. He has people at his disposal. He can get anything done."

Including an abduction and twilight speed race around downtown? "You may be letting your fondness for comic books get the best of you."

"This man is a comic-book villain in the flesh. He's evil. He's large. He's bald."

"Well, that proves it."

"Don't make the mistake of underestimating him, Dan. He's been around a long time, and he's taken down people who were richer and better connected than you. He's a force of nature. He will eat you alive."

Ok, now this high drama was starting to get to him. "All I want is information. This whole mess started as a campaign finance case, and his nonprofit appears to be at the heart of that. Mr. K thought he was connected to it. Sweeney might be able to tell us something useful."

"He's not going to give you anything useful, Dan. Not without exacting a price."

He pulled into the parking lot outside the SweeTech office complex. "You seriously think I would pay him for information?"

"He won't want money. He has tons of money. He'll want—"

"My first-born child?"

Jimmy stared at him, completely serious. "Your soul."

He pushed the transmission into Park. "I'll avoid any contracts that have to be signed in blood."

———————

INSIDE THE LOBBY, DAN INTRODUCED HIMSELF AT THE

security desk. A few minutes later, a woman in high heels and a tight black skirt appeared.

"I'm Prudence Hancock."

"Pleased to meet you." Short hair, layered, swept. Earring on the left, not the right. Skinny and dressed to kill. "You work for Mr. Sweeney?"

"I'm his executive assistant."

"And what exactly does an executive assistant do?"

"Anything Mr. Sweeney wants me to do." She led them to the top floor, explaining that her boss's office was the penthouse suite, consuming the entire floor, accessible only by this private elevator. "He likes a lot of room to spread out."

A reference to his weight? Or his ego? "How long have you worked for him?"

"Six years."

"Worked your way up from the secretarial pool?"

Her lips pursed slightly. "In the first place, we don't have secretaries. We have assistants. And I have a Business degree from Yale and a Masters in Computer Science, so…no."

"My apologies. How did you get interested in computing?"

"Asa Lovelace was my hero as a child."

Was it intimidating to hear that someone's childhood hero was someone he'd never heard of? A little. But then, everything about this conversation was a little intimidating. "I can't place the name…"

"Daughter of Lord Byron. But more importantly, a pioneer in the field of computing. Some say she virtually invented computing. Of course, she received no fame or fortune for it. White males took all the credit."

They entered the elevator. "I'm surprised you're willing to work as someone's assistant."

"What job could be better? Mr. Sweeney is a god."

He and Jimmy exchanged a look.

He recalled Jimmy suggesting that Sweeney might be

threatened by a female mayor. "Is your boss on board with your…feminist ideals?"

"He supports me one hundred percent. Contrary to sexist clichés, Mr. Sweeney has no trouble with strong women. He does, however, dislike stupid women using their gender as a substitute for talent."

And was that his assessment of Camila Pérez?

Prudence continued. "Mr. Sweeney came to my assistance when…when I really needed it. My family and I needed it. I'm still grateful. But this position has allowed me to be on the cutting edge of new tech. Mr. Sweeney practically invented cloud computing, and now he's at the forefront of the coming revolution."

"Which is?"

"Quantum computing. You think computers are amazing now? You ain't seen nothin' yet."

They stepped off the elevator—and entered something that looked like no lobby he had ever seen. This was not a tile-floor generic corporate waiting area. This was more like the foyer of the Taj Mahal. Venetian marble walls. Original art illuminated by tiny raised spotlights. A shell mosaic on the floor in the shape of the SweeTech logo.

Jimmy let out a slow whistle. "Very schway."

Prudence adjusted her glasses. "Something wrong, Mr. Pike?"

"No. I just hate to walk on this. Should I take off my shoes?"

She laughed. "It's meant to be walked upon. Unless you'd like me to carry you."

"That won't be necessary."

"I'm stronger than I look."

"I'm pretty strong myself."

"Must be all that kitesurfing."

He looked up slowly. "Perhaps…"

"I'm a fan of kitesurfing myself. Have you tried psicobloc?"

"Deep-water rock climbing?"

"The purest form of rock climbing. No gear, no safety net, just you, a pair of climbing shoes, a chalk bag, and extremely deep water. Have you tried it?"

"No. People say that's most dangerous activity in the world."

She shrugged. "I'm an adrenaline junkie."

He quickly scanned her whippet-thin frame. "And it requires an enormous amount of physical strength."

"That I have," she said, opening a transparent glass door. "Martial arts training since I was four."

They stepped into an enormous office space that was just as ornate as the lobby outside, maybe more so. Light streamed from windows that covered the entire back wall, top to bottom. The desk was almost as long as the office—rosewood, if he wasn't mistaken. Probably cost in the high five figures. The office had been exquisitely decorated in something resembling a Jules Verne vision of the future. A little steam-punk, a lot of money.

He felt a rumbling of the floor tiles. He was reminded of the moment in *Jurassic Park* when the hero first senses the tyrannosaurus is approaching.

"Daniel Pike. So good to finally meet you face to face."

The man approaching was large, almost huge. Not exactly fat, though certainly not trim. Impressive. Massive. He wore an all-white suit. The only spot of color was a black tie. Bald head. Strong hands. Short legs.

Sweeney took tiny steps, but he moved quickly, shaking both men's hands. "You're Mr. Alexander?"

"I am."

"How is that husband of yours?"

Jimmy was slow to respond. Were they supposed to pretend they were old friends? "He's doing well."

"Probably overworked and underpaid, like every ER doc, right?"

"That's what he says. How do you—"

"I own the hospital."

A slow double take. "You do?"

"Not many people know that. I keep it quiet. The hospital was in financial trouble a few years back and I was able to help. Modernized it. Made sure they had the tech needed to survive. But I'm afraid we're still not paying the ER docs what they deserve."

"Well...we get by."

"I'm sure. Why don't you bring Hank around to see me sometime? I use many physicians in my global operations. Maybe I could find him something...less stressful than ER work. And more profitable."

"I'll mention it to him."

Sweeney gestured expansively, pointing toward his enormous desk. Two chairs rested on the opposite side. "Please. Sit with me."

They followed his lead and took the chairs designated for them. Prudence stood about a foot behind them, as if ready to fulfill Sweeney's every command. Or to keep an eye on them. Or to prevent them from leaving.

"May I get you gentlemen something to drink, Mr. Pike?"

He smiled. "A little early for me."

"Oh, I didn't mean alcohol. Perhaps an oolong tea? Best stuff in the world, and good for you. Full of antioxidants. I have a samovar made fresh every morning. Or a fruit juice, if you prefer? I have a mango pineapple blend that is the tartest restorative you've ever tasted."

"We're fine, thank you. Can I ask about your involvement with CRED?"

"Right down to business, that's how you operate, right? No beating around the bush. I like that." Sweeney leaned into his chair. Despite the fact that Sweeney was not particularly tall, seated in that chair, the man seemed to loom over them. Was it on a raised platform, perhaps? "CRED is a nonprofit organization designed to keep our political system honest."

Jimmy cleared his throat. They had agreed in advance that he would play "bad cop" in this conversation, but at the moment, he seemed reluctant to start. "Some people say it's an attempt to keep our political system under your control."

"Some people see bogeymen under ever bedsheet. There's nothing wrong with people of means being involved in politics. We have the same right as anyone else, don't we?"

Jimmy nodded. "And far more clout."

"I earned this clout. No one ever gave me anything. I built my business up from nothing. Started with a small Radio Shack franchise, and now I run one of the top tech firms in the nation. Biggest in Florida."

"They say you're a billionaire."

"Several times over. What of it? I've used that money to help this city and this state. I employ more than ten thousand people. I've added hundreds of millions to the annual economy. I took a city that some said was dying and turned it around, made it less dependent on tourism. I became a natural leader in this community. Far more than any elected official. Politicians come and go, rarely lasting long and rarely accomplishing much. I've been here for decades, and I'll still be around decades from now, still on top, still setting the course."

"Some people think you're hungry for power."

Sweeney rose slightly. "Do you care about the future of this country, Mr. Pike?"

It seemed like he'd heard that question a lot lately. "Of course I do, but—"

"Then look around you. Look at the state of the world. We need real leaders. Not bleeding hearts who only care about their approval ratings. People who are willing to make hard choices even when they aren't popular. As a nation, we rank twenty-seventh in health care. Kuwait is the richest country in the world. We're not even in the top ten. And do you know why? Because our leaders are weak. Self-interested. Too worried about being popular to be smart. How long can we go on pretending that nothing is wrong? We are being destroyed—by mediocrity."

"Is that why you dislike Camila Pérez? Because she attracted a lot of attention that you felt she hadn't earned?"

Sweeney smiled. "I believe that's what you lawyers call a leading question. I never said I disliked her."

"I've heard it. From more than one source."

"In many ways, I admire her."

"You refer to her as 'La Cucaracha.'"

Sweeney sighed. "That's simply a reference to her relative lack of power. People like her attract a lot of attention, but don't have much say in what actually gets done. In this world, people become famous even though they've never contributed anything of value. Children are led by so-called influencers, people whose only skill is posting selfies and tweeting. I wanted to make a real difference in this town. And I did."

"To be fair, my client has accomplished a great deal in her few years in office."

Sweeney made a snorting noise. "Cut away all the PR and hype, and what has she actually accomplished? Splashed some girly paint downtown. Built a park. Great for PR spreads, but she hasn't improved the economy in the slightest. She's all sparkle, no diamond."

"You want to push her out of office."

"I don't have to push her out. She's done it herself. She wouldn't be in this mess if she hadn't been led by her loins. Any fool could see that banker was bad news. Basically, an alt-right gigolo."

It took him a moment to catch up. "Wait a minute. Alt-right?"

Sweeney tucked in his chin. "Don't tell me you didn't know."

He looked at Jimmy, then looked back. "This is the first I've heard about a link between Mansfield and the alt-right."

Sweeney made an exasperated sigh and tapped on his laptop. "You do have investigators at this alleged firm of yours, don't you?"

"Well…one."

Sweeney punched a few keys, put a flash drive into his computer's USB drive. "Here. Take my entire dossier. As you'll see, Nick Mansfield was an unpleasant piece of work. Extremist. Dangerous. Any savvy politician would avoid him." He pulled out the flash drive and passed it across the desk. "Your client, however, slept with him."

He took the drive. Probably all bogus information, but it would be irresponsible not to look. "I think Camila refused to be your puppet. So you decided to eliminate her."

Sweeney slowly laid his hands down on the desk. His eyes seemed heavy-lidded. "Is that what you came here for? Am I to be your trial scapegoat? Will you try to convince the jury that the richest man in the city decided to melt four powerless losers?"

Several points of interest in that statement, but he decided to remain on target. "I'm not making anything up. Your organization started an investigation into campaign financing on its own initiative, then gave the results to the DA."

"We had no choice. Withholding evidence of a felony is a federal crime."

"You didn't have to start the investigation. You chose to do so."

"Only a criminal fears investigation."

"I didn't say anyone feared it, I said—"

"Are you criticizing me for being a concerned citizen?" He leaned forward across his desk. The facade of geniality seemed to crack. "We need more concerned citizens. We need more watchdogs. We're very much in danger of seeing this nation taken from the real Americans and given to the pretenders and the dead weight."

"And by real Americans, you mean…"

"Don't try to make this racist. I'm talking about the people who worked hard to forge a nation out of a wilderness. That's the spirit we need today. Not people who lounge around binging Netflix shows all day, then expect a handout to pay their bills."

"Mayor Pérez is Latinx. And a woman."

"And don't try to turn this into male chauvinism. I love women. Strong women. Like Prudence here. She never expected a handout and wouldn't take it if it were offered. She's living off her accomplishments, not her ability to generate photo ops and sound bites." He shifted his gaze to Jimmy. "Or to put it another way, Prudence is Catwoman. Pérez is Vicki Vale."

He didn't need Jimmy's DC Comics expertise to follow that reference. Catwoman was the tough sexy one, almost Batman's equal. Vicki Vale was the weak-broth Lois Lane knockoff.

But more importantly, how did Sweeney know Jimmy was a comics buff?

"This is not the first CRED project," Sweeney continued. "More than once our investigations have exposed corruption and led to politicians being removed from office. We are performing a public service and most people appreciate that. The exception being, of course, those who get caught with their hand in the cookie jar."

"Nonetheless, it does appear that you wanted to cause problems for the mayor."

"She only has problems because she's guilty. And so far as I can tell, the DA has dropped the campaign finance charges anyway, so what's your beef?"

"They've only put those charges on the back burner

because they become irrelevant if the mayor goes down for murder."

"Do you seriously think I had anything to do with that? I didn't own that bakery. I didn't sleep with that gigolo. And I certainly didn't melt four men. Stupidest way I ever saw to dispose of someone. Like an elaborate death trap from the old Adam West *Batman* show."

"I love that show," Jimmy murmured.

Sweeney stopped suddenly—then laughed. "Yeah. Actually, so did I." He placed his hands behind his head. "We're running a sale on our laptops this week. Probably the last model before we go quantum. Dan, you need a computer?"

He smiled. "Do you take Groupons?"

"I was thinking of it more as a gift. A token of respect to the St. Pete attorney with the winningest record."

"You're familiar with my record?"

"Mr. Pike, surely by now you realize that I am familiar with everything that goes on in this city. And that includes the man some say is the sharpest defense lawyer in the state."

"Oh, there are many good—"

"I admired the way you handled the defense of Gabriella Valdez, for instance."

"You're familiar with that?"

"Of course. It involved many of the city's most important citizens. Let me ask you a blunt question. Do you really need this Pérez case in your life right now?"

"Sorry, not following."

"Only a few months ago you were fired by a top law firm. Your career was in tatters. Some still consider you washed up. A has-been. And now you want to take on this unwinnable case? You want to take on me?"

This wasn't going anywhere. And it was becoming supremely uncomfortable. "I think maybe it's time for us to—"

"You got that little girl adopted. Now that was good work."

He froze. Sweeney was talking about Esperanza Coto. Jazlyn's adopted daughter. "Yeeeees…"

"Such a smart girl. Energetic. Strong." He paused. "I hope she grows up to be a Catwoman. Not a Vicki Vale."

He eyed the man carefully. "What exactly are you saying?"

"Only that I hope she grows up…" He sighed again. "Perhaps I should leave it at that. I hope she grows up."

He rose from his chair, hoping his knees weren't shaking. "Don't you threaten that girl. Don't you dare."

"You care for her. As if she were your own."

"What of it?"

"I think you care about your client, too. More than you let on." He smiled. "Of course, you can't do anything about that while the case is pending. You'd be disbarred. But later…" He shrugged. "Be careful of women, Mr. Pike. They will destroy you, if you let them."

"I don't consider women a threat."

"Have you read your Bible? Eve. Delilah. Jezebel. They will expel you from paradise, sap your strength. If you allow it."

"I have an ethical obligation to represent my client to the best of my ability."

"Because your boss told you to? Don't you get tired of having your strings pulled?"

"I don't know what you're talking about."

"I'm talking about the mysterious Mr. K." He glanced downward. "Mysterious to you, anyway."

"Are you saying you know who K is?"

"Oh, I've known about K for a long time. We've crossed swords more than once. And I'm getting a wee bit tired of it." He steepled his fingers. "K represents all that's weak about this country. And I represent strength. He represents the past. I represent the future."

So many questions flew through his head he couldn't keep track of them. Much less ask them all. "I can see that you're not going to tell me anything of value."

"I can tell you about the mayor's juvenile arrest record."

He felt as if a gigantic vacuum had sucked all the air out of the room. He didn't know what to say. He looked at Jimmy, who appeared equally perplexed. "That record was expunged. How do you know about it?"

"As I told you, I know everything. And everyone."

"Have you bought off the judge?"

"Don't be absurd. I would never do anything so crude. I don't need to. Information is far better at gaining influence than money. Knowledge is power. When you have knowledge, you can get anything you want."

Dan felt his knees weakening. He willed them to stop, but it wasn't working. "What's your bottom line?"

"The bottom line is simply this. I run this city. I will continue to run this city. Your client didn't want to work with me. Now she's out of office. And she will remain out of office. If you interfere with my wishes…"

"Then I'm your enemy? You're not going to push me around, Sweeney. Did you send that car that almost killed me?"

Sweeney just smiled. "Prudence, see these two gentlemen out, would you, please?"

"Of course, sir."

She stood between them. "Follow me."

He didn't go. "Answer my question, Sweeney. Did you send that car? Am I your enemy?"

Sweeney propped his feet up on his desk. "That, Mr. Pike, all depends on you."

CHAPTER TWENTY-FIVE

As Dan sat on the sofa in Judge Hayes' office, he couldn't shake a profound feeling of unease. The judge agreed to hear the motion *in limine* in chambers, recognizing the sensitive nature of the matters to be discussed and the extremely high profile of the defendant.

He and Maria had debated long and hard whether to raise this matter. They weren't certain the prosecution knew about Camila's juvenile arrest. But in his experience, it was usually a mistake to assume anything could be kept quiet for long. That was even more true in a murder trial, and even truer when the defendant was one of the most famous people in the city. Better to address it head on and try to keep it out of the trial, even though the odds were against them.

Despite the in-camera filing and his attention to every possible aspect of privacy—Sweeney knew about this motion. He not only knew about it, his sneering expression suggested that he knew he wasn't supposed to know about it. He billed himself as the man who pulled all the strings in this town. It was starting to look as if the billing was accurate.

Did this mean there was a leak at the courthouse? Or worse, that some member of his team was working for

Sweeney? Who? Maria? Jimmy? Garrett? He couldn't believe it.

But someone let the word out. And until he found out how the magic trick was accomplished, he couldn't safely assume that any of their trial secrets were actually secret.

"Am I right about that, Mr. Pike?"

He looked up abruptly. The judge was speaking to him. But he hadn't heard a word of it.

"Yes, your honor," Maria said, answering for him. "It's all in the brief. It's comprehensive."

"I agree with that." Judge Hayes slid a pair of reading glasses onto his face. "A pleasure to read, too. Mr. Alexander's work, I assume?"

She nodded. "Jimmy writes the best briefs in the state, if you ask me."

"You may be right about that. Could we get him to teach a CLE, now that Florida requires its attorneys to extend their educations?"

"I'll mention that to him." Out the corner of his eye, he saw Maria give him a sharp look. Wake up!

"I also thought the brief was well-written," Jazlyn said. She sat in an upholstered chair cater-cornered to the sofa. "Which doesn't mean I agreed with a word of it. But I can appreciate the forthright style."

"Which I suppose is our cue to talk about the merits of the motion," the judge said. "I've read your brief too, Miss Prentice, so I think I understand the issues. The defendant has a juvenile record for assault. Expunged later, but still there, just the same. The defense understandably would like to keep that from the jury, stating that it is potentially prejudicial but not probative. The prosecution feels it is extremely probative. Does that about sum it up?"

"Admirably." He needed to get his head in the game. "This is no different from any other evidence of past crimes. Judges keep it out because it can unduly influence jurors, too ready to believe that if a person erred once they must have committed the crime in question. As you undoubtedly know, the trend is very much toward excluding this kind of evidence."

"I've allowed it before," the judge said.

"I know you have." Thanks to Garrett's superb research. "But only in specialized situations when there was genuine reason to believe that it was relevant, like when the same MO recurred. We don't have that here."

"I completely disagree," Jazlyn said. "The fact that your client has a temper is keenly relevant."

He shrugged. "Everyone has a temper."

Jazlyn twisted her neck. "Not like your client does. I have a long line of witnesses ready to testify about how often and how badly she's lost it."

"Most of those are political opponents."

"Some of those are political opponents. Some worked in her office."

"She has a high-stress job. She needs to blow off steam. It doesn't mean anything."

"Completely disagree. Look at the crime we're talking about here. This is not your typical crime of passion. Someone physically dragged four men into an oven. Who does that? Someone turned on the heat and watched while four men were burned alive."

"You don't know that the killer watched."

"Don't quibble. You know what I'm saying. These are not the acts of a normal person with a normal temperament. These are the acts of a psychopath, or someone so completely fueled by rage that they were capable of executing a horrific deed. Showing that the defendant has a temper above and beyond that of a normal person, and that she's had troubles due to it in the past, is very much relevant."

He shook his head. He admired Jazlyn, but this time she was dead wrong. "This minor-league incident happened when

Camila was sixteen. Which of us didn't do something stupid when they were sixteen?"

Even the judge chuckled a bit at that.

"We're not talking about smoking weed in the bathroom, Dan. We're talking about a physical assault. Battery. The victim went to the hospital."

"Camila was also wounded."

"Not like her victim."

"She defended herself."

"With extreme force."

The judge raised his hands. He seemed to be in a relaxed mood today, more amused than angry. He couldn't help but wonder if that was because Camila was not present. "Ok, people, stay calm. I've got the general idea."

"It was *not* a minor incident," Jazlyn said, under her breath.

"I understand. But I'm not going to crucify anyone over a catfight. Girls will be girls."

Jazlyn tucked in her chin.

"I get why you want this evidence admitted," the judge said. "And I'm not saying it's completely irrelevant, either. But it certainly does not prove that she committed these particular murders at the bakery."

"It's the first step."

"But it may be the wrong step. And it may leave any verdict you receive open to challenge on appeal. Do you want that?"

"Of course not."

"So why don't we play it safe and keep the questionable evidence out of the trial. Give them less to gripe about later."

Jazlyn thought for a moment. "What if my esteemed colleague submits evidence about how calm and peace-loving the defendant is?"

He jumped in. "I'm allowed to put on character evidence."

"Exactly. If he can do it, why can't I?"

"My evidence will be to establish her character, the character that made her the leader of the city. Your evidence will be to destroy her character."

The judge returned to the fray. "Are you planning to put on a great deal of character evidence, Mr. Pike?"

"No. I think her record speaks for itself. But to be fair, I haven't mapped out the entire defense. Much of what goes into our case will depend upon what my esteemed colleague puts on during the prosecution case."

"So how about this. I'm going to make a provisional ruling. For now, this evidence is excluded at trial. But if the defense does anything during their presentation that the prosecution feels opens the door to their right to respond, you may raise the issue again and the court will reconsider it."

Jazlyn tilted her head to one side. "Fair enough. I guess." Since that was the best she was going to get. "Thank you, your honor."

Judge Hayes nodded. "Anything else to consider at this time? We're getting close to our trial date."

No one had anything more.

"Good. Let's get out of here. It's almost five. I expect the lady needs to be getting home."

Jazlyn slowly rose to her feet. "Excuse me? Why?"

The judge looked up, lines etching his forehead. "Aren't you a mommy now?"

"Well...yes."

He straightened some papers and opened the door for her. "Well then. I expect you need to get home and start dinner."

IN THE HALLWAY OUTSIDE THE JUDGE'S OFFICE, DAN CHATTED with Maria and Jazlyn. They both had stricken expressions on their faces.

"What the hell was that?" Jazlyn asked.

"That," Maria explained, "was an old-school chauvinist pig being an old-school chauvinist pig."

"And then some," Jazlyn said. "I've got half a mind to file some kind of complaint."

Dan would not oppose. Chauvinist or not, Hayes was a hanging judge who statistically leaned toward the prosecution. "I'll support your complaint."

"Problem is, he might be replaced by someone worse. Sexism is rampant in the justice system." Jazlyn shook her head. "No, it's too late in the game, and a judicial complaint might be seen as a trial tactic. I'll ride this horse to the end. He was right about one thing, actually." She glanced at her watch. "I do need to get dinner started. I promised Esperanza baked squash and tofu. It's her favorite. Thanks for the recipe, Dan."

"Remember, tarragon, not oregano. Tastes better. And add a littler turmeric. The curcumin in turmeric is good for the memory."

"I'll leave it out then. Perhaps I can forget this day happened."

CHAPTER TWENTY-SIX

DAN KNOCKED ON THE DOOR. HE THOUGHT HE HEARD scuffling inside, followed by the rapid-fire pattering of footsteps.

Benji opened the door. "Oh. Dan. I didn't expect you."

"I texted Camila."

"Guess she forgot to mention it. Come in."

He followed her inside. Socks, no shoes. No clipboard. "You two busy?"

They sat in the living room. "Just going over Camila's schedule."

"Is there that much to go over?"

"Not really. But she's come to depend upon me. She still thinks of me as her chief-of-staff. And I'd rather be helping her than that blowhard currently occupying her office. Denton hired someone else to be his chief-of-staff. A man, naturally."

"I hope you haven't got extensive plans…"

"You told Camila to keep a low profile. And by her standards, she has. But as you know, the video of her press conference has been tweeted and retweeted all across the universe. Women's groups are asking her to speak. Not just in Florida. All over the country."

"I think it would be best if she declined. Until the trial is over."

"Which is what I said. But no one tells Camila what to do."

"How well I know that."

Camila entered the room. House slippers. Hair loose. No makeup. Jeans. This was perhaps the first time he had ever seen her dressed so casually, unless you counted when he saw her in jail. "How goes my crusading knight?" she said, smiling and taking his hand.

"Slaying dragons as best I can."

"Can you spring me from captivity? I feel like a caged bird in here."

"Not yet. As far as I'm concerned, you should be out of the public eye until the first day of the trial." They both sat on the couch. "Which sadly, is almost upon us."

"Any breakthroughs?"

"Nothing major. Garrett has done some great research and I think I can poke a few holes in the forensic testimony. But what I don't have is a credible alternative suspect. Even if I could find someone who might conceivably kill Nick Mansfield—why kill the other three? What links them together?"

"Have the police managed to identify the others?"

"Only two. Jonathan Primo and Sean Callahan. Ever heard of them?"

She pondered a moment. "The names do ring a bell."

Benji snapped her fingers. "Isn't Callahan the guy I sent to the office, I don't know, several months ago. The plumber?"

The light dawned in Camila's eyes. "Tall guy. Ripped. Square jaw."

Benji grinned. "That was the one."

"Oh, yes." She laughed. "We had some kind of problem, didn't we? I remember he lit into me in the office one afternoon."

"And Primo?"

"The professor. Major pain in the neck. Threatened to expose some non-existent skullduggery."

"You disliked him?"

"Very much. But not badly enough to bake him."

"Someone did. Are you seeing how bad this is for us? Two newly identified victims—who both have connections to you."

Camila nodded. "Have you considered the possibility that the selection of victims was…random?"

"What do you mean?"

"A serial killer. Someone who kills for pleasure, for gratification, not for a traditional motive."

"There's another possible explanation," Benji said. "Smoke screen. Disguise the reason for killing one victim by tossing in three strangers. Police go nuts trying to link them, so they overlook the obvious suspect for one of them."

Another possibility. Which he might well use at trial. "I'll find out as much as I can about Callahan and Primo. Any more thoughts on the bakery, Camila?"

"Worst investment of my life."

"Can't argue with you there. How did you happen to buy it?"

"I like to invest in the community, and I got a great deal on the place. Previous owner had to move in a hurry. I picked it up for a song." She fell back into the couch. "Wish I'd kept my money."

"I'm probably going to be buried between now and trial. Do you need anything? Can I do anything for you?"

Camila's raised eyebrow made that question sound more suggestive than he had intended. "I think I can manage. But let me say this so there will be no misunderstanding later. I want to testify."

"That's an incredibly bad idea."

She waved his objections away. "I know what you're going to say. It's too dangerous. They'll tear me to shreds on cross."

"They will."

"But the jury will expect me to speak. I am their mayor, after all. They know I can handle myself. If I don't take the stand, they will assume I am hiding."

"In a way, you are. Not in the guilty way. In the common-sense way. Because no defendant comes out of a cross looking good. Especially not when it's handled by someone as sharp as Jazlyn."

"Nonetheless. It is my right, and I wish to do it. If I am to have any future in politics, the people must hear my story."

"Your primary concern should be avoiding the death penalty, not grooming your political image."

"I'm focused on both. What's the point of surviving this if I do nothing with the rest of my life? I will not be stifled by these people who want to crush me. I am stronger than that. I will show them my resolve."

He knew he wasn't going to talk her out of this. But he didn't like it. "We don't have to decide today. Let's wait until the time comes. See how the trial is going."

"I will not change my mind."

On the one hand, he admired her strength. On the other hand, he feared she was committing suicide.

"If we fail," she continued, "I will not blame you. I know you will do the best for me that you can, and I will accept the consequences."

"And if we win?"

Her face brightened. "I want you to take me kitesurfing."

He tilted his head. "It's dangerous."

She grinned. "Story of my life."

CHAPTER TWENTY-SEVEN

DAN AND HIS TEAM HUDDLED AROUND THE ONLY BOOTH AT Beachcombers, hidden in the back corner. Beachcombers had some snacks, but it was basically a bar, and a fairly seedy one at that. He liked it because it was near the marina where he kept his boat, and because it was open 24/7. And in truth, he kinda liked the seediness. It appealed to his inner beach bum. Lots of Jimmy Buffett music. Even though he had made a point of surrounding himself with the best things in this life, he could have been a Parrothead in another. Beachcombers reminded him where he came from.

"I've read your trial plan cover-to cover, Maria. As usual, you've done a magnificent job."

She batted her hand in the air. "Thank you, sir."

"Seriously. This is incredibly useful. If you assume that long-range strategy planning is better than my usual approach."

"Making it up on the fly?"

"Basically."

"We have such an unusual, even…outré crime, I don't think the jury will believe there are a host of people who could've committed it," Maria explained. "We'll have more success if we narrow the range and suggest the crime was politically motivated. People were killed not because of who they were but because someone wanted to incriminate Camila. That seems more credible, given the circumstances. They created a heinous crime scene that couldn't be ignored. And they left clues pointing straight to Camila. The prosecution followed their lead without seriously considering other possibilities."

"I like it. But you're dodging the central question. Who did it?"

"Because I don't have an answer to that question. And let's face it, we don't have to prove that someone else did it. We just have to prove there is reason to doubt Camila did."

"As long as she remains cool and collected, I think any rational person would have trouble believing she committed a crime like this."

"Don't assume the jury won't be able to conceive of Camila as a murderer. There's a gigantic amount of cynicism out there. Especially when it comes to politics."

"And lawyers," Garrett added. "And both will be sitting at the defense table."

On that sobering note, all four took another drink.

"Also, kudos on the research, Garrett."

"Does this mean I get a raise?"

"Take that up with Mr. K. But I appreciate the good work. Your witness outlines are excellent, too. Makes my job a thousand times easier."

"That motion *in limine* could still come back to bite you," Garrett warned. "Make sure you stay clear of any testimony about Camila's temperament or demeanor."

"Will do. Jazlyn's got a long list of co-workers. She's hoping that eventually someone will slip in something about the mayor's tantrums. You think there were that many?"

"My research suggests so. Many people complained about it. A few HR reports. Camila would fly off the handle and…well, by all accounts, behave in an unprofessional manner."

His face hardened. He sensed there was something Garrett was thinking but not saying. "What are you suggesting?"

Garrett drew in his breath. "Okay, I'm only going to say this once, but I feel it's my obligation. Are we sure we're on the right side of this?"

"We're on the essential side of this. Everyone is entitled to a defense. Otherwise the system doesn't work. Defense attorneys are all that separates the country from a fascist state run by cops and bigwigs like Sweeney."

Garrett raised his hands. "I don't need the sixth-grade Civics lecture. I'm just saying there is a significant amount of evidence against Camila. And no other credible suspect. You know—Sweeney isn't completely wrong."

"You believe Camila is a threat to the American way of life?"

"No. But this country is failing. We're not as strong as we once were. Maybe it's time we started rethinking things."

"And pass the reins to rich white males?" Maria said. "Because that's what Sweeney wants."

"There's a middle ground. Preserving our values without completely undermining the American character."

"I'm sure. But we need to focus on the case, not the politics surrounding it." He adjusted his gaze. "Jimmy, heard anything useful down at the courthouse?"

"Lots of gossip. But not much I'd call useful. I don't sense the DA is planning any dirty tricks."

"Jazlyn doesn't go in for that."

"Agreed, but her boss is calling the shots. Still, I think it will stay on the up and up."

"Good to know."

"On the other hand, Judge Hayes' clerk, Meredith, tells me the judge does not like Mayor Pérez at all."

"She said that?"

"No, of course she didn't say that. But Meredith has worked for him almost fifteen years. She says Hayes didn't vote for her."

"Big surprise."

"And wishes he hadn't been assigned this case. The sooner it's gone, the happier he'll be."

"He could dismiss the charges."

"Natural twenty! But we both know that won't happen."

And he had no idea how the judge's hostility would play out in the courtroom. But he probably shouldn't expect any favors. Not that he ever did. "Anything else we need to discuss?"

"Yeah," Jimmy said. "How do we keep Sweeney from interfering with the trial?"

A thought that had troubled him as well. "I think he was just blowing smoke. I mean, seriously—what could he do?"

"Buy off the jury. Buy off the judge—who may already be on his payroll. Blow up the courthouse. Have us assassinated. I don't think there's anything that man wouldn't consider. He thinks he's the big cheese in this town, and he doesn't like Camila Pérez sitting on the Iron Throne."

"Sweeney talks big, but at the end of the day, I don't see him taking major risks just to influence a trial. Why would he? The papers are acting like it's a slam dunk, like she's all but convicted."

"True," Garrett said. "Most of my friends dropped the adverb 'allegedly' from their discussions of this case a long time ago."

"We'll do our job, and do it well, because that's how we roll. If you'll excuse me"—he tossed a twenty onto the table —"I'm going to wander back to my boat. We should all get a good night's sleep. Long days ahead."

They exchanged greetings and parted.

He walked outside. The cool sea air was bracing. He loved

this town, night or day. He loved the sun beaming down and the wind whistling through the palm fronds. But he also loved the stillness of the night, the lapping of the water, the quiet song of the seagull.

He stepped onto the street. Just a short walk and he'd be back at the marina. Five minutes from now, he'd be tucked—

He heard screeching tires behind him.

He whirled around. A car was racing down the street, much too fast. He couldn't tell which lane the car was in. Both, basically. Right down the middle. Going at least a hundred.

Straight toward him.

He dived away at the last possible moment. He could feel the rush of air as the car sped past. His face ground down into the pavement, scraping one side of his face, reopening the old wound.

Was that the same car as before, the one that abducted him and took him for a thrill ride? He thought so, but it was hard to be sure in the darkness. And no chance he could get a license plate number.

He hobbled off the street onto the sidewalk.

The car slammed on its brakes at the end of the street, executed a controlled jackknife, and came back for him.

What the hell? He wasn't even on the street any more. What—

The car jumped the curb. No question—it was coming for him.

He needed to get someplace a car couldn't drive, and he needed to get there fast.

He could feel blood tingling on his cheek. He'd cut himself worse than he realized, but he didn't have time to perform an analysis. The marina was at least three hundred feet away. And there was nothing between it and him except pavement and dirt.

And a few trees.

That was his only hope.

He watched carefully as the car approached, trying to time it perfectly. Just as the car was almost upon him, he leapt to the right.

But not quite fast enough. The right side of the front hood caught his leg. It felt like it had been shattered. He rolled for several feet, dirt and mud mingling, getting in his face and nostrils and teeth.

He wasn't sure he could walk. But at least he wasn't dead. Yet.

If he could just get to the nearest tree…

He knew he couldn't climb. But if he stood behind the tree, would the driver risk hitting it? He hoped not.

He hobbled in that direction. Sword blades of pain raced up the injured leg. It did not want any pressure. But that couldn't be helped.

He got behind the tree.

The car slammed to a halt. Not a hundred feet away from him.

A dirt cloud billowed between them.

He peered at the windshield but couldn't see anything. Same driver, different driver? He had no idea.

He pulled out his phone and made a show of dialing 9-1-1. He knew where the police were this time of night. They could be here in five minutes. Maybe less.

The driver-side window rolled down. A gun emerged. "Final warning, lawyer!"

He ducked, but not before the gun fired. The report split the night, so loud it shattered his senses.

The car backed away, not turning until it was so far away he couldn't read the plate. Then the driver swerved, floored it, and disappeared.

He collapsed on the ground, nursing his injured leg. He wasn't sure if it was broken. But he wouldn't be kitesurfing for a while.

In the distance, he heard a siren.

It was going to be a long night, and a long time before he was sleeping on his boat.

Last warning, the driver had said, leaving no doubt what this was about. The attack wasn't random. This was someone who wanted him to lose Camila's case.

Or someone working for someone who wanted him to lose Camila's case.

And if they were willing to do this—what wouldn't they do?

He planned to save Camila from the hangman's noose. But it would be a bitter victory if it ended with his neck in there instead.

THE TWITTERING CLOUD

CHAPTER TWENTY-EIGHT

CAMILA STUMBLED INTO THE BATHROOM AND FLICKED ON THE light. Time to put her face on. Which meant opening her eyes. Even though it was five a.m. But she was accustomed to getting up early. She liked to have time to think before she started her day, and she didn't like being rushed.

How much to do? Her instinct suggested that her makeup should be subdued. She didn't want the jury to think she was artificial. They would see her live and up close, not from a great distance or through a camera lens. She wanted to be pleasing—but not too pleasing. There could be no suggestion that she was putting on a fake front to win over the men or anything like that.

She leaned into the mirror. Just enough paint to take off the rough edges, she decided. She was still young. She didn't need to hide anything—actually, no one did, so far as she was concerned. The female jurors might feel the same way, and she didn't want to alienate them. If they felt ordinary and she came off looking like Angelina Jolie, it would not engender their sympathy. She wanted them to feel they wanted to take her under their wing and protect her, not scold her for being brazen.

There was so much to consider. And all she was doing was putting on her face. Men had no idea.

At this rate, by the time she had to decide what to wear, she might be completely overwhelmed.

She needed coffee. She shuffled into the kitchen and pushed a button. She had loaded the coffeemaker the night before, so she'd have java in five. The Keurig would be quicker, but that never tasted as good to her as coffee that had actually percolated. And those spent cups were a blight on landfills.

Had to pass the time somehow. She picked up her phone.

She saw a new text waiting, sender Unknown. That was unusual. She didn't give this number to anyone other than a close circle of intimates and co-workers.

She tapped the screen. The text message popped up.

I WILL RAPE YOU AND CUT YOU AND THROW YOU IN THE OVEN LIKE YOU DID YOUR BOYFRIEND

She almost dropped the phone.

How—

She used her thumb to scroll through the previous messages. There were dozens of them, maybe hundreds. Somehow, her number had gotten out. And been distributed. To people who hated her.

She switched to her Facebook app, then Twitter. It was all the same. Her newsfeed was flooded with hate, memes and fake news articles about her, none of them remotely true. Some had links to webpages that looked like newspapers, with headlines exposing her "crimes."

Twitter was worse. She didn't know you could use words like that in the Twitterverse without being banned. Of course, there were probably all fake overnight accounts, so they didn't care if they were banned.

She fell back against the kitchen counter and suddenly realized she was trembling, head to toe. She could barely stand. She gasped for air.

Come on, Camila, she told herself. You're tougher than this.

But the trembling would not stop.

Where the hell was that coffee?

Was it too early to call Dan?

She heard a buzzing, and against her better judgment, she lifted the phone and looked.

YOU WILL BE PUNISHED FOR YOUR CRIMES, BITCH. YOU MELTED THEM. I WILL MELT YOU

DAN STARED INTO THE BATHROOM MIRROR. NOT THAT HE HAD much choice. The so-called bathroom on *The Defender* was little larger than a coat closet, and the shower took most of the space. There was nowhere else to look. But when he stared into that mirror, he felt as if he barely recognized the face. Who was that man? And why did he look so worried?

Sure, his life had been threatened, and last night some speedster had demonstrated just how serious the threat was. His leg wasn't broken, but it still hurt like hell. He liked to tell himself the driver was only trying to scare him—again—but he was not completely convinced. If he hadn't leapt at just the right moment, he would've been flattened. If he hadn't shielded himself behind that tree, he would be dead.

Someone wanted Camila convicted. And felt the surest way to make that happen would be to take out her attorney.

He couldn't let that get to him. Camila was counting on him to save, not only her, but her future. Her potential. All the good she might do in the world, if this concerted effort to take her out failed.

What had happened to him? He had made a name for himself handling tough cases and winning far more than he lost. But he also knew that to a large degree—he distanced himself from the cases, and especially the clients. He compartmentalized the work. He cared about the justice system, about preventing innocents from being railroaded by the government. But individuals....

When he joined Mr. K's firm, for the first time, he gained a sense of being part of a team, working with others in a concerted effort to help people and make the world a better place, all the stuff lawyers frequently said they were doing but too infrequently did. And he was no different, until he started working for Mr. K. Until he met Esperanza, the young girl he'd represented in that first case. She depended upon him to save her. And he did everything possible, not for an abstract concept or ideal, but for her.

Once that paradigm shift occurred, everything changed for him.

And now he was feeling exactly the same way about Camila. Maybe for different reasons. But just as powerfully.

Maybe even more so.

He didn't want to let her down. He cared about her.

And that was another cause for concern.

Ever since this case began, people had accused him of being sexist. He pretended it didn't bother him, but it did. He'd always thought of himself as progressive. He'd marched in equal rights demonstrations. He'd lobbied for equal pay. He understood the importance of consent in relationships and never pressured anyone. Anytime he'd been in a position to hire, he made sure women were equally represented. He didn't discriminate. To the contrary, he preferred the company of women.

And yet...

He did have a tendency to notice women's appearances before he noticed anything else. Saying that was hardwired into his heterosexual DNA didn't make it better.

He did tend toward flirtatious banter with women he would never use with men.

He did adopt a protective attitude at times. Patronizing? Paternalistic?

He'd read all the theories about the "male gaze." Did he look at women through blinders, a heterosexual male perpetually on the hunt, sexualizing women even when there was nothing sexual about the situation? He knew about the Bechtel test. His life wasn't a movie and he had no idea what women said in private conversations, but when was the last time he had a conversation about a woman that made no reference to her appearance?

He peered back into the mirror. Did he feel so strongly about this case because Mr. K had convinced him Camila had the ability to usher in a better tomorrow? Or because she was smoking hot and he wouldn't mind getting close to her?

He reached into the basin and splashed cold water on his face.

Get your act together, Pike. You don't have time for soul-searching self-scrutiny. First and foremost, you need to win this case. Camila is depending upon you. And she—

He stopped the thought half-formed.

And she was a worthy individual who deserved a fair trial. End of story.

Maybe.

CHAPTER TWENTY-NINE

DAN WALKED FROM THE METAL DETECTORS TO THE FIRST-floor elevators. He still limped somewhat, but he hoped if he kept a slow steady pace, no one would notice. These elevators were as old as the courthouse, and most times he just took the stairs. But not today. His leg didn't need any extra pressure. And since he was about to address the prospective jurors, he thought maybe it was best not to work up a sweat.

Mr. K had insisted on hiring security to keep an eye on him, and the other members of the team and Camila. But they kept a discreet distance. He didn't want the jury to think he was an egomaniac who traveled with an entourage.

And he didn't want whoever was behind that attack to know how badly he'd been shaken by it.

Just before the elevator doors closed, another local attorney, Greg Conrad, slid inside. As soon as he spotted Dan, he grinned.

"Here for the mayor's case?"

"Yup. Jury selection."

Greg whistled. "That's going to be a challenge."

"More for my client than me. But she'll hold up."

"No doubt. You might remind her that it's always important to stretch before a workout. Don't want to get a cramp at the wrong moment."

Whaaaat?

The bell dinged and the doors opened. "Good luck in court, Dan. Remember—four's a crowd."

He squinted, trying to make sense of the encounter. But he couldn't. He would just have to remind himself of a fundamental fact—Greg was a jerk.

He made a beeline toward Judge Hayes' courtroom. He didn't see Maria. But he did spot an African-American woman he recognized from the coffee shop. Claudia? Claudine? She locked eyes with him and made a tsking noise, shaking her head back and forth.

"Mm, mm, *mm*."

"I'm sorry. Is there a problem?"

She held up her hands. "None of my business." But he could tell she was desperate to say more. He paused and waited. "Didn't your mam tell you the difference between right and wrong?"

"I taught myself the difference between right and wrong. Are you suggesting it's wrong to provide a defense to the accused?"

She looked at him as if he were completely clueless. "You just be careful, that's all I'm sayin'. You don't know what diseases people got these days."

Why did he suspect everyone else knew something he did not? He didn't like this at all, but sadly, it was nine o'clock and he needed to be inside the courtroom.

Jazlyn stood inside the door talking to one of her associates.

"There he is, right on time," the younger man said.

Jazlyn nodded. "Morning, Dan. Are you okay? Your face—"

"I'm fine. Fit as a fiddle."

"That's because of all the time in the gym," the other man

said, then laughed as if he had made the funniest joke in the world. He kept walking.

Both Maria and Camila were already at the defendant's table, huddled around Maria's laptop.

"Give it to me straight," he said. "What's going on?"

"She's been attacked," Maria said, not looking up.

He rushed beside Camila. "What, at your house? Are you okay?"

Camila frowned. "Define 'okay.'"

"I don't mean physically attacked," Maria explained. "Something far worse." She pivoted the laptop around so he could see the screen.

The browser was on a social media page. The headline was large enough to read from a distance.

MAYOR CAUGHT IN THREESOME AT GYM

He lowered himself into a chair. "Someone tell me what this is."

"Fake news," Camila explained. "It's all over Facebook, all over Twitter, all over YouTube, and featured on dozens of webpages accessible from hundreds of links all over the Net."

"When did this start?"

"Last night, apparently, but it expanded exponentially every time someone clicked on it. By this morning, it was in the news streams of everyone in the city."

"Everyone?"

"Everyone with a computer or a cellphone."

He fell back into his chair. "Everyone." The photo beneath the headline was blurry but it did appear to be Camila. Though photographed from behind, she appeared to be nude. Another naked woman embraced her, and a third person, a man, leered at them.

"Photoshop?"

"Or Gimp. Same thing, but free. More than adequate to handle this."

"Who's the woman?"

"It's supposed to be Benji, my secret lover masquerading as Chief of Staff. But it isn't. Look at those sculpted French nails. Benji would die first."

"And the man?"

Maria arched an eyebrow. "According to the article, it's you."

"What?"

She read from the article. "'…caught in a torrid embrace with her attorney, known for his history of sexual exploits.'"

He tucked in his chin. "I have a history of sexual exploits?"

"The story is implying you're a demented pervert screwing your client, which would not only get you disbarred but would completely undermine your credibility in court."

"And we're in a gym?" He paused. "And I'm just watching?"

Maria put a hand on her hip. "Seriously? That's what you're most worried about here?"

"I'm just asking. Why a gym?"

"Because it sounds public and shameless."

Now he understood the comments he'd been hearing since he entered the courthouse. "Every juror in the pool will see this."

"With the possible exception of a few grandmas, yes."

He pressed a hand against his forehead. "Is there more?"

"More than you can imagine." Maria took him on a quick tour of all the sites she had tabbed this morning. The headlines were varied and amazing. The only common denominators were that all the stories were supported by doctored photos and promoted a sleazy negative view of Camila Pérez. Apparently suggesting she was a murderer wasn't enough. Someone had to convince everyone she was a deviant as well.

MAYOR CAUGHT IN BED WITH UNDERAGE GIRL

DID OUR MAYOR DO THIS HOMELESS MAN?

MAYOR   LAUGHS   AT   HANDICAPPED PANHANDLER
PEREZ LETS HER CAT DIE OF STARVATION

"That's the worst one of all," Camila said. He could see she was trying to keep her face stoic. But this was an onslaught she didn't need, coming at the worst possible time.

"How can you rank them? They're all bad."

"Being a pervert is bad. Letting a cat die is unforgivable."

"Have you ever seen anything like this before?"

"Of course. This is a standard element in modern American campaigning. Opponents hire hackers to launch Twitter-bots. Self-replicating programs that spread crap all over social media. Then they create fake webpages designed to look like legitimate news outlets. The social media posts have links to lead people to the webpages."

"Clickbait."

"Exactly. They can actually make money selling advertising on fake news webpages. The more clicks, the more money they get. Destroying reputations is profitable."

"Can't you complain? Get the posts removed?"

"You can try. Twitter will take down defamatory posts or freeze accounts. But remember, these are self-replicating—and vengeful. You get rid of one, they replace it with ten more. It's like playing Whack-A-Mole. You can't stop it."

"We need to learn who's behind this."

"Good luck. These people are expert catfish. They masquerade as people they aren't. They use false names, accounts, and bounce through dozens of servers all over the world between launch and destination. Tracing to point of origin is time-consuming, expensive, and all but impossible."

He felt his phone vibrate. He pulled it out of his pocket—and saw a News Alert about Camila's wild sex orgy on North Beach.

Camila frowned. "I've been getting those all morning."

He scrolled through his messages and realized that he had

been too. He just hadn't noticed because he hadn't looked at his phone.

"They must have a great mailing list covering most of the adults in St. Petersburg—in other words, the jury pool. Possibly hacked the City Hall databases—that would be my guess."

"I'll complain to the judge."

"You think that will help?"

"At the very least, he might delay the trial. Or take away the juror's phones."

Maria laid a hand on his arm. "Dan—don't make them hate us."

"He'll have a revolt on his hands if they have to surrender their phones," Camila agreed. "They'll refuse to serve and march out *en masse*."

"Why so many posts? Doesn't that undermine the credibility?"

"The variety is purposeful," Maria said. "Something for everyone. If you're hung up on sex or homosexuality, here are some posts to turn you against the mayor. If you have a handicapped person close to you, here's a reason to hate the mayor. And if you love animals—which would be almost everyone—here's a reason to send her to death row."

"Someone put a lot of thought into this."

"Yes. Someone."

"Sweeney?"

"He would have the resources to orchestrate something like this. But he's not the only one who has an interest in seeing Camila convicted."

"The murderer?"

She touched her nose. "Ding ding ding."

CHAPTER THIRTY

JUDGE HAYES DECLINED TO DELAY THE TRIAL. HE ALSO declined to take the juror's cellphones, fearing that such a move might induce withdrawal symptoms. Then he denied a repeat motion for change of venue, looking genuinely irritated to be revisiting the topic. He did agree to allow the lawyers to question jurors about their exposure to clickbait and social media. He also agreed to expand his usual media restrictions to include the Internet and any posts or webpages relating to the mayor.

But what good would that do? They couldn't unsee what they'd seen. Prejudice was an insidious weed. Most people didn't think of themselves as prejudiced. But most decision-making is instinctive, not conscious. And people also tend to believe that "where there's smoke, there's fire." Once you've seen a series of doctored photos portraying the mayor having lesbian sex in public, it's hard to put it out of your mind.

This attack would probably only work with a female defendant. An alleged orgy wouldn't necessarily break a male candidate. In some quarters, it might improve his ratings. But women were held to a double standard in a nation that expected virginal public personas.

He chatted with Jazlyn while they waited for the judge to return to the bench. "Are you satisfied?" she asked.

"Not remotely. This reinforces my original opinion that the case should have been moved to another jurisdiction."

"A jurisdiction that doesn't have social media? Where would that be? Upper Slobbovia?"

"Anyplace would be better than here."

"Did it occur to you that this could work in your client's favor?"

He looked at her as if she were speaking a foreign language. "How could all this tawdry slander help Camila?"

"Because it *is* tawdry slander, and most people will recognize it as tawdry slander. A smear campaign. Come on, an experienced politician having a threesome at a public gym? Sure."

"But people love gossip, and whether it's true is secondary to the cynical satisfaction they get from hearing and repeating it."

"We'll see. One thing is for certain. The jurors will be looking at you differently."

"Me? Why?"

"Did you look closely at that threesome photo?" She smiled. "That guy that's supposedly you is seriously well-endowed."

"It's not me."

"I know. But if the women in this town think it is…you're going to get a lot more swiping right on your eHarmony profile."

He returned to the defense table and sat beside Maria. Where was the judge? He hated waiting. Trials were hard enough without delays intensifying the tension. "Any news?"

"I asked Garrett to look into the malicious posts. He got Mr. K to authorize hiring our own team of hackers. Someone to track down the IPs of the Twitterbots that started this."

"Let me know what they come up with."

"I'll text you the deets."

Camila leaned in. "Even if we find the source, what can we do? Has a criminal law been broken?"

"Probably not. We could try suing for slander."

"Which would give them a public forum to put my morals on trial. We would be playing into their hands."

She could well be right. "Look, let's learn as much as we can. Then we'll decide on a course of action."

Camila frowned. "As you say."

Judge Hayes finally entered the courtroom. He looked somewhat off his game, perhaps understandably. This trial had already proven complicated and atypical, and it hadn't even begun yet. The judge called the panel of venirepersons, the prospective jurors, and gave them general preliminary instructions. He asked a few questions to weed out those who were obviously disqualified—those who knew the parties personally, those who didn't believe in the justice system, and those who would never under any circumstances apply the death penalty. This was all done in the interest of fairness, but it also meant the jury tended to lean toward those who favored extreme punishment. It also provided an easy out to anyone who didn't want to serve.

Eventually it was time for the lawyers to inquire. They could always remove a juror for cause if true prejudice or conflict of interest appeared. They also each had a limited number of peremptory challenges—the ability to remove a juror for any reason or no reason at all. The only consistent exception, thanks to the Supreme Court, was race. Lawyers were not entitled to remove jurors based upon their race, or to alter the racial balance of the panel. In the past, too often, prosecutors wanted minorities off and defendants wanted them on, thinking them more likely to acquit. As a result, today, if you removed a juror of color, the judge might well ask for a constitutionally acceptable basis.

Given that the defendant was Hispanic, Dan knew this

could prove important. There were many differing theories about juries and who you did and did not want on them, and most of these theories—some would say stereotypes—involved race, gender, education, or age. Educated liberals were good for the defense, more likely to take seriously the standard of "beyond a reasonable doubt." Muslims, Jews, and other minority religions were good as well—so long as the defendant was not a member of an opposing religious group. Young urban women liked to think of themselves as iconoclasts. They were more likely to go against the grain, to stand up to the majority and create a hung jury. This was good for the defense, since prosecutors rarely retried. But Camila needed an exoneration if her career was to have any hope of proceeding.

Also, women tended to be hardest on other women.

Or was that just another sexist stereotype he had convinced himself was fact?

Jazlyn asked the standard questions, ensuring the jurors had a proper sense of the gravity of the situation and were willing to convict those proven to have committed crimes. She excused a mother because she had three children of school age and feared this case would keep her away from home too long. And she removed two Hispanic women, though she explained privately that she did it because they considered the mayor a heroic figure and a trailblazer for their people. Hayes allowed it.

And then it was the defense's turn to ask questions. Jury selection was his least favorite part of a trial. He would be happier if they just called twelve people at random and started. At least today he had help. While he asked questions, Maria would be carefully watching the jurors, recording their answers, and scanning for tells. In the gallery, Jimmy would use his phone to look up their Facebook pages and see if he could detect hints to their political leanings or personalities. Were they nice family people? Members of liberal organizations? Photographed with friends of other races? Or posing with a rifle? Marching with the alt-right?

His most difficult conversation was with a white woman in a black blouse and dark red lipstick. Beauty-shop hair. High neck. Stiff posture.

"Would you mind if I asked if you voted for my client in the last election?"

The woman stiffened even more. "I believe we have private ballots in this country for a reason."

"Fair enough. I don't mean to pry. But I do need to know if anyone has any preconceived objections to her that have nothing to do with the case."

"I can keep an open mind."

He thought for a moment. He didn't want to alienate the woman, or anyone else. But if he didn't press, he wasn't going to get anything useful. "That sounds like you're saying you do have some negative thoughts, but you will sideline them during the trial."

"I didn't say that."

"I know you didn't say that, but that was the impression I got."

"I can't help your impressions."

She was making this a thousand times more difficult than it needed to be—which also suggested she needed to go. But he pressed onward. "Since you seem to be familiar with the mayor, can you tell me anything you dislike about her?"

She hesitated. "If you must know, I hate that paint she splashed all over downtown. So garish. Like a kindergarten."

More than one head in the gallery bobbed. He hoped it wouldn't hurt Camila's feelings. She'd probably heard it all before. "And anything positive you can say about her?"

"She's a snappy dresser." Pause. "And I admire any woman her age who…visits the gym regularly."

Was that a compliment…or a reference to what she read this morning in her Twitter feed?

He removed the woman from the jury.

By mid-afternoon, he'd used all his peremptories and removed two more jurors for cause. Jazlyn had done the same. The judge swore in a panel of eighteen, twelve primary jurors and six alternates who would listen to the trial but would not deliberate unless they were needed to replace one of the twelve. Once again Judge Hayes cautioned them to avoid the media and any mention of the parties or the case.

He pounded his gavel. "Very well. Opening statements will begin tomorrow morning at nine a.m., followed by the prosecution witnesses. Wear comfortable shoes. It's going to be a long day."

CHAPTER THIRTY-ONE

DAN SLEPT POORLY THAT NIGHT. HE WASN'T SURE WHY. THE
weather was perfect. Cool, gentle breeze, no noise. The boat
practically rocked him to sleep. He just couldn't clear his
head.

His brain kept flashing back to the murderous Jaguar and
the attempt on his life. He'd been frightened by it more than
he cared to admit. Worse, it was clouding his brain, possibly
preventing him from make the usual observations and connections that helped him uncover the truth.

And he was worried about Camila. Pretrial jitters always
made him insomniac and dull-witted. Of course, if a time
ever came when he wasn't nervous before a trial—it was probably time to quit. Those jitters gave him an edge. They guar-
anteed he went the extra mile and prepared and reviewed and
checked and double-checked. Those jitters built his reputation. Possibly aged him prematurely. But they were an essential
part of his success.

———

NEXT MORNING, JUDGE HAYES RECONVENED THE JURY AND

called the court into session. As the prosecutor, Jazlyn was first to address the jury.

"Ladies and gentlemen of the jury. To quote a great American patriot of another era, these are the times that try men's souls. Every day we're greeted with news stories about terrorist acts, mass shooting at schools and theaters, cold-hearted killings so shocking that you can't help but wonder what has happened to this world. In most cases, we can comfort ourselves by noting that…it happened somewhere else. But the stories keep coming closer, don't they? Mass shooting at an Orlando nightclub. Mass shooting at a Parkland school. And now this incident—not a shooting, but perhaps in some ways more horrific, because of the cruel and deliberate means by which the murders were enacted."

If this went on much longer, he would have to object. The court typically gave counsel considerable latitude in their opening and closing statements, and Jazlyn would say she was simply waxing poetic, setting the stage. But her comments could also be seen as a call to action, an implicit suggestion that the jury should convict, not based upon the evidence, but to draw a line, to stem the tide of violence.

"I know from yesterday's questioning that all of you are familiar with the terrible and unnatural crime visited upon this city recently. Four men were drugged, dragged into a large industrial oven—and baked alive. The evidence will show that they died of heat stroke and related problems, that they suffered for a long time before they died, that their flesh was seared from their bones. I say this not to horrify you—though what human would not be horrified—but to impress upon you the importance of the task you are about to undertake. I represent the government, yes, but more importantly, I represent the people. I represent everyone who wants a better future for this nation."

Jazlyn proceeded to provide a general outline of the prosecution case. Since this was an opening statement, not an argument, she was not supposed to argue. Instead she outlined what she anticipated "the evidence will show." But of course, she did that in a manner that was little different from argument. She highlighted the horror of the crime and the cruel nature of the person who committed it.

She also outlined the evidence tying Camila to the crime. She hinted at the "teeming mass of forensic evidence," but left the details for the experts to explain later. She noted that Camila owned the bakery and that she knew, employed, and had an "intimate relationship" with one of the victims, Nick Mansfield. "Hell hath no fury like a woman scorned." And of course, she mentioned the "C" etched in blood, Mansfield's "last desperate attempt to identify his killer."

After she worked her way through the witnesses and most of the evidence, Jazlyn stood front and center before the jury and brought it to a conclusion. "As the prosecution, we hold the initial burden of proof in the case. We do not run from this burden. To the contrary, we embrace it. No one should be charged with a crime, much less tried, unless there is substantial evidence of guilt. But I can assure you that in this case, the evidence is more than substantial. Most would call it overwhelming. Damning. Inescapable. And at the end of the trial, I believe you will see it the same way."

She paused, casting a backward glance toward the defendant's table. "Whether you agree with me or you don't, here is my one promise: I will not lie to you. I will not lie, and I will not allow my witnesses to lie. I will not engage in any sort of... trickery or showboating. I will let the facts speak for themselves."

"Is she casting shade on me?" he whispered. Maria hushed him.

Jazlyn continued. "Consider the sources. None of the witnesses I'll call to the stand has any motivation to lie. On the other side of the courtroom...the story is different. Over there, they have every reason to lie. One of the main reasons we have juries is so disputes can be resolved by objective finders of fact, people who can cast a sharp eye on what is said and uncover the truth. Don't let the smokescreen prevent you from doing your job. Don't let irrelevancies prevent you from seeing clearly. From using common sense. From doing your duty. Thank you."

He pushed himself to his feet. After that rousing oratory, he wasn't sure whether he should speak or salute. Jazlyn had obviously put a lot of thought into it. Though she was above average in front of a jury, he would not call her a great orator. But this time, she had outdone herself. She had probably been practicing this speech for a long time, refining the content, carefully choosing the right words, and practicing her delivery. As always, hard work paid off.

The defense had the option of saving opening statement until it was time to put on their case, after the prosecution closed—but he thought that was tantamount to suicide. You don't waive chances to talk to the jury, or let the jurors go days without hearing any rebuttal to the prosecutor's opening. Yes, this was a statement, not an argument, but he would still poke holes in Jazlyn's presentation every chance he got.

As he approached the jury box, he wondered if he should recalibrate his presentation. Since Jazlyn had warned them against "showboating," perhaps he should tone it down, take the sober, nothing-but-the-facts approach. Since she had come off like Cicero, maybe he should adopt a more regular-guy, common-man approach.

Nah. He'd stick to the strategy Maria had worked out and the style that had worked for him his entire career.

"Good morning. Thank you for being here and serving on this jury. I know you were summoned, but I also know you could probably have avoided service if you'd wanted. Instead, you're here, doing your duty, taking on a tough case. So thank you."

He walked to one end of the box. He hoped they focused

on his words, but making the presentation less visually static usually helped. "Let me start with something that might surprise you. I don't disagree with most of what Ms. Prentice just told you. Surprised? I'll go even further. I agree with most of what she just told you. This was a horrible crime. And she's right—someone should be punished. And you know what— she's right about what's going on in this nation. It is scary. We have serious issues that need to be addressed. But here's where I differ from the prosecutor. I don't want you to become so emotionally involved in the need to solve America's problems —or this case—that you lose sight of what you're here to do. You're here to determine whether my client, Mayor Camila Pérez, committed these murders. And the fact is—she did not. And the prosecution will not prove otherwise.

"I was glad to hear Ms. Prentice acknowledge that she has the burden of proof. We do not have the burden. I don't have to prove anything. I will, because the prosecution evidence is so weak, but I don't have to. And at the end of the day, you're not here to take your best guess about who committed the murders. You're only here to determine whether the prosecutor has proven my client's guilt beyond a reasonable doubt. If she has not, you must find my client not guilty, regardless of what you think might have happened."

He considered taking a witness-by-witness walk through the people he could call to the stand, but he feared that would be boring to a group of people who were already showing signs of waning interest. That was one of the downsides to speaking second. He decided to make his talk briefer.

"We do have problems in this nation today. But we're not going to solve them in this courtroom. Wish we could, but we can't. Here's what we can do. Prevent someone from being unjustly destroyed. Has it struck anyone as wildly coincidental that this horrible headline-grabbing crime occurred the way it did? I mean, a bullet would've done the job—but would not have attracted so much media coverage. A rural location would've been less risky, but this bakery was sure to be connected to the mayor. And I know some of you saw the barrage of trashy memes and fake news that hit cyberspace yesterday. It's almost as if someone wants my client out of the way. Who would target a politician? And why?"

He paused. The questions would have more rhetorical impact if he left them unanswered.

"If we want real change in this nation, then we have to dismantle the good ol' boy network, the entrenched forces that don't want change, that benefit from the world remaining just as it is. Someone sees Camila Pérez as a threat. Because she represents change. Because she represents the hope of a better tomorrow. If you also want a better tomorrow, then you should resist this deliberate smear campaign and demand evidence—evidence that will not be forthcoming."

He knew he was pushing his luck, but Jazlyn hadn't objected yet. Better to end it before she did.

"One last thought. Despite what some say, the role of the defense lawyer is not to get people off the hook. Only juries can acquit. Our job is to make sure justice is done. You can't expect cops to do that, or even prosecutors. Their job is hard enough already. The defense is here to guarantee the rules set forth in the Constitution are actually observed. We make the system work. We make sure everyone gets a fair day in court. And we do our best to prevent the innocent from being convicted. Every time you hear me object, every time you hear me argue, don't think of me as the guy who's interfering. Think of me as the guy who's standing up for my client's rights. And your rights. And every American's rights. Especially the right to be innocent until *proven* guilty."

CHAPTER THIRTY-TWO

DAN WAS RELIEVED JAZLYN DID NOT ATTEMPT TO REINVENT
trial strategy on the first day. She followed the tried-and-true
template for criminal prosecution. First item on the agenda
was proof of crime, which in this case, meant proof of death
by unnatural causes. There was no dispute about the fact that
four men died a gruesome death in that oven, but it was still
an essential element of the crimes asserted against Camila,
and if Jazlyn didn't cover it, she risked being shut down by a
motion to dismiss.

Jazlyn started with the medical examiner, though she had
many other experts ready to testify on the subject. Where do
you find experts on death by baking? He didn't even want to
know.

The medical examiner, Dr. Zanzibar, took the stand first.
Blue suit. Pocket protector. Bow tie. Stiff as a board. Jazlyn
quickly established that he had been called to the scene of the
crime soon as the corpses were found by a uniformed officer
investigating a revolting odor emanating from the bakery.
Zanzibar performed an initial investigation on site, then took a
closer look at the corpses in his morgue. Although he examined all four bodies, Jazlyn focused most of his testimony on

Nick Mansfield. Presumably, that was where Jazlyn thought she had the strongest case against Camila. Ultimately, it didn't matter if the jury found Camila guilty of one murder or four. One was enough to earn the ultimate sanction.

"Could you please explain what caused these deaths?"

He nodded. "It's not entirely different from the heat stroke that arises after extreme physical exertion, or when people have been out in the sun too long. Or go to sleep inside their cars on a hot Florida day. All of which can be potentially lethal."

"But why?"

"Your body always wants to maintain an ideal temperature of about thirty-seven degrees Celsius. When the outside temperature is higher, the body tries to maintain that ideal temperature by increasing its rate of heat dissipation through mechanisms that involve significant increases in blood flow to the skin. Unfortunately, that means the amount of blood available to other organs decreases. A sharp decrease in blood flow to the brain can cause unconsciousness and eventually death. It's simple thermodynamics, really."

Which probably meant nothing to most of the jurors, but certainly indicated that the witness knew what he was talking about. "How hot does it need to be before this process starts?"

"Not as hot as you might imagine. The interior of this oven was probably uncomfortable in a matter of minutes. Plus, these men were touching it, so they would experience burns even before their bodies began to go haywire. Most people have accidentally touched a hot pan or stovetop briefly. Imagine if that happened but you were unable to jerk your hand away."

He noted several disturbed expressions on the faces of the jurors.

"Would the bodies sweat?"

"Of course. That's the body's first line of defense, as it tries to push the heat within the body to the surface. The sweat cools the body—for a time. When your skin temperature is warmer than the outside temperature, you can also lose heat. That's what we call dry heat loss. But that would not have happened here. The oven interior became too hot, too quickly."

"How quickly?"

Zanzibar's testimony was typically unemotional, but even he appeared affected by thoughts of the interior of that deadly cauldron. "At forty degrees, the body tells the muscles to slow down. That's when fatigue sets in. At forty-one degrees, the body starts to shut down. Cells deteriorate. Organ failure begins. The body can't even sweat anymore, because blood flow to the skin will cease. The body will feel cold and clammy—while the skin may actually be cooking. Or melting."

"Is that when heatstroke sets in?"

"Yes. Hyperthermia."

"How quickly would that occur?"

"Given how fast the oven heated—perhaps five minutes."

"Did the men live long?"

"No." He took a breath. "Thank goodness. If heatstroke is not treated immediately, the likelihood of survival is virtually nil. Heat and organ failure would be painful, but the body would shut down and they would lose consciousness long before they were actually dead. Which is a mercy. This was a hellish way to die, but probably not a prolonged one."

He could see the jurors' pained expressions. They knew the nature of the crime before the trial began, of course, but hearing a witness talk about it at length was far more disturbing.

"What other symptoms did they suffer?"

"I can't speak with certainty since I wasn't there. But based upon my examination of the remains, I believe that before death they suffered delirium, convulsions, and possibly entered a comatic state. Various forms of trauma and electrolyte abnormalities. All of those symptoms are pathophysio-logical inflammatory responses determined by the intense heat, as is multiple organ failure. On at least one of the victims, organs actually burst, plus a blood vessel eruption near the surface caused a skin rupture, possibly aided by weakening of the skin due to contact with the oven heating elements. As a result, blood splattered."

"Beside Nick Mansfield?"

"The victim in question was positioned to his right."

"What was the actual cause of death?"

"There are multiple possibilities, and the corpses I examined were so damaged it's difficult to make a precise determination. But in all likelihood, it was the loss of blood to the brain. Intercranial hypertension, cerebral hypoperfusion, and neuronal injuries. But I want to stress that all of that might have been augmented, or possibly preceded, by what was happening in the rest of the body. Arterial hypotension. Multi-organ ischemia. At the cellular level, exposure to this degree of heat at will inhibit DNA synthesis and transcription and cause protein degradation, cell-cycle interruption, metabolic changes, and cytoskeletal alteration. The autopsies revealed marked petechiae and ecchymosis on the thymus, as well as hemorrhagic diathesis, brain and pulmonary edema, cerebral edema, massive blood aspiration, and internal bleeding in multiple organs. No one could recover from that."

"Doctor, I fear the jury may not understand all your medical terminology. Can you give them the bottom line?"

The doctor shrugged. "The four men baked to death."

Jazlyn finished her questioning. He had not originally planned to cross at all. He and Maria both thought the sooner they got Doctor Death off the stand, the better. One thing Zanzibar mentioned triggered his interest, though.

"You said the victims might have suffered from delusions?"

Zanzibar nodded. "Very likely. In the brief time before they died. I don't know the circumstances that led to them being placed in that oven, but I think we can all agree that it was probably not voluntary."

Especially since they were drugged, but he knew another witness would testify about the tox screen later. "What conclusion do you draw from that?"

"They were already in an agitated state. Then confined in a rapidly heating deathtrap. Anyone might panic, hallucinate. But combine that heat with the biological distress—and delusion seems much more likely. Possibly a hypnotic state. Certainly impaired judgment."

"Thank you. Nothing more." And good riddance to Doctor Death.

CHAPTER THIRTY-THREE

DAN WASN'T SURE WHY DR. ZANZIBAR HADN'T ALSO TESTIFIED about the toxicology findings. He was certainly qualified, although it was the primary focus of his assistant, Dr. Elias Abraham. Perhaps Jazlyn thought it would have more weight coming from a specialist. Or perhaps she thought the jury would like a break and a chance to clear their heads after all the horrific testimony about heat stroke and baking to death. Or maybe she thought it might be smarter to put on a younger, better-looking doctor.

Or maybe that was just him, once again, making judgments about people based upon their appearance.

Damn those feminists. Once they get into your head, you can't get them out.

Dr. Abraham took the stand. Goatee/mustache combo. Weak left eye. Hunched shoulders. Left-handed.

Jazlyn quickly established his credentials and asked about his toxicology findings.

"What I discovered in all four corpses was virtually the same. Variations in quantity, but not in substance. Mansfield showed the greatest concentrations, which is one reason we believe he was the last victim lured into the oven. But they all showed traces of the same drugs."

"Would you please explain to the jury what those findings were?"

"Ketamine. All four were exposed to ketamine."

"And what is that?"

"It's most common use—at least it's most common legal use—is as a horse anesthetic. Veterinarians use it when they perform surgery. But it has a mind-altering effect on humans."

"It produces a high?"

"It does, but perhaps more importantly—it is thought to be one of the few true aphrodisiacs."

He noted several eyebrows rising in the jury box, and not just from the men. They'd all heard rumors about oysters and marijuana, but this was new.

"What do you mean? What's an aphrodisiac?"

"I mean it heightens sexual experience. Pleasure. According to some sources, it produces an orgasm more intense than anything most people will ever experience naturally."

"Is that the only effect?"

"No. In time, it produces a hard, deep sleep. The kind nothing will rouse you from, not till the drug wears off."

"Was that all you found?"

"No. The bodies also showed traces of MDMA—ecstasy. Also amphetamines, mixed with alcohol. It would appear that all four victims drank a heady cocktail before they were placed in the oven. The inevitable unconsciousness may have been the key to getting them into the oven."

"Would they have remained unconscious…when the temperature rose?"

"Impossible to know for certain. But based upon the concentrations of drugs found in the bloodstreams of the corpses, I would say yes—in at least two of the four cases.

Perhaps three. The last victim put in there—Nick Mansfield—seems to have regained consciousness."

"He would've known what was happening to him?"

"In all probability. But of course, he was helpless to do anything about it."

"Do you have any idea how the victims might have received these drugs?"

"A flask was found at the scene of the crime, in the main lobby of the bakery. We tested it and found traces of ketamine, alcohol, and MDMA. Presumably the victims drank from the flask. Within twenty minutes, they'd be hard asleep. Faster if they experienced a sexual climax."

What a day that must've been, he thought. Best sex ever, dreamless sleep—and then you awake to find your flesh cooking.

"Where is that flask now?"

"I don't know. I was in our evidence locker, but it has disappeared."

Jazlyn turned toward the defense table. "Do you know who took it?"

"No."

"Who would have a motive to remove this evidence?"

"Objection." He rose to his feet. "Calls for speculation." He knew that missing evidence was always an embarrassment to the prosecution, but he didn't appreciate the suggestion that he might've had something to do with it.

"Sustained," Judge Hayes replied. "Anything else from the prosecution?"

"No more questions. Your witness, Mr. Pike."

He toyed with letting Dr. Abraham go uncrossed, but then again, if he rooted around a little, he might stumble across something useful. At any rate, it was worth a try.

He squared himself in front of the witness, careful not to let his limp show. That leg still hurt like the blazes. "Your whole testimony appears based upon the assumption that the victims, and Nick Mansfield in particular, were given drugs by someone else. Were there any signs of violence at the bakery?"

"Some overturned chairs. Evidence of bodies being dragged."

"You're not answering my question. Is there any evidence that anyone was forced to drink from the flask?"

"Not that I'm aware of."

"They could've taken it voluntarily."

"I couldn't say."

"Because they probably wanted that all-time-high orgasm you were talking about."

"Again, I couldn't—"

"Have you ever encountered instances of people doing stupid things to get high? Or to get laid? Or to have a great orgasm?"

Dr. Abraham appeared supremely uncomfortable. "This is outside my area of expertise…"

"Have you heard of autoerotic asphyxiation?"

"Well…yes."

"People choke themselves, or have others choke them, because they believe that near-death strangulation will result in a more powerful climax. Some people believe that was what led to David Carradine's accidental death."

"I have heard of that."

"You know that some people risk death just for the thrill. For the heart-thumping orgasm."

"We are all driven by sexual drives. It is inherent in our DNA."

"And of course, drug addicts are constantly risking death, taking dangerous drugs, to get a high."

"That is true."

"For all you know, these men might have voluntarily taken these drugs. They might have mixed the brews and brought it themselves."

He saw the doctor's eyes dart toward Jazlyn and also

spotted her tiny but detectible shake of the head. Don't fight him, she was cueing. Which was good advice. She needed her experts to remain above the fray. She'd do the arguing for them later.

"My job is to report on my scientific findings. Not to speculate about people's motives."

"Then I'll ask the jury to disregard all your testimony with respect to motives. You don't know how those men came to take the drugs, and you don't know why they took the drugs."

"That's true."

He knew that wouldn't really get him much, especially after the other police witnesses took the stand. But at least he felt like he was doing something. And it might buoy Camila's spirits. Which would be good.

Because he knew this trial was about to get much worse.

CHAPTER THIRTY-FOUR

DURING THE LUNCH BREAK, DAN AND MARIA AND CAMILA discussed what had happened so far. They had all been watching the faces in the jury box, but Camila seemed particularly astute in her observations—even though he had warned her never to appear to be staring, or to do anything that made the jury feel uncomfortable. She thought the jury looked smart and attentive, and she was encouraged by the fact that they didn't avoid making eye contact with her. They were understandably curious, but not skittish. Or to use her words, there was no sign that they had already decided to convict her.

He spotted Prudence Hancock, Sweeney's assistant, entering the courtroom and seating herself on the back row of the gallery, not far from the plainclothes security officers K hired to keep an eye on him. Jimmy noticed as well, and his bug-eyed expression suggested that he didn't like being on the same side of the courtroom with her.

Had Lex Luthor sent her here on some dastardly mission? He texted:

Ray gun wouldn't get past metal detectors

Jimmy texted back:

Unless made of plastic—Lex is genius

Camila turned to face the gallery, and unless he was mistaken, Prudence appeared to duck.

Did she not want to be spotted by the mayor?

Jazlyn spent the early afternoon calling a series of police officers to the witness stand. The first was Bryan Dietrich, the unfortunate soul who was the first to discover the corpses. His usual beat was patrolling the Crislip Arcade area, an assignment that rarely involved anything dangerous or complex. On the morning in question, however, he encountered something dramatically different.

"It was the smell that led to the report," he explained. Baby face. Missed a loop with his belt. White undershirt. "That's what I was supposed to be investigating. I thought it was probably a dead animal. Maybe a skunk. Something like that."

"How did you go about your investigation?" Jazlyn asked.

"I had to force entry. The door was closed. Padlocked. The registered owner was a corporation called Petersburg Preservation, and at the time, I had no idea who owned it." Of course, as Jazlyn mentioned in her opening, the owner was Camila. "I called the number listed with the Secretary of State, but no one answered or called back."

"Did that surprise you?"

"It did. There were signs that renovation was about to begin, so I expected someone to be in charge. But I never saw anyone there or heard from them. So, based upon the public nuisance, I was forced to enter the premises."

"What did you discover?"

He shook his head slowly, as if the question brought the memory too vividly back to his consciousness. "The stench was unbearable. This wasn't my first rodeo, and I've seen some bad stuff, but when I got a whiff of this—I almost passed out. I ultimately put a cloth over my nose and mouth just so I could bear it."

"What did you find?"

"Bit of a mess in the lobby. Overturned chair. Litter. I thought maybe an animal had gotten inside, knocked things around a bit. But the odor became a much more intense as I approached the kitchen."

"What did you find there?"

"The source of the smell appeared to be the oven. Big industrial-sized thing, designed to cook several tiers at once. Clamp handle on the door. No way to open it from the inside, but easy from the outside. I opened it…" He fell silent.

"Officer Dietrich, please tell the jury what you found."

He took several seconds before answering. "Turned out the oven was big enough to accommodate more than bread. It was big enough to contain four adult bodies."

"Is that what you found?"

"I found what…remained of four men. They had been burned. Caked blood on the floor and the walls. What wasn't burned to a crisp was…" He drew in a deep breath. "Melted."

"Do you have a clear memory of what you saw?"

"I will never be able to get that image out of my head. And believe me, I've tried."

"Did you see any sign that the victims attempted to escape?"

"They were trussed up, knees to nose. Trapped."

"Were there any signs that anyone had…made use of their hands?" She was trying not to lead the witness, but they all knew where she was going with this.

"Only one. The corpse nearest the oven door, the one who was later identified as Nick Mansfield. His fingers touched the base. He appeared to be…drawing."

"In his own blood?"

"Or someone else's."

"And what did he draw?"

Dietrich took another deep breath. "Looked to me like the letter 'C.'"

JAZLYN FOLLOWED WITH TWO OTHER POLICE WITNESSES WHO mostly just filled in the blanks, covering a few items Dietrich could not.

A member of the CSI team named Glen Austin testified about what was found on the premises. Portly. Monotone. Dark circles around his eyes. The only items of interest were the flask and the vial.

The second police witness worked in the records lab and looked like he rarely got out of the basement. Thick glasses. Spit curl. Small bruise on right hand. He was the one who eventually learned that Petersburg Preservation was a holding company one hundred percent owned by the defendant. He opined that, as the legal owner, she would undoubtedly have a set of keys.

The jury also heard from Dr. Brenda Palmer, the finger-print expert. He had examined Palmer during the Gabriella Valdez case. She'd been pushed to take her evidence further than she should and he'd burned her badly. He could tell she was not happy to back in the courtroom with him. As might be expected, there were a host of fingerprints in the bakery, particularly on the doors and countertops. And some of those matched Camila.

On cross, he tried to make this seem as insignificant as possible. He smiled as he approached Dr. Palmer. Pant suit. Small scar behind left ear. Stud earring, also on the left side. "You would expect the owner of the building to have visited once or twice, wouldn't you?"

"I can't say that I find it surprising."

"And there were many other fingerprints around the place, weren't there?"

"I detected at least forty-seven distinct sets of prints."

"Can you time-date the fingerprints?" This was a loaded question. During the Valdez case, the doctor had claimed she could establish a rough timeline of when prints were laid down. He had destroyed the whole theory on cross. He doubted she would try that again.

He was right. "Not with any degree of accuracy. We generally assume that those with greater oil residue are more recent, but that can vary depending upon the degree of contact. How long, how hard."

"Can you give the jury any idea when the prints from my client were made?"

"I feel comfortable saying it was within a month of when I conducted my examination. Anything more specific would be speculative. They were good, strong prints, but as I've said, there are multiple possible explanations for that."

Palmer was playing it safe. Which was just the way he liked it.

"Did you find her prints on the flask?"

"We found no prints on the flask."

"And the vial?"

"Same thing. No prints."

"What about the oven?"

"We did find prints on the oven, but they were blurred and indistinct, probably due to the high temperatures."

"So as far as you're concerned, there's no evidence that my client was even in the kitchen, much less near the oven."

The doctor drew in her breath—then smiled. Once burned, forever cautious. "I did not find a clear set of prints on the oven."

Good. Jazlyn might've established that deaths occurred, but there was nothing strongly tying Camila to the deaths.

Yet.

Of course, the prosecution was just getting started.

CHAPTER THIRTY-FIVE

DAN HAD MIXED FEELINGS ABOUT JAZLYN'S LAST WITNESS FOR the day, Detective Jake Kakazu. He suspected Jazlyn had saved him for a reason. Given Kakazu's many years of experience, he had undoubtedly testified on many occasions and acquired a certain competence, if not expertise. Plus he was smart, though not a smart aleck. She wanted the jury to go home feeling like the prosecution was doing its job—and the defendant was probably guilty.

Smart witnesses were always dangerous, but the detective was a straight shooter and would not willingly be part of any wrongful prosecution. He preferred crossing someone he respected.

Jazlyn quickly established that Kakazu had been called to the scene of the crime, arriving less than an hour after Dietrich discovered the bodies. He sealed the area and called for forensics, then contacted the medical examiner's office to ask what to do about the four corpses decaying in the oven.

"Did you notice anything unusual about the crime scene?" Jazlyn asked.

Kakazu raised an eyebrow. "Finding four corpses in a

bakery oven is always going to be on my Top Five List of Unusual Discoveries." A few of the jurors flashed a wry smile.

"Let's take it one step at a time. Anything unusual in the lobby area? Where customers would enter."

"The place was covered with dust. It was difficult to breathe. I get allergies."

"Anything else?"

"As you know, one of the chairs had been overturned and one of the tables had been cleared. Everything on it had been swept to the floor. I didn't think anything of it at first..." His eyes wandered to the defendant's table. "...but I eventually was persuaded that someone might've had...a moment of passion on the table."

Jazlyn batted her eyes. "And when you say 'moment of passion'...are you talking about sex?"

"Yes. Two people had sex on the table."

"You found evidence."

"The CSIs found traces. Dried seminal fluids and such. Not enough to get a DNA sample. But enough to make it clear someone had used the table...in a non-traditional way."

"Would that be before or after the oven cooked the victims?"

"We found the fingerprints of one of the victims, Nick Mansfield, just under the rim of the table."

"Just beneath it?"

"Yes. As if he had been...gripping the edges." He glanced at the jury box to see if they were following what he was implying. They were not. "As if his sex partner had been on top, straddling him, and he gripped the tabletop to hang on."

Okay, now the jury was on board. Though the elderly woman on the back row offered a sour frown.

"Do you know when this sex act occurred?"

"Based upon the forensic samplings, we believe it occurred about an hour before the oven became a murder weapon. And given evidence of an aphrodisiac on the premises..." He shrugged. "Looks like the last victim, Nick Mansfield, got turned on, got lucky…and then got extremely unlucky." He shivered a bit. "Talk about unsafe sex."

"Any other fingerprints?"

"Only Mansfield's. We assume that the other person in the room wore gloves. Or wiped her prints off afterwards."

He jumped to his feet. "Objection to the use of the feminine pronoun."

Judge Hayes gave him a patronizing look. "Do you think he was having sex with a man?"

He remembered Jimmy saying Hayes had performed gay marriages. "It's possible. At any rate, I object to anything that points prejudicially to my client."

Jazlyn jumped in. "The evidence *all* points—"

"We're not even talking about evidence here. We're talking about the absence of evidence. The absence of fingerprints doesn't point toward anyone."

The judge grudgingly agreed. "I'll sustain the objection."

Kakazu rephrased. "I'm sorry. The other person in the room that presumably gave him the flask might have worn gloves or wiped their prints off."

Jazlyn nodded. "And the vial?"

"It held the ketamine, which is not the easiest thing to obtain. Possibly stolen from a veterinarian's office, though thanks to the glorious thing that is the internet, it is possible to get the stuff online. Dark web."

"Did you examine the kitchen and the oven?"

"I did. The oven door was open, as Officer Dietrich left it. Most of the kitchen seemed ordinary, if you ignored the stench. It was only after you stuck your head in the oven that you felt as if you'd stepped into the Twilight Zone."

Jazlyn handed him a photograph. Fortunately, the photo was not in color. "Can you identify this?"

"Yes. That's the interior of the oven. Just as I found it. I took this photo myself."

Jazlyn handed him one more exhibit. "Can you explain what this is?"

He glanced at it, then answered. "This is the same photo, but an enlargement focusing on Nick Mansfield's right hand. As you can see, he was able to touch the surface. Just to be clear, the lower surface would have been hot, but it was not the source of the heat. The heating elements were on the sides."

Which they were pressed up against.

"Is there anything unusual about this photo?" She put an enlargement on a large television screen, as she had the other exhibits. The jurors winced. One covered his eyes.

"If you zero in on his hand, you'll see that he appears to have drawn something with his finger. He had a brief opportunity to draw in a liquid surface until it became so hot that the blood coagulated."

"And the drawing?" Steering him back to the subject.

"You can see for yourself. He's making a semi-circular line in the blood. You can also tell that he had to make an effort to touch the surface, which was already painfully hot."

"And the drawing?"

"He's making the letter 'C.'"

Jazlyn stared at Camila, just in case someone wasn't quick enough to recall the first letter of her first name. "Interesting."

Jazlyn let that sit with the jury for a while before she continued. "Have you been able to identify the four men in the oven?"

"Three of them—and all have connections to the defendant."

"Objection." He rose. "That's not what the witness was asked."

"Sustained," the judge said diffidently, as if he really didn't see the point. They were sure to get there soon enough.

"How did you discover the identity of the victims?"

"That was a problem, initially. None but Mansfield had ID

on them. Presumably the killer removed identifying traces. One was a man named Sean Callahan. He was an unemployed plumber. Seemed to work intermittently as a handyman and had done some work at the mayor's office. We traced Callahan by searching through missing persons reports till we found someone who matched the victim in the oven."

"And the third victim?"

"Jonathan Primo. College professor. History department. We believe he was the first one dragged into the oven, although they all appear to have arrived within twenty-four hours of one another."

"How did you track him down?"

Kakazu smiled. "Facebook."

"How did you manage that?"

"Although none of the corpses were in the best condition, Primo's face showed the least damage. We were able to make a detailed facial recognition scan, adjusting for burn damage, reddening, swelling, and so forth. The software makes a record of the details of the face—distance between eyes, between nostrils, height of the cheekbones, and so forth. Then we ran the data through the faces in Facebook photos, starting with pages belonging to people in the St. Petersburg area."

"And that worked?"

"Like a charm. Took a while, but eventually we got a hit. That's the cool thing about detective work today—people are surveilling themselves, uploading selfies and posting constant status updates about their every movement. Makes our job a lot simpler."

Once again, Jazlyn steered him back to the case. "You looked at the Facebook pages of all the victims after they were identified, didn't you?"

"Yes."

"Find anything of interest?"

"You mean the video, right? Callahan had posted a video

he took with his iPhone. Shows the mayor—well, you should see for yourself."

After she entered it into evidence, Jazlyn played the video on the screen for the jurors.

He had already seen it, of course, but it was no less damning the tenth time around. In fact, it was much worse, because he watched it with a room full of people who held Camila's future in their hands. He had tried to keep the video out, arguing that it violated wiretapping laws because Camila didn't know she was being recorded, but given the gravity of the charges, and the fact that it was not being admitted to prove the truth of the matter asserted, the judge let it come in.

The video started *in medias res*. The altercation had already begun. Callahan had put his phone in his shirt pocket, so it caught Camila at eye level.

She was angry. Loud, aggressive, violently angry. She was in his face and shouting, so close to the phone that she appeared in distorted close-up, making it even less flattering. She was screaming, pushing, threatening. Her voice was so loud that most of the time it was hard to make out the words, though a few choice phrases emerged. "Son-of-a-whore." "Cheapass bastard." "Brokedick loser."

Toward the end, she screamed, "Do you think you can get away with this?"

In the video, Callahan held up his hands, as if to protect himself. "I'm not trying anything."

"No one gets away with this. Not in my office. Not to me and my people!"

"Maybe I should just leave."

She moved even closer to him. "And don't come back. Ever."

"I'm going to leave now."

"You'll leave or I'll throw you out!"

"I said, I'm leaving."

He backed toward the door, but she grabbed his arm.

"You will pay for what you have done. Do you understand what I am saying? You will pay for this!"

The video ended abruptly. The lights came up in the courtroom. The jurors looked at one another, rubbing their eyes as they adjusted to the light.

The entire courtroom was silent. And all eyes were on Camila.

That video made her look dangerous. Crazy, even. Crazy dangerous.

Jazlyn turned toward him. "Your witness, Mr. Pike."

He could read the expression in her eyes. *Good luck.*

CHAPTER THIRTY-SIX

DAN DECIDED TO START SLOW AND BUILD. IDEALLY, YOU wanted a cross to end with your strongest point, your most impressive indictment of the witness's testimony. The problem was, you could never be sure what that might be. You took your shot, hoped for the best—but outcomes were never completely predictable. Especially with a witness as smart as this one. Kakazu already knew where the holes in this case were. He wouldn't overreach, he wouldn't say anything he couldn't support—and he probably would see Dan's attacks coming long before they arrived.

"Detective Kakazu, do you seriously think any halfway intelligent person would choose to murder people in a bakery she owned? I mean, wouldn't that be about the stupidest possible move?"

"In my experience, criminals are often stupid. Especially when their temper gets control of them. And that client of yours has a temper. As we all saw."

"You did not find my client's fingerprints on the flask, correct?"

"She might've worn gloves."

"In Florida? This time of year?"

"It's possible."

"Did you find any gloves on the premises?"

"To borrow your phrase, leaving the gloves would be the stupidest move possible."

"So the killer was stupid enough to leave the flask, but not stupid enough to leave the gloves?"

"I suspect that she forgot about the flask when she got wrapped up in the hot sex."

"You have no evidence that my client engaged in sexual activity on those premises."

"Someone did."

"But you don't know who. And there were no prints on the flask, right?"

"She might've wiped the flask after she touched it."

"And that wouldn't make Mansfield suspicious? Watching someone wipe the flask clean?"

Kakazu shrugged. "He wouldn't be the first man who ignored red flags when he thought he was about to get—I mean, you know. When he believed a sexual encounter was imminent."

"And the vial? Did you find my client's fingerprints on it?"

"You know we didn't. Completely clean."

"The only spots you found my client's prints were on the doorknobs and the countertops, correct?"

"Correct."

"And it would be impossible to visit, as she must've done before buying the bakery, without touching those places."

"Probably true."

"And since she left prints on those occasions…she must not have been wearing gloves, right?"

Kakazu tossed his head back and forth for a moment, then answered. "I'll give you that one."

Hallelujah. Ten minutes in, he'd made one point. "You said repeatedly that one of the victims, Nick Mansfield, had an intimate relationship with my client. I must've missed the evidence, though. What's your proof?"

"You've stipulated that they dated."

"A single dinner date. Is that what constitutes an intimate relationship in your mind?"

"It's a logical assumption. We have several witnesses—"

He cut Kakazu off. "Have these witnesses testified?"

Kakazu glanced at Jazlyn. "Not yet."

"Then why don't you let them speak for themselves. We don't need a hearsay sneak preview. All you know for certain is that the two went out once, right?"

"Okay."

"And you have no idea how intimate they were during the date."

Kakazu glanced again at Jazlyn. "So far."

"You misled the jury. You suggested they were physically intimate, but you have no evidence to support your assertion."

"I never used the word physical. There are many kinds of intimacy."

"We all know perfectly well you led the jury to believe they were sex partners."

"To the contrary, I am content to allow the jury to form their own conclusions, based upon the fact that they went out once, she has a passionate temperament, and she apparently had sex in an abandoned bakery."

"Objection. Motion to strike. He has no evidence my client was the woman in the bakery before the murders occurred."

Jazlyn stood to respond. "The witness did say 'apparently.'"

"Your honor, may we approach?"

He knew they were about to argue, which meant rehashing Kakazu's statements, and he didn't want them repeated in front of the jury. At some point, it didn't matter whether evidence supported a statement. If it's repeated often enough, people start to assume it must be true.

The two lawyers walked to the bench. Judge Hayes covered the microphone. He seemed torn. "You did, in effect, ask the witness for his interpretation of the evidence."

"I asked if he had evidence of intimacy. He responded by repeating his self-serving and baseless assumption that they did and may have repeated the act in the bakery."

"Detective Kakazu is a fifteen-year veteran of the force," Jazlyn said. "He has insight on these matters. He's effectively an expert witness."

"Not today he isn't. He's a fact witness. He was called as a fact witness. And that means he should be reporting the facts. Not giving his slanted interpretations."

"If you're going to ask these argumentative questions," Jazlyn said, "you have to expect him to respond in kind."

"The only thing I expect your witness to do is answer questions. Not be part of an orchestrated smear campaign."

Judge Hayes drew in his breath. "I will agree that the witness was called as a fact witness and should not be arguing or interpreting the facts."

"Thank you."

The judge raised a finger. "But that means that you need to stop trying to use him as a springboard for your closing argument. Fact-based questions beget fact-based answers. Argumentative questions lead to argumentative answers. Understand what I'm saying?"

He did. "Thank you, your honor."

They left the bench. "The objection is sustained. Please continue the questioning."

The judge was probably right in one respect. Trying to argue with this witness was futile. He had too much experience to be intimidated by a defense lawyer. Time to try something new. "You mentioned that Nick Mansfield's finger touched the base of the oven."

"Yes. And drew the letter 'C.'"

"There you go again. Interpreting, instead of stating the facts."

He shrugged. "Sure looks like a 'C' to me."

"Wouldn't it be more honest to say it's somewhat C-shaped?"

"Wouldn't a 'C' always be C-shaped?"

"The question is whether the victim was deliberately drawing a 'C,' or whether a momentary twitch or spasm caused a movement vaguely in that shape."

"I listened to the testimony of the medical experts," Kakazu said. "I heard nothing about twitches or spasms."

"Do you think he might possibly have squirmed a bit? Like when the oven got up to a hundred degrees?"

"To me, that's all the more reason to not touch the surface —unless you have a definite purpose. I still think it's a 'C.'"

"But you don't know for certain."

"I wasn't there. But it looks like a 'C' to me."

"Even if you think it was a deliberate effort to draw something, you can't say with certainty that he was drawing a letter. It might have been the start of something else."

"Yeah. Like her full name."

"Objection. Motion to strike."

Jazlyn bounced to her feet, but the judge waved her down. "Don't bother. Sustained."

"Isn't it true that you have no way of knowing what Nick Mansfield was trying to write or draw?"

"I know what I think."

"No, you're guessing, trying to make your scant evidence point to the only suspect you ever seriously considered."

"Mr. Pike." The judge looked stern. "Now you're being objectionable."

"Sorry, your honor." Which he wasn't. "Let me rephrase. You don't read minds and you never spoke to Nick Mansfield. So you don't know what, if anything, he was doing with his finger in the blood. And why assume it was a letter? Perhaps he was drawing a crescent moon."

"Looks like a letter to me."

"The top half of an 'S'? An unfinished 'G.'"

"That's not what I see."

"Even assuming it's a 'C,' do you know how many words in the Oxford English Dictionary start with a 'C'?"

Kakazu beamed. "4,364." He glanced at the jury and winked. "This isn't the first time he's asked me."

"I'm pleased to see you did a little investigating. Of something."

Kakazu winced. "Ooh. Burn."

"But you never seriously considered any suspect other than my client, did you?"

"With respect, sir, her guilt has been obvious since the crime was discovered."

"Objection."

The judge shook his head. "I think you asked for that one."

Kakazu continued. "The rest of the investigation has just been filling in the blanks. Completing the story. But we already knew the ending."

He let it go. He had one more subject to tackle, then he was going to mercifully terminate this keenly unproductive examination. "I'd like to ask you a few questions about the video you showed the jury. You say you found that on one of the victims' Facebook pages, right?"

"The late Mr. Callahan, yes. He shot it with his iPhone, then uploaded it."

"Was that the only video on his page?"

"No."

"But that was the only one you showed the jury."

"That was the only one that shows the mayor screaming like a maniac."

"Is it possible she had a good reason?"

"I'm sure she thought so."

"Is it possible the man did something so horrible anyone would've been upset?"

Kakazu considered. "Most people are better able to keep their heads together, even in negative circumstances."

"Have you ever lost your temper?"

"Me?"

"Yeah, you, the detective with fifteen years on the force. Ever lost your cool?"

"Once or twice."

"Does that prove you're a cold-blooded killer?"

"Obviously not."

"In fact, it's impossible to judge whether someone's reaction is reasonable without knowing what instigated the situation, wouldn't you say?"

"That reaction was over the top, no matter what explanation she trots out."

"What if the man threatened your daughter?"

Kakazu stopped short. He knew Kakazu had two daughters and like most daddies, he loved them dearly. "Your client doesn't have a daughter."

"She has people she cares about. Answer the question. If someone threatened your daughter, would you calmly attempt to reason with them? Or would you bite their head off?"

Kakazu thought a long time before answering. "In that situation, I might be prone to overreact."

"Thank you for your honesty. One more thing—why didn't you show the jury the entire video?"

Kakazu stiffened. "What?"

"Is there something you didn't want the jury to see?"

"I don't know what you're talking about."

"Do you know what metadata is?"

"Vaguely…"

"Well, iPhones store metadata with every photo or video they take. I'm told you can turn that off, but almost no one does. This is why iPhones can tag people and add locations and such." He paused. "It also stores the length of the video. And your video was originally one minute and twelve seconds longer than the video you showed. I can put our expert on the stand if there's any dispute about this."

He could see Kakazu glancing at Jazlyn, begging for answers. "I'm sorry. I don't know anything about this."

"Did you extract the video from the phone?"

"No. CSI tech-heads do stuff like that."

"Do you dispute that the video was edited?"

"I know I didn't edit it."

"Is there anyone in the courtroom who can explain how this video was doctored before you played it to the jury?"

Another glance at Jazlyn. "I don't think so."

"Do you know what editing tools were used?"

"No."

"Can you establish the chain of custody regarding the iPhone or the video copied from it?"

"I didn't know we'd be getting into this."

He addressed the judge. "Your honor, at this time I renew my motion to exclude the video as evidence. I'll submit a brief detailing our findings, but bottom line, something was cut and I rather doubt that was done accidentally. Since the jury has already seen the video, we'll ask that they be instructed to disregard it."

In fact, he could've turned this into a terrific motion for mistrial, but Camila forbid it. She wanted this business over with. He could blow all the smoke he wanted, but anything that kept her out of office one day longer than necessary, she opposed.

Judge Hayes blew out his cheeks. He clearly didn't like this —but he couldn't overlook possible evidence tampering. "I'll ask for briefs from both parties. If the video has been tampered with…I'll take it from there."

"Thank you, your honor. I have no more questions."

The judge glanced at his watch. "We've had a long day. Let's shut 'er down. That will give you time to submit your expert's information to the prosecution and give them a chance to respond. I want your briefs first thing tomorrow morning. I'll rule as soon as possible. Court dismissed."

Back at counsel table, Maria flashed him a "thumbs up."

Camila waited till he sat down. "This is good for us, right?"

"It's not as good as if Kakazu had broken down in tears and confessed that he turned on the oven. But yes, I think this was our best play."

"I watched the jury while Jazlyn played that video. They didn't like what they saw."

"They don't understand the context."

"They understand that it shows me being exactly what the entire internet currently says I am." She placed her head in her hands. "Combine memes and sneaky-cam videos, and you get the death penalty."

He laid his hand on her shoulder. "That's going to change. Right now, we're doing damage control. Picking at the prosecution case. When we put on our case—" He smiled. "They're going to meet a very different Camila Pérez."

CHAPTER THIRTY-SEVEN

JAZLYN STOPPED HIM IN THE HALLWAY OUTSIDE THE courtroom. He wasn't surprised.

"What the hell was that?" Her voice wasn't loud enough to attract attention, but for her, this was practically shouting.

"That was me doing my job."

"By suggesting that I doctored evidence."

"I never said that."

"Practically. Why didn't you tell me about this before? I would've gotten to the bottom of it before the trial began."

He smiled but did not reply. He considered telling her, but ultimately, he didn't think giving her advance notice was best for the defense. The suggestion of evidence tampering buttressed their theory that this case was politically motivated.

"Don't you understand that when you make these insinuations, it impugns my reputation?"

"I'm on record acknowledging that you're a fine prosecutor."

"But a crooked one?"

"I've never said anything like that."

She took a step closer. "I know we're on opposite sides of the courtroom. And I know you're obligated to defend your client." Her voice dropped. "But I also thought we were friends."

"I hope we will—"

"And friends don't pull crap like this on one another. This is beyond the pale."

"Jazlyn, please. Let's—"

She turned her back on him. "Excuse me. I have a brief to write."

She walked away wordlessly, cold as ice.

DAN TOOK CAMILA HOME AND SPENT SOME TIME WITH HER, making sure she felt as strong as anyone could possibly be when their life was on the line. As he left, she hesitated, standing close, peering into his eyes.

Was he misreading the signals? Imagining them? Flattering himself?

Didn't matter. She was his client, and as long as this case was active, nothing remotely romantic could take place.

Afterward....

Back at the office, Maria and Jimmy buzzed about the kitchen assembling some kind of frozen something while Garrett noodled at the keyboard. But he wasn't playing his usual Brubeckesque jazz riffs. This piece was slower and had more sustained notes. Somber. Almost mournful.

"Is that a dirge?" he mumbled to Maria as she passed by. "Are we having a funeral for the case?"

"Don't be silly. He's just in a mood. We all need a vacay."

Jimmy passed by stirring a pot, head bobbing from side to side. "This has definitely not been a good day."

"Because you're stirring your sauce with a metal spoon?"

Jimmy glared. "No, Gordon Ramsey. Because our client looks guilty."

"You think so?"

"I know so. The jurors think so too. They may not have made up their minds yet. But that video, plus that business with the 'C' sketched in blood, didn't help at all."

"That could be anything."

Maria raised her hands. "Dan, stop already. It's a 'C.' It's clearly a 'C.' Everyone thinks it's a 'C.' And every time you suggest it might be a twitch or a crescent moon or something, you sound desperate. Better to come up with an alternate explanation for the 'C.'"

"Like what?"

Silence permeated the kitchen.

"I thought the video was the worst," Maria said. "She looked like a banshee about to take her next victim."

"Oh, come on. It wasn't that bad."

"It was bad. It made an impact. They'd never seen their mayor behave like that."

"Ok, so she has a temper. Everyone does."

"Not like that."

"Having a temper doesn't mean she'd be crazy enough to bake four men in an oven."

"And yet," Jimmy said, "someone was crazy enough to do it. I'm guessing it wasn't a calm, even-tempered soul."

"I don't buy it. Camila is too smart. Too career-oriented."

Maria tapped him on the chest with a spatula. "You're not seeing clearly, Dan. Because you're sweet on our client."

"I'm sweet on all our clients."

"Not like this."

"We've never had a case like this. No one has."

"You're changing the subject." She grinned. "Our cool aloof warrior-king has a crush on the mayor!"

"I do not."

Jimmy gave him a stern look. "No sex till after the case."

"I know that! I mean, I'm not saying—I don't—"

"Uh huh." Jimmy continued stirring. "Would it be presumptuous of me to suggest that it's unwise to develop an attachment to someone who may well be living behind bars in a few days?"

"Yes, actually, it would." He changed the subject. "Has anyone figured out how Sweeney found out about the motion *in limine*?"

"That man gives me the creeps. He's a Lex Luthor clone—"

A mechanical female voice cut in. "I don't have a response for that."

Jimmy looked puzzled. "What? Why?" He stopped. "Oh, I get it. She thought she heard her name when I said 'a Lex—'"

The blue ring appeared atop the black box. "Would you like to hear a song from your playlist?"

They answered in unison. "No!"

He tried to steer them back to the case. "Do we have a leak?"

Garrett stopped playing and cleared his throat. "We do."

All eyes in the kitchen moved to their senior partner.

"I'm not saying it was one of us," Garrett continued. "I'd stake my career that it wasn't, in fact. Even if one of you disliked Camila or thought she was guilty"—he paused —"which would not be an impossible assumption, you still wouldn't betray the team. But the fact remains. Word got out."

"Any idea how?"

"We've had this problem before. Remember during the Gabriella Valdez case? Someone leaked info from a confidential client conference."

He remembered all too well. "And?"

"And now a leak from an *in camera* motion we filed. What do the two have in common?"

He thought a moment. "The courthouse."

"Someone there could easily plant a listening device in a client consultation room."

Jimmy leaned in. "I don't believe it."

"And there's another possibility." Garrett turned toward the cylindrical black box on the countertop. "Alexa, are you listening to our conversation?"

The blue ring accompanied the female voice. "I only listen after I hear the wake word."

Garrett smiled. "But how could she hear the wake word unless she's listening? You see what I'm saying, Dan?"

"Are you suggesting that our leak...is Maria's Amazon Echo?"

"It's not impossible. Amazon has admitted that they have thousands of employees working on improving their digital assistants, in part by listening to voice recordings captured in the homes and offices of Echo owners. Those recordings are transcribed and stored on a computer, analyzed to improve Alexa's responses. Any computer record can be hacked. You may have heard about the Oregon couple who discovered that hours of their conversations had been recorded, stored, and sent to a friend. It was supposedly an accident."

"You don't believe it?"

"I have no idea. The point is, Alexa is not only listening, she's retaining records of conversations she hears. We need stronger privacy laws. Europe has the General Data Protection Regulation, but in the US we have nothing. Privacy activists have filed a complaint with the FTC arguing that these voice-activated devices violate the Federal Wiretap Act."

"That seems extreme."

"The reality is, we've voluntarily put millions of live mics in our homes, and we don't have the final say on when they're active or who gets to listen. The mic can record your daily activities and location history. Your preferences and routines. We're giving artificial intelligence enormous amounts of information that could be used against us."

Maria reached toward the wall. "Okay, I'm unplugging Alexa."

"And while you're at it, take off that Fitbit."

Her eyes widened like balloons. "No!"

"It makes records too. About your location and activities. That's how it knows whether you've hit your walking goals. That data is stored on a cloud and could be hacked."

Maria sounded as if she might burst into tears. "But I love my Fitbit."

"For that matter," Garrett continued, "we're all carrying little computers in our pockets that we call phones, even though people rarely use them to make calls anymore. It's well known that the FBI can activate them and use them as listening devices. Even if they aren't turned on. Ditto for your laptops. The Feebs can peer right through that camera lens."

Maria lowered herself into a chair. "Okay, you're making me very paranoid."

"So now you know why I'm playing dirges. It's an elegy to our personal privacy. Which we have largely given up in exchange for high-tech convenience."

Maria looked as if her life were over. "But I can't give up my cell phone…"

"No, you can't. We need to be able to contact you, text you, send you documents instantaneously. And that's the point. The only reason our phones can perform these miracles…is because they know where you are and what you're doing. They're listening. They're watching. They're keeping tabs on you." He paused. "And storing information that could be used against you."

CHAPTER THIRTY-EIGHT

DAN WONDERED IF THE TRIAL GODS WERE CONSPIRING WITH Garrett to creep everyone out, because the first prosecution witness of the morning fanned the flames he'd stoked the evening before.

Bret McCoy was a telecommunications data-mining expert, which was apparently a fancy way of saying he hacked cell phones and knew everything there was to know about them. He had helped the prosecutors draft the search warrants they used to obtain information, not only from Camila's phone, but also from the phones of others who were in the pedestrian shopping area at the approximate time the oven was activated.

"It's called a geofence warrant," McCoy explained. Big man, former wrestler. Curly hair. Hipster threads. "A tool we use to collect information about people suspected of crimes. We specified an area and a time period and sent the warrant to Google."

"Did Google reply?"

"Yes. Fortunately, the defendant used an Android phone. Apple claims it doesn't collect this kind of information. But Google does. In Sensorvault."

The jury looked mystified but intrigued. Many probably had Android phones. "What is Sensorvault?"

"That's a Google database. Huge thing. Connected to their Location History service. Started in 2009."

"Is this on all Android phones?"

"It is, but it's not on by default. Google prompts users when they set up their phones. They can choose whether they want it activated."

"Do most people use Location Services?"

"Almost everyone. Because they want Google Maps. They want real-time traffic alerts and such. And that means Google has to know where they are. Google can collect that data any time the phone is on, even if you're not currently using an app that requires location services. They use it for commercial purposes. For instance, to target ads. They know when you've been in an advertiser's store—or a competitor's."

"And Google will provide this information to law enforcement?"

"Yes. Sensorvault turns all those cellphone user locations into a digital dragnet that law enforcement can access. Federal agents were the first to use this, back in 2016, but since then, many local and state departments have also used it. Last year, Google was getting 180 requests a week."

"Did your warrant produce any useful information?"

"Yes. I collected the data in a spreadsheet to help everyone see the bottom line." After admitting his spreadsheet into evidence, Jazlyn put it up on the screen so the jurors could view it. "I realize not everyone here is a techie like me, so staring at numbers may not be your idea of a great time. I highlighted the most important parts."

"What conclusions did you reach?"

"This data provides information on all devices recorded at or near the bakery at the time the murders took place. We can say with absolute certainty that Camila Pérez was in the area at the time the murders took place. She was there when the last victim was lured onto the premises. She was there when the sex act took place in the lobby." He paused. "And she was there when the oven was turned on."

He checked the faces in the gallery. Their sober expressions were not difficult to read. Even if they didn't understand the document, they understood what he was saying.

"Were there any witnesses who saw her there? I mean, human witnesses?"

"Absolutely. At least fourteen people spotted the mayor in the shopping area and took pictures. Several uploaded photos to Instagram."

"How far is the pedestrian mall from the bakery?"

"Less than a block."

"Did the defendant ever come any closer to the bakery?"

"Absolutely." Jazlyn put a location map on the screen. "See the blinking red dot? That's the defendant. The square outlined in blue is the bakery. You can see that, about the time of the murder, she went straight there."

"Thank you. Your witness, Mr. Pike."

He glanced at Maria as he rose, hoping she had some miracle line of attack, because he certainly didn't. These tech devices were the modern equivalent of expert witnesses. In some ways, they were worse, because you couldn't cross-examine a Google database. You could barely understand it.

He plunged right in. "You're aware that my client made a public appearance at the shopping mall at the time in question, right?"

"I've heard that. I don't have any personal knowledge of it."

"She gave a speech and cracked a bottle of champagne, christening a new minority-owned business. Wouldn't that explain why she was in the area?"

"Maybe part of the time."

"And it would explain why people were able to take her picture."

"Perhaps."

"In fact—and for some reason you failed to mention this to the jury—those Instagram photos you mentioned were all taken at the mall. Not the bakery. Right?"

"That's true. But the mall wasn't the only place she went."

"But it explains why she was in the neighborhood."

"Or shows she was creating an alibi."

"After she performed her job, she walked around, which is what people are supposed to do at a pedestrian mall. None of this proves she committed murder."

McCoy stood his ground. "My data shows that she walked directly to the bakery."

"Is that surprising? She owned it."

"My point is that she was there at the approximate time the murders took place."

"Emphasis on the word 'approximate.' You cannot tell the jury precisely when the murders took place, can you?"

"I'm not the medical examiner. But I read his report, and he placed the activation of the oven in a two-hour framework. My data shows your client was at or near the bakery during part of that time."

"Did the medical examiner come up with the two-hour slot before or after you presented your data?"

"My data shows she was there at five in the—"

"And if your data showed she was there at four, would the coroner have made it a three-hour window?"

Jazlyn rose. "Objection. He's calling into the question the integrity of the prosecution witnesses."

"That's my job," he muttered.

"Specifically," Jazlyn continued, "he's impeaching the testimony of the medical examiner, who is not in the court-room to defend himself. Mr. Pike had a chance to cross-examine the medical examiner and he raised no objection to this aspect of his report then."

"Your honor, I hadn't seen yet how the time-of-death window expanded to include the time when they think my client was in the area. It smacks of prosecution conspiracy. Possibly even witness and evidence tampering. Again."

Jazlyn's neck stiffened. "Again I object. And I ask that counsel's offensive and possibly unethical remarks be stricken from the record."

Judge Hayes waved them forward and covered the microphone. "First of all, chill. Both of you. You're not impressing the jury and you're not helping your case. Mr. Pike, these jurors are smart enough to put two and two together. They don't need you to indulge in name-calling. They—"

Jazlyn interrupted. "It's more than that. He insulted my —"

The judge erupted. "Little lady, I will thank you to not interrupt me. Ever. You will respect this court. Otherwise, you will not be welcome here."

Jazlyn tucked in her chin.

The judge took a breath and continued. "I'm going to overrule the objection. This is cross and tearing at your case is hardly unexpected. But I will warn you, Mr. Pike, that this will not immunize you from later ethical complaints if you engage in slander relating to members of the law enforcement community or the bar. Toe the line."

"Yes, sir."

Jazlyn found her voice. "I want to file that ethical complaint right now. I want—"

The judge cut her off. "Oh, don't get your panties in a twist. If I were you, I'd focus on your case. If you flop on something this high profile, there won't be enough McToo in the world to keep you in your job."

He watched Jazlyn's face flush red right before his eyes. He knew exactly what was running through her brain. She wanted to call him on his patent sexism. But while that might give her some personal satisfaction, it probably wouldn't hurt Hayes much in the long run.

She bit her lip and nodded.

The judge waved them away. "Let's get this done. I'm hungry."

He continued his cross. "You've claimed my client was at the bakery during a vague two-hour period when you think maybe the murders occurred. Did she actually go inside?"

McCoy hedged. "That I can't say for certain. This location tracking isn't that precise. Only good to about two to three hundred feet. She might've gone in. She might've stood outside. I know her prints were found inside."

"But you don't know that they were left on the day of the murders."

"That is outside my area of expertise. But if she was present when the murders took place—"

"Then she might've been completely unaware she was a few feet away from a horrible crime."

McCoy smiled. "Involving the bakery she owned and three men she knew and had serious grudges against."

Out the corner of his eye, he saw jurors nodding in agreement. "Motion to strike."

Judge Hayes shook his head. "You opened the door to that, counsel."

He couldn't conclude on that note. "There's no indication my client went anywhere else during that time period. Is there?"

"No."

"Or did anything else. Didn't meet henchmen or bury bodies."

"No."

"Didn't go to a bar and get plastered."

McCoy agreed. "No, after her time at the bakery, the location data indicates she went home and remained there until the end of the time period covered by the geofence warrant. Presumably she went to sleep." He folded his hands. "And slept with the calm satisfaction that comes from completing a job well done."

CHAPTER THIRTY-NINE

DURING THE BREAK, IN CHAMBERS AND WITH A COURT
reporter present, Judge Hayes revisited the motions and objections Dan raised regarding the video. Jazlyn claimed she knew
nothing about any editing of the video. Her tech people said
there was no way to reconstruct or recover the edited portion.
Even phone whiz Bret McCoy had been unable to find it
online or on a phone or cell tower or cloud. As far as anyone
knew, it was gone.

"I can't exclude evidence based on it being incomplete,"
the judge explained.

"You can if what remains presents a prejudicial portrait."

"But I don't know that is the case. I can't make that judgment without the missing piece. There's no one around to
explain what was in it. Except, of course, your client."

"Who has a constitutional right not to testify."

"But if she chooses not to testify, and there are unanswered questions, she has no one to blame but herself."

"Are you trying to pressure me into putting her on the
stand?"

"Far from it. Here's the reality, Mr. Pike. Most evidence is
imperfect. We never have as much as we'd like. If the defen-

dant wants to help clear things up, great. She's under no obligation, but she also can't whine that the jury didn't get right
what she chose not to explain. When the jury deliberates, it
has to make the best of what portion of the big puzzle they
got. So I'm not going to instruct the jury to disregard. But
when I release the jury to deliberate, I will include an instruction explaining that a portion of the video is missing and we
do not know what was contained in the missing portion. And
that they may consider that fact in their deliberations."

It wasn't ideal, but under the circumstances, it was probably the best he could hope for.

Jazlyn didn't say much. Did she think it was best to remain
quiet when she was winning? Probably she was just grateful
the judge didn't call her "little lady" again.

OUTSIDE IN THE HALLWAY, HE STOPPED JAZLYN BEFORE SHE
disappeared. He reached for her arm, but she shrugged
him off.

"Hey, look. If I was out of line in court, I apologize."

She gave him a harsh look. "If?"

"I was just trying to discredit the witness. It would be
malpractice if I didn't."

"Excuses, excuses."

"I never at any time meant to suggest that you would be a
part of anything crooked. I know you better than that. But
this is a tough case. Careers are on the line."

"Mine is. Your client's is. But yours isn't. You'll sail on
from this case to the next, gliding along like the superstar you
are. You're the Teflon lawyer. Nothing sticks to you."

"That's not fair. I know how hard you've had to work to
get where you are."

"Because I'm a woman?"

"That's not what I was saying."

"But that's what you meant. You knew how hard it was for me to rise in the department because I'm female and the world is still ruled by sexist pigs like you and that despicable judge I have to suck up to." Her eyes widened. "And I'm sick of it!"

"Hey, hey, easy." He wanted to reach out, but he knew that would be a mistake. "You don't hear me calling you 'little lady.' Or making reference to your panties."

"The first thing you notice is how a woman looks. Then you check for a ring to see if she's married. If she passes the first two tests, you try to get her back to your boat."

"That's…not…"

"It's what you did to me."

He couldn't very well deny it. "I also appreciate that you are extremely smart. And honest. And talented. I treat you like an equal. Just as I do Maria."

"Maria is useful to you. As I am, at times. It's not the same thing."

"I'm working day and night to keep Camila off death row."

"Because you've got the feels."

"Because I was assigned her case."

"Maybe. But you're taking it so hard because you've got the feels."

Wait a minute. Is that what all this was about? "I can assure you nothing is going on between Cam—"

"Yet."

He sighed. "Could we at least remain civil? There's still a lot of trial to get through."

She pursed her lips. "I might be able to manage civil."

"Friendly?"

She showed him the back of her neck. "Don't push your luck."

HE MET THE REST OF THE TEAM FOR A QUICK LUNCH BEFORE the trial resumed. Since they didn't trust the courtroom consultation rooms or anyplace that could be bugged, they sat at a stone picnic bench not far from the courthouse. Jazlyn had indicated that she had one more witness and then she was done. Which could mean that some of her witnesses didn't turn out to be as strong as she had thought. Or it could mean that she believed she had the case in the bag, so she didn't need them. He hoped it was the former.

Garrett spoke. "As you know, we hired a hacker and I've been working with him, trying to find the source of the fake news barrage targeting Camila."

"And the results?"

"Varied. Some of it is just ugly people being ugly. But the vast majority of it, including the round that initiated it, came from a single source. After threading a backward path through about a hundred different servers all over the world, we were able to trace it to a single account."

Was the man deliberately trying to build suspense? "And the owner of that account?"

He pointed across the table. "Camila Pérez."

Camila's eyes widened. "You think I posted that bull about myself?"

He shrugged. "Could possibly be someone hijacking your phone or laptop. Using your IP address. Perhaps someone in your office."

"I haven't been to the office." She leaned across the table. "You think I did this myself, don't you? Conservatives are always cynical. They think it means they're smart. Even though it doesn't."

"Frankly, I don't know what to think. I'm just reporting my findings."

She turned toward Dan. "Your friend wants me out of office. Just like Sweeney."

Garrett shook his head. "This has nothing to do with politics."

"Everything has to do with politics. I should never have allowed you to work on my defense team. Dan, I want him gone."

"Wait a minute," he said, raising his hands. "I know you and Garrett are on the opposite sides of the political spectrum, but I also know he would never throw a case for political reasons. Or any other reasons. We are your lawyers and we are all backing you one hundred percent."

Camila looked furious. "Does not look that way to me."

He turned back to Garrett. "Why would Camila post trash about herself?"

"You know what they say. There's no such thing as bad publicity."

"This stuff was pretty damn bad."

"Maybe she hoped to turn herself into a martyr. A victim. An object of pity. 'Though targeted by arch-Republicans, she overcomes the lies and triumphs, catapulting herself into the national spotlight.' Something like that."

"I would never do that," Camila said. "Never! Dan——?"

He tried to intervene. "Are there any other possibilities? You understand this tech stuff much better than I do. Could someone disguise their posts to look as if they were coming from Camila?"

Garrett thought a few moments before answering. "Do I recall you telling me that Sweeney gave you a thumb drive?"

"Yeah. It was just documents."

"Did you attach that drive to your computer, Camila?"

She nodded. "I wanted copies."

Garrett spread wide his hands. "There's your alternative answer. Malware."

He shook his head. "I checked the file. There was nothing on it but documents."

"Nothing you could see. But malware apps are usually

invisible. No one would deliberately infect their computers. Theoretically, that thumb drive could've contained an invasive viral program that spread through your computers and allowed Sweeney's hacker to cut through the firewall. That would explain a great deal. How he seems to know all our secrets. And it might explain these posts. They were in fact posted from Camila's computer—just not by Camila. By someone else accessing the computer through a back door."

Camila fell into her chair, the wheels behind her eyes obviously turning. "My office computer is networked to all the other computers in my office."

"Does that include your home computer?"

"Of course."

"Your phone?"

"And my tablet."

"If this is true, there would be no secrets from Sweeney."

Jimmy threw down his pen. "That's it. Last straw. I am officially turning off all my devices. This world is getting too scary."

"How would you access the court clerk's office? How would you transmit documents out of the office?"

"I can live without all that."

"How would you read the Dungeons & Dragons subReddit?"

Long pause. "You're right. Big Brother owns me."

"I think what we're learning is that we're vulnerable. And we shouldn't be. We can't afford to be. Especially not in a case like this. Garrett, is there any way you can investigate this possibility?"

"I'll talk to our hacker. But I think we'll have to hire someone else, someone even more expensive."

"Do it. I'm confident Mr. K will pay the bill."

"On it."

"Technology is convenient, but I don't want to lose a client over it." He glanced over at Camila. "Especially not this one."

CHAPTER FORTY

DAN CHECKED ONCE, TWICE, THREE TIMES BEFORE HE CROSSED the street to the courthouse. Maybe he was being paranoid. But that was the problem with having someone try to run you down. It left you somewhat unsettled.

And it isn't paranoia if the threat is real.

Probably the next assassination attempt wouldn't happen in broad daylight. But then again—who knew? It was a matter of public record that he would be at the courthouse today. If that Jag seriously wanted to take another shot...

He steeled himself and crossed the street. Damn this all to hell, anyway. He was into extreme sports. He met every challenge with a steely eye and grim determination.

And now he was getting chills about crossing the street.

Back in the courtroom, he noticed that the gallery had swelled. Was word out that the next witness was a big deal? Or perhaps that the prosecution was about to rest? Whatever the reason, the number of reporters, busybodies, and looky-loos was on the upswing.

He spotted Prudence, Sweeney's assistant dominatrix, or whatever she was. Why was she back in the courtroom?

After a few preliminaries, Jazlyn called her final witness,

Frank Esposito. Frayed suit, ten years old at least. Crumpled collar. Brown belt with black shoes.

Jazlyn quickly established his role as the mayor's campaign manager. "Were you a member of the mayor's staff?"

"No, independent. Contract labor. She just brought me in to handle the paperwork. Campaign finance is my specialty and these days you need a specialist because the laws are crazy complicated. Once the controversy arose, of course, she brought me in to do a full rundown, get everything in order, answer the allegations."

"What was the problem?"

"The usual. Bad loans. Shady PACs. And missing money."

"What would cause money to go missing?"

"Once you've eliminated math errors, there's only one explanation." Pause. "Someone had their fingers in the cookie jar."

He noted how different Esposito's tone was compared to when he'd met the man privately. And he couldn't help but notice that the man kept glancing out into the gallery. Where Prudence sat, watching.

"Did you have any idea who might be behind the missing funds?"

"Not back then. I had no way of knowing. I could only speculate."

"What are the possibilities?"

He shrugged. "There were only five signatories on the bank account. Camila Pérez and four staff members."

"Objection." He rose. "We're not trying the campaign finance charges today. This is a homicide trial."

"It's relevant," Jazlyn replied calmly. "One of the victims worked in this office, as did the defendant. Goes to motive."

The judge nodded. "I'll allow it. Tie it up as soon as possible."

"I will, your honor." Jazlyn continued. "Mr. Esposito,

we've established your relationship with the defendant. Did you know any of the victims?"

"I knew all three of the victims who have been identified."

"Let's take them one at a time. Did you know Nick Mansfield?"

"Of course. He hung around the mayor's office for a while."

"What was his position?"

"I'm not sure. He wasn't full-time staff. Wrong gender for that. I think he was more of an errand runner." He paused. "And of course, the mayor's personal boytoy."

That got a reaction from the jury. "Can you explain what you mean by that?"

"You know. They were a thing."

"A couple?"

"I don't if they were officially dating. He didn't make public appearances with her. Probably wouldn't have looked right, him being younger and so skeezy. I think it was mostly, you know. Sex."

He had to shut this down, if at all possible. "Objection. Both to the language and the topic. Does the witness have personal knowledge of any sexual relationship?"

"I don't know." The judge looked at Esposito. "Do you?"

"I didn't watch them, if that's what you mean. I'm not into that."

"Did the defendant tell you about a sexual relationship?"

"No. But it was well known about the office."

"Hearsay. Renew objection. Motion to strike."

"I think I will have to sustain that," the judge said. "Proceed."

Jazlyn continued. "Did you have any reason to suppose the two were seeing each other after hours?"

"Yes. I saw them leave together on more than one occasion. I heard them mention getting dinner once. And I helped her arrange the rehab thing."

Jazlyn looked surprised, although he knew perfectly well she wasn't. "Can you explain what you mean by the rehab thing?"

"The kid had a problem. Well, he had a lotta problems, far as that goes. Cheap hustler. Little better than a gigolo, I thought. And he was a junkie."

"Do you know specifically what his problem was?"

"I think he was into heroin."

"What did you do for him?"

"At the mayor's request, I arranged for him to go to a facility upstate. One of my cousins went there, that's how I knew about it. Mansfield spent a week in house." He paused. "Wasn't long enough."

"And who paid for this?"

"The mayor, of course. He could never have afforded it. I advised her against it. I knew it would show up if she were audited, plus I thought it was money down the drain. But she was stuck on the kid."

"That is a lie," he heard Camila whisper. "I was just trying to help."

He put a finger across his lips. Not now. Later.

"When you say she was stuck on him—"

"Head over heels. Could barely breathe when he was in the room. Guess he was really good, if you know what I mean."

"Objection," he said, rising. "Speculation."

The judge nodded. "Sustained." Not that it much mattered at this point.

Jazlyn resumed. "Was that why the relationship ended? The drugs?"

"Oh no. She forgave that. But he cheated on her."

The reaction from the jury box was audible.

"And how do you know this?"

"She told me. She wanted me to bill him for the rehab, to try to get her money back. Which was hopeless. She was just trying to get back at him. She said she'd caught him screwing someone else."

Camila dug her pen into a legal pad. NOT TRUE! OBJECT!

But he couldn't. It wasn't hearsay, since the defendant was allegedly the person who said it and it was obviously against her interest. And making a big futile fuss would only draw more attention to already damaging testimony.

"Did she say who the other woman was?"

"No. And just for the record, she didn't specify that it was a woman. But she did say it was someone she knew. Which I think made it sting all the worse."

Jazlyn let that sink in for a few moments, then proceeded. "You mentioned that you knew the other victims. Did you know Sean Callahan?"

"The plumber? Oh yeah. I was there the day she had the big meltdown."

"The...meltdown?"

"Yeah. The one on the video. I was there. Saw it happen. She really lit into him."

"Why?"

"Don't ask me to explain it. I mean, I think she was unsatisfied with his work, but come on. Most normal people don't react like that over a mediocre plumbing job. There was something personal going on. I think they were doin' it too."

He rose. "Is this going to be more rampant speculation?"

The judge nodded. "Given the prior testimony, I think that's a fair question. I will instruct the witness to stick to what he has seen and heard."

Jazlyn resumed. "What is the basis for your suggestion that the defendant and the plumber were having sexual relations?"

"I saw them holding hands."

Camila threw herself back in her chair.

He gave her a stern look that he hoped spoke volumes. No reactions! The jury is watching you!

Jazlyn continued. "Anything else?"

Esposito shrugged. "The way they looked at each other. The way they acted around each other. I think she saw something she liked when he came to fix her pipes, and then he ended up...really fixing her pipes. And you saw how she behaved in that video. Is that how you treat a worker you barely know? Or is that how you treat someone who fixed your pipes—and then stopped taking your calls?"

"Objection." He let his mounting anger show. "This is becoming a tabloid tv show, but one with a complete lack of evidence. The witness supposedly saw them holding hands so now they're hooking up?"

Judge Hayes drew in his breath. "I will repeat my earlier admonition that the witness should restrict his testimony to what he has seen and heard. No speculation, extrapolation, or imagination."

Esposito nodded. "Yes, your honor. Sorry about that."

He didn't look very sorry. And he kept glancing out toward the gallery.

"And what about the third victim? Jonathan Primo. The history professor."

"He was writing a book about the mayor. Actually, it wasn't just about her. It was more a history of St. Petersburg, the city and its government. But as the current mayor, obviously, she would play a significant role. And he'd discovered some things she didn't like. She asked me whether she could prevent him from publishing."

"What did you tell her?"

"I told her I'm an accountant, not a lawyer. Last I heard, we had the first amendment in this country."

"Did she indicate what she didn't like about the book?"

"This guy, Primo, had been through the financial records. In some cases, even deeper than I had. I cared about how much money there was and where it went. He only cared about where it came from. He discovered that Pérez was still taking money from gangs. Drug money. That's how she was building her war chest for a second term."

The response in the courtroom was so loud the judge resorted to banging his gavel twice. "If you can't maintain proper decorum, the bailiff will escort you out of the courtroom." Pause. "Please continue."

Esposito did. "As you know, during the Valdez trial, the mayor admitted taking some gang money before her first run, but said she thought it came from legit businesses and as soon as she learned otherwise, she stopped accepting cash from them. Except she didn't. It was all on the QT, and it all came through checks that made it look as if it came from honest business enterprises. But she was still taking drug money. Huge contributions from Southside Imports, which is just a front for the Southside drug-running business. And this guy Primo knew it."

Camila crumbled a yellow sheet of paper in her hands. She looked as if she might explode.

"What did she plan to do about Dr. Primo?"

"I don't know. We just had the one conversation. But she's not the type to take things lying down. If you think the plumber got reamed..." He whistled. "I hate to think about what that poor academic got."

"I think we all know what he got," Jazlyn said, closing her notebook. "And now we understand why he got it."

CHAPTER FORTY-ONE

Dan didn't let a second pass between the time Jazlyn sat and the moment he stood. He marched straight to the witness stand and stopped barely a foot away, as close as he thought the judge would allow. He wanted the jury to feel his contempt for Frank Esposito.

"Mr. Esposito, who's paying you off?"

The witness blinked several times. This was probably not the opening question when Jazlyn rehearsed him. "I—I don't know what you mean."

"Are you being paid to testify today?"

"No."

"You just volunteered?"

"I was subpoenaed."

"But your story has changed dramatically since I spoke to you."

"I'm not aware of any changes."

"I am. I'm also aware that you keep glancing out into the gallery. Why is that?"

"I don't know what you're talking about."

"Is someone watching you? Making sure you deliver?"

At this point, Jazlyn intervened. "Your honor, I have to

object. If Mr. Pike had some evidence of witness tampering, he'd put it on. But he doesn't. He just doesn't like what the witness said."

"I didn't like it because it was a tapestry of lies."

Judge Hayes pointed a gavel. "She's right, counsel. You may attempt to impeach all you want. But the man has said he's not being paid to testify and you have no evidence to the contrary, so move on."

He took a deep breath, trying to calm himself. He probably wasn't doing Camila any good here, but he was convinced this man was lying and he wanted the jury to get that. Whether they shared his belief or not, they were going to observe his outrage. "When we spoke before, you didn't mention the alleged relationship with Sean Callahan."

"I don't believe the police had identified that victim yet. I didn't know it was relevant."

"Do you have any actual evidence that those two did anything? Other than supposedly holding hands?"

"I didn't see it with my own eyes. But I definitely got the vibe."

"I don't want to hear about your vibes. Did you see them act romantically toward one another?"

"I only saw what I testified about."

"For all you know, the argument on the video was about plumbing. Not romance."

Esposito craned his neck. "If that's how she reacts to bad plumbing, I'd hate to see what she does to a cheating lover."

"Motion to strike."

"Sustained."

"Mr. Esposito, do you know what happened before the fight?"

"Not sure what you mean."

It was always dangerous to ask a question on cross when you didn't know the answer. But if there was a chance he could learn more about that video, he had to take the risk.

"The metadata indicates that about a minute of footage was trimmed from the start of the video. Since you were there, do you know what happened during that minute?"

"All I remember was the shouting."

"And nothing more?"

"Maybe she came on to him. Tried to get something going in the storage closet."

Once again, his remarks seemed calculated to characterize Camila as sexually loose. Maybe he was just capitalizing on the fake news stories and slanderous social media. But wasn't that what men like Sweeney always did when they wanted to tarnish a woman's reputation? Never mind the facts. Make her look like a whore. "I didn't ask you to speculate. Your eagerness to do so, to trash the defendant at any opportunity, undercuts the credibility of your testimony."

"Objection," Jazlyn said. "Let's let the jury weigh the evidence for themselves."

"Sustained," Judge Hayes said. "But I will, once again, ask the witness to restrict his testimony to personal observations, and I will instruct the jury to disregard any statements that are not based upon personal observations."

He plowed ahead at line-drive speed. Surely if he kept at this liar, something would give. "And then we have Jonathan Primo, the third victim, who you claim also had an alleged dispute with my client."

"There's nothing alleged about it. Pérez came to me and told me about it. But for her, I wouldn't know that guy's book even existed."

"Being upset about a book hardly proves she killed the author."

"Gives her a motive."

"To hire a lawyer. Not to murder someone."

"Sure. It's just a coincidence she had a motive to kill at least three of the victims, and they all ended up frying in an oven."

"Objection!"

Judge Hayes waved Jazlyn to the bench. All three huddled.

The judge covered the microphone. "Madame Prosecutor, if you can't get your witness under control, I'm taking him off the stand."

"I've tried your honor, but—"

"Don't give me that weak-sister crap. You want to play with the big boys, then strap on a pair and grow up. One more outburst and I'll instruct the jury to disregard everything the man said."

The judge became more offensive with each conference. But if there was any chance he might shut down this witness, he couldn't get in the way.

"May I speak to the witness, your honor?" Jazlyn asked.

"Briefly. And not about any substantive matters."

"Understood." He couldn't hear what was said, but he did notice that Esposito was more subdued afterward. For about fifteen seconds.

He resumed cross. "Do you have any personal knowledge whether the claims Mr. Primo made were true?"

"No. Like I said, I care where the money goes, less so where it comes from. But of course, the mayor's connections to gang money are well known."

"In the past. Not the present."

"If you say so."

"And that wasn't the cause of the problem with the DA's office?"

"No. They were concerned about a sketchy loan and some PAC collusion."

"And you have no idea what happened to the missing funds, do you?"

A second after he asked the question, as soon as he saw the expression on Esposito's face, he wished he could take the question back. But he couldn't.

They'd laid a trap for him. And he fell right into it.

"Actually, I believe I do. She spent the money on a demolition team. To take out the bakery."

A leaden silence blanketed the courtroom.

"But—I thought she was planning to remodel and reopen."

"So did I. And then I got this bill. Not for renovation. For demolition. Seems she hired guys to raze the joint. Told them she was going to rebuild from the ground up."

"But—when—"

"Demolition was scheduled to start on Monday. Of course, that ended when the place became a crime scene. But that's why all that scaffolding was there. She was tearing the place down." He paused. "Including the oven."

And the corpses within it. He knew how the jury would see this. First she killed those men. Then she planned to destroy the evidence.

"If that cop hadn't wandered in beforehand, the demolition would've started on Monday morning. There would be no crime scene to be found."

"The demolition team would've found the bodies."

"Maybe. Maybe not. Maybe she would remove them first. She's a cold character. You asked me what came before the video started. You should've asked what happened after. She practically broke Callahan's arm. And when he threatened to file a complaint—she got right up in his face and said, 'You'll be sorry you treated me like this. You're gonna burn.'"

His lips parted. "Your honor, I object. This is entirely new—"

The witness continued, not waiting for a ruling. "Course at the time, I thought she meant he was gonna burn in hell. But now I realize different. She was creating her own hell. She was gonna burn him in the oven. Him and all the other men she hated."

THE PERCEPTION FILTER

CHAPTER FORTY-TWO

SWEENEY LAID HIS HANDS IN PRECISELY THE RIGHT POSITION ON the edge of the bookshelf, then turned to his visitor and smiled.

"You understand—very few people have seen what I'm about to show you."

The other man in the room returned a crooked smile. His nervousness was apparent, but that was always true on the rare occasions he met Sweeney face-to-face. Probably worse today, but such matters were hard to measure. "I'm honored."

"Indeed you are." He depressed the hidden button with his middle finger. They both heard a tiny clicking sound. A panel released. The bookcase itself popped slightly outward.

"A bit theatrical, I know. But that's what I love about it. The revolving bookcase that reveals a secret room. It's like something out of a Gothic novel. Or *Abbott & Costello Meet Frankenstein*." He pulled the bookshelf out. None of the books tumbled, since most were facades firmly attached to the shelf.

The room beyond seemed cavernous. Twice as large as the sitting area, which was larger than most offices.

"And this is where I keep my treasures," Sweeney said, with a generous sweep of his arm. He moved his considerable body into the room and the other man followed, gazing in amazement.

The paint was an off-white, eggshell perhaps, and the floor a rich pinewood. But the walls were covered with art. Paintings along all three visible walls, plus a few smaller pieces of statuary on the ground. Each painting had its own overhead lamp, spotlighting it perfectly.

The room seemed to shimmer. This was a magnificent gallery, amazing and breathtaking. Though Sweeney had excellent art in the elevator lobby, even an uneducated rube could see that these works were more magnificent.

And for his eyes only.

"This is...something else."

"Indeed. I'm glad you have the eye to recognize it. Sometimes number-crunchers aren't the best judge of fine art."

"I majored in art history," the man said quietly. "Then I had to figure out how to pay the bills."

"I understand." Sweeney moved across the room, gazing at a huge mural depicting a battle between mythological figures. "The work outside is adequate. But this is where I've put the best. Some of these pieces have...shall we say, gone missing? Best to keep their current location quiet. I never wanted everyone in the world gawking at my treasures, uncultured masses drooling and pretending to appreciate. As Ms. Dickinson said, how awful to be public, like a bog."

"So...you'll never make these available to a museum or gallery?"

"Oh, never say never. I have plans. Big plans. I never think small. Small plans are for small people."

The other man smiled awkwardly.

"Look how far the Sacklers got just by snapping up Dalis when he was young and they were affordable. I'll give credit where due. They recognized the future value when others were making fun and calling Dali a talentless publicity hound.

And now those paintings are the core collection of the finest museum in St. Petersburg."

He paused, turning a full circle, gazing at the work on the walls. "But this. This defines an entire era. An era that has yet to be defined by critics."

"The modern era?"

"Yes. But what is it? Are we Post-Modern? Post-Post Impressionistic? Post-Cubist? Pre-Global? Critics think they make these decisions. Critics and academics. But not this time. This era will be defined by me. I've already laid the seeds. Give it another ten years, and everyone will understand that the most important art of this time came from the artists in this room. And when that happens—who will have the most valuable collection in the world?"

"You will."

"Of course. I'll hold the trump cards. I always do." He tilted his head slightly, as if noticing his companion for the first time. "Which I suppose brings us back to the mundane matter at hand. You did good work in the courtroom."

"Thank you, sir. I tried."

"Pissed the judge off royally. But I'm not sure that's a bad thing. Sexist dinosaur. Should've retired ten years ago. Thinks he doesn't need my support. This case will ultimately hurt him almost as much as it does sweet little Camila." He did another pivot. "Prudence tells me the jury rather enjoyed your testimony. You came off as honest and scrappy. Insuppressible. They tend to root for an underdog. Americans always do. Until you become too successful. Then they love to watch the fall."

He turned back to his art, as if momentarily distracted. "You've been helpful to me and I appreciate that."

"The feeling is mutual."

"I don't just mean today. When you found the discrepancy in the mayor's books, you came to me first. That was helpful. I like to have the inside track."

"Least I could do."

"Of course, I passed the word to my people at the DA's office. Once I learned everything I needed to know."

"That investigation started the ball rolling."

"Yes. And four dead bodies certainly accelerated it. Fortunately, one of my men was the first on the scene. He was able to…tidy things up. While there was still time."

A pause ensued. Then, abruptly, a smile spread across Sweeney's face. And a few moments later, he chuckled. Then laughed. Loud deep laughter echoing through the largely empty gallery. "Did you really suggest that Camila Pérez was whoring around with the plumber?"

"I did, sir. And I saw heads nodding when I did it. I think the jury bought it."

Sweeney shook his head. "The Big Lie technique, I suppose. The more outrageous the story, the more likely people are to believe it. Because after all, no one would ever say something that outrageous unless it were true."

"That's the theory. Same for the gang-money stuff."

"Well, she started that ball rolling herself. You know— they've been prying into your financial records."

"They have?"

"Pike isn't an idiot. He knows you changed your story, or certainly enhanced it. The obvious explanation would be a payoff. But they're not going to find any evidence of that."

"I don't expect any money from you, sir."

"Good thing. Much too dangerous. But if you need a favor somewhere down the road…you know where to come."

"I will remember that, sir." He swallowed. "But—you've already done what matters most to me."

He nodded. "I understand. Your feelings are admirable. Your loyalty. There's too little of that in the world today, if you ask me."

"I'm kind of old school, sir. Loyalty is what I'm all about."

"I'm sorry my man wasn't there soon enough to remove

the body. But he did remove all possible means of identification. His phone, his wallet. His teeth. Skin and hair were burned. His prints were on one piece of evidence...but oddly enough, that has gone missing. His DNA is not on file in any law enforcement database. Your secret is safe."

"I appreciate that, sir. And if there's ever anything I can do—"

"Like what? You want to prepare my taxes?"

"Well..."

"I'm joking. I have a fleet of men who handle that. Haven't paid income tax in sixteen years. Despite being the richest man in the city."

"Impressive."

"Prudence will continue to monitor, but I don't think you'll be needed for the prosecution's rebuttal case. And Pike wouldn't dare put you on the stand."

"I wouldn't think so, sir."

"Let me renew my promise." He turned slowly and looked the much smaller man directly in the eye. "No one will ever learn the identity of the fourth person in the oven."

Esposito looked up, tears welling in his eyes. "Thank you, sir."

CHAPTER FORTY-THREE

DAN WAS IN CAMILA'S LIVING ROOM TRYING TO COMFORT HER, but he wasn't having much luck. The temper he had heard so much about in court was on full display, and he didn't seem to be able to rein it in.

"That lying dog! That complete son-of-a-bitch!" She paced back and forth across her living room. "I let the man work for me! I paid him! And this is how he repays me!"

"Apparently someone else paid him more."

"This is not a court of justice. This is a court of killers. And they are all conspiring to make me their next victim."

"Garrett and several others we hired are investigating—"

"Find the payment. Follow the money."

"We're working on it."

"Don't just work on it. *Do it!*"

He stood. "Camila, we're doing everything possible and then some. But you can't hope for miracles. Esposito is not a stupid man. We have to assume he's covered his tracks and he's not going to have a sudden change of heart and recant his testimony. We have to build our own case. We have to prove his lies were lies."

"Another reason you must put me on the witness stand."

He had objected to Esposito's final jab suggesting Camila threatened to "burn" Callahan, and the judge instructed the jury to disregard the remark—but how could they? After Esposito finished testifying, Jazlyn rested the prosecution case. Tomorrow morning, the defense would start putting on their case. Whatever that might be. Maria's strategy was to make all the charges appear politically motivated, but that was harder now that Esposito made Camila out to be a lusty vengeful shrew. "Sadly...I think you're right. The Fifth Amendment isn't going to get us anywhere. The only person who can refute those charges and rehabilitate your character is you."

"I don't know why you would even resist. I can handle myself. I can explain what actually happened."

"You're assuming that if you explain everything, the jury will believe you. But it doesn't always work that way. You're on the defensive, just by merit of being charged with a crime. Once the defendant is on the witness stand, the burden of proof effectively shifts. It's no longer the prosecution proving you guilty beyond a reasonable doubt. It's you trying to convince the jury you're innocent. Jurors will perceive everything you say as a desperate attempt to escape punishment for your crimes."

"I have committed no crimes."

"Some people assume anyone accused has committed some crime, even if it isn't the one they're currently on trial for. You're mounting an uphill climb, even before you've begun. Plus, you'll be cross-examined."

"Can't be worse than a political debate."

"Oh yes it can. People are at least semi-respectful in debates. In cross, they go for the jugular. And Jazlyn is very good at that. She has a knack for slicing people to shreds before they realize she's even taken out the blade."

"She does not scare me."

"She should. She scares me sometimes."

Camila stopped a moment. "The great ladies' man is scared of a woman?"

"I have never been a ladies' man. But I respect a gifted opponent, and that's what she is."

"You and she dated once, no?"

"No. Well...depends on who you ask. At any rate, it didn't go far."

"Her choice, or yours?"

"Mutual. Prosecutors can't date defense attorneys."

"All things are possible when the heart is aching."

"Yeah, well. Didn't happen."

"Defense attorneys can't date their clients either, right?"

"Definitely."

"And yet...I see the way you look at me. When you think I don't notice."

He turned slowly, eyes narrowed. "I...don't know what you..."

A grin crossed her face. It was pleasant to see her finally smiling...but also unsettling. "Later. When this is done. If I am not incarcerated. Put me on the stand. First."

"Not first."

"They are anxious to hear from me. Give the people what they want. First principle of politics."

"Trials have more to do with showbiz than politics. And the first principle of showbiz—make 'em wait. Build anticipation."

"They will wonder—"

"Let them wonder. Don't seem overeager. We need to lay a foundation. Didn't you read Maria's strategy plan?"

"Twice. She is a smart woman."

"She is, and she's right about this. First, we'll put on Benji. She's fiercely loyal to you, and she can clear up some of the business with Nick Mansfield and Sean Callahan. Then Culpepper. She can deal with the business about the bakery and the demolition. Then, once we've had credible witnesses explain that most of Esposito's insinuations were completely ungrounded, we'll put you on the stand to explain what really happened. Instead of a weak bunt, you'll be batting cleanup. That's how we get the grand slam."

Camila thought for a moment. "That does make sense. I suppose I can wait. But you will put me on the stand."

He held her by the arms and looked directly into her eyes. "I will. That's a promise."

Her eyes narrowed. "There was one part of that ugly man's testimony that was true. You do not want to be on the wrong side of my temper."

He gave her arms a little squeeze. "Of that I am certain."

WHEN HE RETURNED TO THE COURTROOM, DAN FOUND MARIA by the front doors, jogging in place.

"Fitbit?"

She nodded, huffing. "Thing's a slave driver. I was looking at my data online this morning. I'm not getting enough steps. Got to keep my derriere in shape."

"Your derriere is in excellent shape."

"You're just being kind."

"That was the first thing I said when—" He stopped short. "First thing I said. First night I met you. Complimented you on how well your jeans showcased your... assets." Another pause. "I think maybe...I should apologize."

"You're a guy. Guys will be guys."

"Yeah." He pondered a moment. "You think all this would be happening if Camila were a guy? If the world was gender-neutral?"

Maria's Fitbit pinged. She slowed her jogging and pressed a hand to her chest. "I'm confused. Does this mean you don't like the way I look in my jeans?"

"No. But it means maybe that shouldn't have been the first thing I noticed."

He started toward the defendant's table, but Jazlyn waved to get his attention.

He held out his hands. "Friends, right?"

"Business associates. We need to talk."

"Ready to throw in the towel?"

"Not even close. But I have been authorized to make an offer."

———————————

TEN MINUTES LATER, HE WAS BACK AT THE DEFENSE TABLE. HE sat between Maria and Camila. "Guess what?"

Camila gave him a look. "Given how much time you just spent with the comely prosecutor, we either have a plea bargain offer or you have a dinner date."

"The former. She started with life, no death penalty, but after some negotiation, I wheedled her down to manslaughter. It's not an intent crime, so it carries a lesser penalty."

"How many years?" Maria asked.

"Fifteen flat. Meaning no chance of reduction, no probation or parole. Fifteen years."

"And to get it," Camila said, "I must plead guilty."

"Exactly."

"That will never happen."

"Which is what I told her. But I am ethically required to present all offers to my client. I gather my client rejects the prosecutor's offer?"

"Your client tells the prosecutor to go screw herself."

He nodded. "That's a no."

"Why would anyone ever agree to that?"

"Because they're scared. Because they don't want to roll the dice at the craps table we call a courtroom. Especially not when the death penalty is on the table. That's the way the system works these days. Discretion is in the hands of prosecutors. Used to be in the hands of judges—and should be—but politicians didn't like that. Crime rates spiked in the 80s and politicians started using "law and order"—often a code phrase for racist appeals—as a slogan to get votes. They passed mandatory sentencing laws, which removed discretion from judges. That's when we started to see our prison populations rise to such extent that today we have the largest prison population in the world."

"But prosecutors do have discretion?"

"They decide whether to bring charges. They deal with their huge overload of cases by offering plea bargains, which defendants accept even when they aren't guilty because they don't want to risk going to court, especially if they belong to a minority group. 96% of all cases filed are plea bargained. So prosecutors know there's a 96% chance the defendant will plead guilty to any charge they bring. Prosecutors can brag about their high conviction rates—and prisons get stuffed to the max with non-dangerous offenders and drug addicts and people who just need help—which they won't get in prison. They become a taxpayer burden because we insist upon this medieval form of punishment."

Maria smiled at Camila. "You've gotten him on his soapbox."

"So I see. You feel strongly about this."

"Given my family history, I don't have any choice. This system is screwed up, and it won't get any better if people refuse to talk about it. Or refuse to acknowledge that there might be a better way of doing things. Instead of throwing non-violent offenders in prison, we should explore other sentencing possibilities. Work release. Halfway houses. Restitution. Drug and alcohol programs. Psychiatric counseling. All of which would be cheaper than incarceration."

Maria cleared her throat. "But getting back to this case..."

"Yes. Sorry. Getting back to this case. The offer doesn't

mean they think they're losing. But they know this trial is getting a lot of attention, and fifteen years will be enough to appease the populace."

"It doesn't even make sense," Camila replied. "Manslaughter? Like someone carelessly turned on that oven?"

"They'll say you were out of your mind. Diminished capacity. You'll have to undergo psychiatric examination."

"Let me repeat. Tell your pretty friend that she can—"

"Got it." He turned toward Jazlyn, caught her eye, and turned his thumb downward.

She understood.

Five minutes later, the trial resumed.

CHAPTER FORTY-FOUR

DAN CALLED BENJI—BEATRICE NAOMI RINGGOLD. SHE TOOK the witness stand, wide-eyed and highly caffeinated. Professional skirt and blouse combo. No jewelry.

"Thank you for being here today, Ms. Ringgold."

"Please call me Benji. Everyone does."

"All right then. Benji." As quickly as possible, he let the jury know who she was—her background, schooling, professional history. She was one of the first to join the mayor's campaign staff, before Camila even announced her candidacy, and in a matter of months she had assumed the position of Chief of Staff.

"Would it be fair to say this is a time-consuming job?"

"It would be fair to say this is an all-encompassing job. A 24/7 job. I have little time for a private life, which is why you don't see any rings on these fingers. But I wouldn't give it up for anything. This has been the most fulfilling work of my life. Being a small part of Camila's plan to bring this city into the twenty-first century has been the greatest honor of my life."

"Do you have a positive opinion of the mayor?" Character testimony was permitted.

"I've never known anyone I admired so much. She's more

than a boss. She's a role model. And a dear friend. A few months ago, I was having some personal problems. She was the first to step up and help."

He turned a page in his trial notebook, not because he needed to, because he wasn't reading it, but to give the jury a moment to absorb what they had heard. After hearing so much negative information about Camila, and probably seeing a barrage of it on social media, he was anxious for them to understand that those who actually knew her personally liked her.

"Were you with the mayor on the day the murders took place?"

"I was."

"Please tell the jury what happened."

"Mayor Pérez was at the mall for the opening of a new business. They went through a little christening ceremony. Then she posed for pictures and signed a few autographs."

"How long did it take?"

"About half an hour."

"What did you do afterward?"

"We went our separate ways. She mentioned that she wanted to do a little shopping. I did too, actually, but I ultimately just went home. It had been a long day."

"Did she mention the bakery?"

"No. I was aware that she had purchased it. But it didn't come up on that occasion."

"Benji, I'm going to ask you about the men who were found dead in the bakery oven. Did you know any of them?"

"Yes, somewhat."

"How did you know Mr. Mansfield?"

"I knew him socially and I heard he was looking for work. The mayor needed some part-time help on financial matters and he had banking experience."

"Did Mr. Mansfield work at the office?"

"For a short time."

"There's been a suggestion that Camila and Mansfield dated. Do you know anything about that?"

"It's true, though it's not nearly the big deal that accountant made it sound like. As far as I know, they only went out once. He was on the rebound from another relationship." They had decided not to volunteer information about the sexting. There'd been too much talk about sex in this case already.

"And his employment at the mayor's office?"

"That had already ended. As I said, it was just part-time and short-term. He was a temp, basically. He was done working before they started dating. Camila did try to help him get off drugs, which was interfering with his ability to hold a steady job."

He nodded. Benji was doing a great job. She obviously liked Camila and wanted to help her, but she didn't seem defensive or overreaching. Just calmly relating events that she —unlike Esposito—had witnessed.

"Did you know Sean Callahan?"

"Yes."

"How did he come to work in the office?"

"That was my fault, too." She cast her eyes skyward. "Miracle the mayor forgave me for that one. City Hall has a custodial staff, but for some reason, they couldn't get this job done. The toilets kept backing up, the mayor's office smelled like a sewer, and I was sick of cleaning a disgusting mess every morning when I got to work. So I called this guy I knew. What a mistake."

"Why do you consider it a mistake? Did he get the job done?"

"Yes, he fixed the sewer problem. He's a wizard when it comes to plumbing. But he cornered the mayor in the hallway and lit into her like a psychopath. Seriously. I was glad there were metal detectors downstairs. This man seemed dangerous."

"When you say he lit into her—"

"Just to be clear, there was nothing personal between them. They were not dating or in any way romantic or intimate. No hand-holding, nothing. I think Mr. Esposito is confused or misremembering that. But Callahan was apparently an extremist right-winger, or fascist, white supremacist, or something. Started telling her she was tarnishing the city and people like her were destroying the country."

"You saw this with your own eyes?"

"I did, and I was horrified. You would've seen it too, if that video hadn't been edited. Someone removed the part that makes the whole scene make sense, that shows the mayor was defending herself, responding to a vicious attack. Maybe she could've been cooler, but if you'd seen the way this man came at her, you'd understand. Most people would've punched his lights out." She drew in her breath. "He called her a 'spick.' He said she and her 'bean-eating friends' were the worst thing that ever happened to St. Petersburg. He said the city would be better off if someone burned the whole Southside to the ground. That's what really ticked Camila off. That's when she read him the riot act and threw him out of the office."

"At the end of the video, Camila seems to threaten him. She says, 'You will be sorry for what you have done.'"

"She was referring to the racial slurs. The threats against the Hispanic community. She has zero tolerance for that. She called HR to make sure Callahan was never hired by the city again. She considered reporting his threat to the police, but ultimately decided not to give him publicity he would probably enjoy, a platform for his racist beliefs. She's a strong woman, and she wanted him to be sorry for what he had done. She believes you have to stand up to bullies, to racists. Otherwise they will run right over you."

"And yet, is Camila normally given to bursts of anger in the office?"

"Far from it. She's normally perfectly calm, cool, and collected."

He pivoted a little, moving closer to the jury box. Two alleged motives explained away, one more to go. "You were also aware of the problem with Dr. Primo."

"Yes."

"You knew him, too."

She pursed her lips. "I knew him better than any of them. We were...seeing each other. A little."

"Dating?"

"Yes."

"Living together?"

"No, but...you know." She glanced downward. "Sometimes he slept over."

"Was this in any way relevant to the charges he was making?"

She choked a bit as she spoke. "I don't know how he did it, but...somehow, he gained access to Camila's campaign finance records." She appeared deeply disturbed. "And I very much fear that was my fault."

"What did he do?"

"I don't know exactly. But he gained access to confidential records. Maybe some night while I slept he got onto my laptop. Maybe he stood behind me one evening and watched me type in my password. I really don't know. But he got the financial information and drew all the wrong conclusions from it. He was more like muckraker than an academic."

"What do you mean when you say he drew all the wrong conclusions?"

"As you heard, Primo traced some of the mayor's funds to gang entities. Specifically, Southside Imports, which was originally a front for a drug-running operation. The original owner has since left the city and the company is now run by a man named Luis González. But what they didn't get is that Luis has worked hard to turn it into a legitimate business. They don't run drugs. They bring in niche import goods from Cuba and other island countries. They specialize in orchids. It's a great company—and entirely staffed by Latinx workers from the Southside, people at high risk for gang recruitment."

"And this legitimate company donated money to the mayor?"

"That's why I say Primo got it wrong. A few years ago, the mayor funneled money to Southside Imports. Off the books. Nothing illegal, but out of the public eye. Luis was having financial problems. Temporary, he thought. Mostly a cash flow problem. But he needed cash fast or his business was going under. Camila gave him a loan, which he pledged to pay back. And did." She shook her head. "No good deed goes unpunished, right? She wasn't taking money from them. She was giving it to them. All they did was pay her back. She was trying to break the vicious cycle of poverty and gangs."

"Did you ever explain this to Dr. Primo?"

"I tried. He wouldn't listen."

He thought for a moment. Benji had explained some of the hearsay accusations the prosecution raised, and rehabilitated Camila's character. But he knew the jury could spin this another way. Benji had Callahan spewing racial threats and Primo accusing Camila of corruption. Those actions could be perceived as motives for murder.

"Did you detect any signs of...animosity from Camila toward these men?"

Jazlyn had been quiet so far, but this question put her on her feet. "Objection. Calls for speculation."

"No," he responded. "I'm asking her to relate her observations, if any."

"You're asking her to offer an opinion."

"I'm asking her to be a character witness, and given the extensive contact she's had with my client—who better?"

Judge Hayes nodded. "I'll allow the question."

He repeated the question, just to remind the jury what they were arguing about.

"No," Benji said. "Far from it. Camila Pérez is the most forgiving person who ever walked the face of the earth. Sure, she opposes racism. And people who espouse hate shouldn't receive taxpayer funds. I'm convinced that in time, she would've been able to show Primo the error of his conclusions. Unfortunately, he was killed before she had a chance."

He didn't think he'd ever get a better place to end the examination, so he stopped it there. "Pass the witness."

Jazlyn did not plunge into the fray, at least not immediately. He thought he knew why. Benji came across as calm and credible. Biased, sure—she obviously loved the mayor. But that too spoke well of Camila—she was such a generous person she inspired a high degree of loyalty. Jazlyn wouldn't get far trying to argue with Benji, or trying to get her to defame Camila. So she skipped the usual cross-ex approaches and instead tackled something entirely different.

Something he hadn't anticipated.

"You will acknowledge that you have seen the defendant lose her temper, correct?"

"I would say her reaction when attacked by Callahan was totally justified."

"We'll let the jury determine that. We witnessed an extreme fit on the video."

"But not the racial slurs that preceded it."

"So you say." Jazlyn pulled a slip of paper out of her notebook. "The defendant has a history of issues with…anger management. Correct?"

Benji appeared stricken. Veins stood out in her neck. "I don't—I'm not sure what you mean."

"Has she ever received psychiatric treatment for this problem?"

He shot to his feet. "Objection. Outside the scope of direct."

The judge pondered a moment, then shook his head. "No, there's been extensive discussion of the defendant's anger, which is keenly relevant, given the nature of the crimes. I'll allow it."

Jazlyn didn't miss a beat. "Please answer the question."

Benji's voice dropped several notches. "She did seek help for her anger issues. But I think that shows what a fine person she is. She had a problem so she got treatment. That's the honorable—"

"You say she got help. Was there more?"

"I'm not sure…"

"Has she been institutionalized?"

"Objection!" he insisted, fearing he was making matters worse, not better.

The judge shook his head. "Overruled. Sit down."

Benji hesitated. "That was…long before."

"Before she was mayor? Yes. But it's a fact, just the same. She was committed to St. Angelo's, a psychiatric hospital near here. Correct?"

"Years ago."

"She must've done something serious to get institutionalized. She was arrested, wasn't she?"

"Objection!" He leapt to his feet. "The prosecutor is delving into matters that were the subject of the prior motion in limine."

Jazlyn fired right back. "The court ruled that if the defense introduced character evidence, I could raise this matter in response. That's exactly what he just did."

"This witness is a fact witness."

"And a character witness," Jazlyn insisted. "He specifically asked her about the defendant's temperament. Whether she normally blew up."

He started to argue, but the judge cut him off with a wave of the hand. "I warned you about this, counsel. The evidence exclusion was provisional, and you did ask this witness to testify about your client's temperament. In all fairness, I have no choice but to allow the prosecution to respond."

"Your honor—"

"Your objection is overruled. The witness may answer the question."

"But your honor—"

Judge Hayes' forehead creased. "I've ruled, counsel. Now sit down or I will be forced to remove you from the courtroom."

He sat down, fuming. This was bad. Very bad.

And it was his fault.

"Who did the defendant hurt?" Jazlyn asked.

Benji looked up with pleading eyes. "It was an accident."

"Who did she hurt?"

Benji forced the words out. "Her younger sister."

What? Camila told him she'd had a fight with a girl. She didn't mention the girl was her sister.

Camila did not look at him.

"How badly was her sister hurt?"

Benji's voice choked. "Bad."

"She almost killed her own sister, right?"

"No! I mean—she didn't mean to."

"She broke her sister's arm. Someone intervened before she could do worse."

"She—She—It wasn't like that!"

"Were you there?"

"No." Benji was almost crying. "But I know Camila. She would never intentionally harm anyone."

"Except, she did." Jazlyn exchanged a look with the jurors. "No more questions, your honor."

"It wasn't like that!" Benji cried. "She's a good person!"

The judge banged his gavel. "If there's no redirect, the witness is dismissed."

He had no intention of redirecting. He needed her off the stand, fast.

Tears streamed down Benji's face. "She's a good person! She just wants to help people!"

But as much as Benji insisted, as he looked into the eyes of the jurors, he knew they didn't believe it. Someone who could lose it so badly she almost killed her sister could do anything. That was the kind of rage that could lead anywhere.

Even to four men burned to death in a bakery oven.

CHAPTER FORTY-FIVE

DAN ASKED CAMILA AND MARIA TO JOIN HIM. HE FOUND A secluded alcove in a corner of the courtroom hallway. This was a conversation that needed to be conducted away from prying eyes.

"Why didn't you tell me you'd been in a mental hospital?" Just as well he couldn't scream, because he felt like screaming. He noted that Camila stood closer to Maria than himself. Women uniting? Wouldn't work—Maria knew just as well as he did that this cross-ex revelation had been devastating.

He could see from her facial expression that she understood how badly that had played with the jury. "I didn't think it was important. My mother thought I had a problem. After the accident. She put me in that hospital for a few days."

"You should have told me about it. What better possible way to discredit you than to reveal that you did time in the psych ward?"

"To be fair," Maria said quietly, "that was bound to come out no matter what."

"But if I'd known, I could've brought it out in advance. Prepared the jury."

"How? You wanted to save Camila for last."

"I could've had Benji mention it. Instead of having it dragged out of her like a guilty secret."

"Well, it's out now," Maria said. "So what? A lot of people get help. That's what you're supposed to do when you have a problem."

"The jury might overlook a little self-improvement time. But that business about hurting her sister. Who ever heard of anything like that?"

"Mmm, everyone who's ever seen *Frozen*?"

Camila looked at Maria wryly. "So that's the Disney princess you think I resemble? The mad ice queen?"

He glared at them both. "This is not a cartoon. This is a death penalty trial."

Camila held up her hands. "What's done is done. I'm sorry. It was all an accident. In the distant past. I will explain everything when you put me on the witness stand. Which I hope will be soon."

"It has to be," he said. "One more witness, then you take the stand. If we let this evidence sit unrebutted too long, it may be impossible to change the jurors' minds about you."

HITTING HER FIFTIES HADN'T SLOWED GLORIA CULPEPPER IN the slightest. She was active, engaged, and ready to take on the world. Colored beads around her neck. Tattoo of the word "WOMAN" in cursive on the side of her neck. And of course, the modestly sized B-cup fake breasts.

"Gigolo." She smiled as she said it. No trace of bitterness, but no trace of doubt, either. "That's what Mansfield was. Nothing more or less. Gigolo. He bilked me for money. And he wanted to do the same to Camila."

"Wasn't Nick Mansfield a banker?" he asked.

"Technically. But I don't think he was very good at it. He could talk the talk. But he'd lost his job and couldn't find another. Maybe he had his fingers in the till, I don't know. Given all the drugs he was on, he may not have known himself. But he had bills and creditors breathing down his neck, and I wasn't interested in paying off my little manchild's debts."

"Did he break up with you?"

"No. I told him to take a hike."

"He subsequently initiated a relationship with my client, right?"

"In time, yes. I worked with the mayor closely on a number of projects for about two years. Our most important initiative was a series of women's shelters."

In the gallery, he spotted Garrett raising his head.

"I feel strongly about those shelters," Culpepper continued. "I should. They saved my only sister's life. She couldn't make herself quit this brute she was with. We were raised by a staunch conservative father who taught us that you stick with your husband, preserve the family—no matter what. And sticking to that credo almost killed her."

Maybe he imagined it, but he thought he saw a flicker behind Garrett's eyes.

"I got her to a shelter and that saved her life. I wanted to provide that same life-saving benefit to others. Mayor Pérez helped me create more facilities to make that happen. Eventually we had a split about the equal rights amendment, but until then, we got some good work done. I'd introduced Nick to Benji at some party. She got him on in their office, and eventually I heard he'd gone out with the mayor. If I'd had any notion, I would've warned her off."

"Do you know anything about the time they spent together?"

She gave the jury a knowing look. "Only that Camila was a lot smarter than I was. She cut it off after one date."

"And when you say she cut him off..."

"Well, I don't mean she decided to shake-and-bake him to

death. She's a politician, for heaven's sake. She's much too savvy to attempt something that risky. Or pointless. And yes, she has a temper that flares on occasion, but there's a huge difference between venting once in a while, which is healthy, and coldly calculating an incredibly cruel murder."

"Objection," Jazlyn said. "Non-responsive."

The judge smiled. "The witness does appear to have wandered off-topic a bit. Please just answer the questions, miss."

Culpepper raised an eyebrow. "Miss? I've been married four times."

Judge Hayes clearly did not like being corrected. "You will not address the court directly. If you have comments to relay to the court, do it through counsel."

"Would you say that if I were a man?"

At counsel table, Maria drew a slashing thumb across her throat. He hoped Culpepper got the message. This was not the time to call the judge on his chauvinism.

Judge Hayes drew himself up. "I do not permit disrespect to be shown to the court by anyone. Counsel, you need to have a talk with your witness. Or I will not permit her testimony."

Before he could reply, Culpepper jumped in. "No need. I'll be a good girl. Let's get on with it."

He hoped that would placate the judge. "There have been allegations that my client has a temper. Do you know anything about that?'"

"I know Camila chewed people out from time to time. So what? Men do that crap and they're called strong and decisive. Women do it and they're called strident and bitchy. That's the world we live in."

No one had objected, so he continued. "Are you suggesting these charges are sexist?"

"I know they are. No one in their right mind would believe the mayor of the city baked four men in an oven in a building she owned. Unless you characterize her as a crazy woman, because we all know how crazy women get, especially if there's some hunky guy involved." She shook her head. "I'm surprised no one has suggested she was having PMS."

He could see Jazlyn wavering, but she remained seated. Maybe she was even considering what Culpepper said. "Could you describe your work with the mayor in more detail, please?"

"What I'm proudest of is the fourteen women's shelters that didn't exist before."

"Has this initiative ended?"

"Not at all. A lot of what we started is still in progress. Problem was, our funds ran dry. That's the key to the bakery acquisition."

He saw the jurors sit up. Now she was talking about something that interested them. "How so?"

"Camila didn't buy that place because she had a hankering to get into the pastry market. She planned to convert it to another women's shelter. That's why the demolition was scheduled. Didn't have anything to do with bodies in the oven. She was building another shelter—this time using her own funds to do it. And—I hope you don't mind my saying this, Camila—but she is not a rich woman. She's given her life to public service, not private profit. Nonetheless, she put a huge sum of money, some of it borrowed, into that shelter. It would be the first in that part of town, and it was needed. That's the kind of woman Camila Pérez is. All this talk about bakery and boyfriends is a sexist distraction. This is a person who genuinely cares about other people, who does more than just talk. She makes things happen. We need more like her. That's why certain people in this community are so determined to bring her down."

He knew he was never going to get a better finish than that. "Thank you. No more questions."

Jazlyn rose, but once again, she took her time before questioning. "You've been a big supporter of women's rights, correct?"

"You know it is."

"And a strong advocate of women in politics."

"And every other aspect of American life. I've been an advocate of equality. I want a nation where all people are treated equally and all people have equal rights, not just whatever subsidiary rights the men in power find it convenient to give us."

"Do you think it's possible that your... perspective has created some bias?"

"What kind of bias?"

"A tendency to sympathize with women. Regardless of the facts."

"Well, I'm not feeling particularly sympathetic toward you at the moment."

He saw Judge Hayes cover his mouth, eyes sparkling.

"Motion to strike," Jazlyn said. "Ms. Culpepper, I think the truth is you give yourself a lot of credit for fighting for equality, but what you are actually advocating is a world in which women cannot be challenged."

Culpepper leaned forward, pointing a finger. "Let me explain to you what I've been fighting for, Ms. Prentice. I was on the front line forty years ago, before you were born, during a time when not only were you not in the district attorney's office, there were no women in the district attorney's office. I'm the reason you exist."

"We're all aware of your efforts—"

"I'm not sure you are. We have all this talk these days about the MeToo movement and Time'sUp, but you know what? Time was up a long time ago. We all stand on the shoulders of those who came before us, and this movement only works because other pioneers fought for equal rights forty years ago. For that matter, there were strong women before my generation who fought hard and laid the foundation for my work."

Jazlyn held up her hands. "We don't need a history lesson."

"I think maybe you do."

"My point is that you are a biased witness, and you're proving my point."

"There is a difference between bias and gratitude."

"Are you suggesting we should allow murderers to go free if they've done good work in the past?"

"No. I'm suggesting that calling our mayor a murderer is ludicrous, and I don't think you're so biased you can't see that."

He wasn't even sure what was happening. This was more like a town hall debate than a cross-examination. But Culpepper seemed to be making her point and giving the jury something serious to think about, so he kept his mouth shut.

"I can assure you that I would not have brought these charges unless—"

"Except you didn't make that decision, did you?"

Jazlyn was taken aback. "I filed the charges in—"

"But the decision to prosecute was made by your boss, right? Your white male boss? The district attorney?"

Jazlyn's lips twitched, but she didn't answer.

Culpepper continued. "And we have no idea who's pulling his strings, do we?"

"I hardly think—"

"The democratically elected mayor is thrown in jail and who takes her place? A man. Who I saw outside the courtroom today giving a press conference, deploring this sad state of affairs, but basically drawing attention to himself. Gearing up for the next election. He's not the only one monitoring this trial. Here's your reality—someone up top wants this mayor put down before she becomes more powerful than she already is. And that's the real reason we're here today."

CHAPTER FORTY-SIX

GLORIA CULPEPPER'S TESTIMONY NOT ONLY PROVED HELPFUL, Dan realized, but perfectly set the stage for Camila to take the stand and speak for herself. Culpepper had all but canonized her, plus planted the idea that this prosecution was politically motivated. That had been Maria's trial strategy from the start, but Culpepper had driven it home more effectively in two minutes than he had done during the entire preceding trial.

He could see that Camila was nervous. Who could blame her? Sure, she'd given a million interviews and speeches and press conferences, but this was the first time she sat before a handful of citizens pleading for her life. Urging them to accept her version of the events rather than the one they'd heard for so long.

He didn't waste much time introducing her. Everyone already knew who she was. His plan was to keep this as short and focused as possible. Let her do what she needed to do and then get her off the stand as quickly as possible.

After the introductory questions, he took her to the night of the murders. "Were you on the premises on the day in question?"

"I was at the pedestrian mall," Camila answered.

"Did you go to the bakery?"

"Yes, I stood outside the bakery for a time. I owned the place and I was preparing to raze it and erect a women's shelter."

Let's get to the point. "Did you kill those men in the oven?"

"Of course not."

"Did you know men were being killed inside the bakery?"

"No. I did not see or hear anything."

"Do you know who killed them?"

"No. I cannot believe anyone I know could commit such a cruel act."

"Were you having the building destroyed to destroy evidence of the crime?"

"No. I didn't know the crime existed. I've dedicated my whole life to helping people. And that most certainly didn't include burning them in an oven."

Okay then. The jury had heard it from the lion's mouth, so to speak. Time to dig into the details. "You did know Nick Mansfield though, correct?"

"Yes. He worked briefly in my office. After his work for us ended—and only after he was no longer my employee—we dated."

"How long did that last?"

"One date. Not a great success, obviously."

"What was the problem?"

She thought for a moment. "He was going through a rough patch. He'd lost his job at a bank. He had a drug addiction. And he was on the rebound."

"From his relationship with Gloria Culpepper?"

"I assume. I never asked him. Didn't feel it was any of my business. But he was definitely damaged. Which does not make for the best boyfriend, especially for someone in the public eye. I ended it before it became something toxic."

"Did you threaten him?"

"No. Never."

"Did he threaten you?"

"Not that I recall. We both got on with our lives. Unfortunately, his ended prematurely. Gloria Culpeper was right about at least one thing—this is only an issue because I'm a woman. When a man in the public eye is seen stepping out with women, that's cool and shows how macho and sexually attractive he is. But when a woman is seen with a man, she's a trollop."

He thought that was okay. Not too pushy, but definitely something to think about. This whole examination was about persuading the jury to rethink their presumptions. "What about Sean Callahan? The plumber?"

"That's an entirely different situation. Contrary to what Mr. Esposito said, we never dated. No hand-holding, nothing. He may have heard Callahan asking me out to dinner. I declined."

"Why?"

"Because I knew almost nothing about him, and what little I knew, I didn't like. Why would I date him? Because he was somewhat handsome? That's more sexual stereotyping based upon prejudice, not fact. When I turned him down, he became agitated and started spewing the racist filth Benji has already described. Was I supposed to take that lightly because I'm a woman? No man would. I told him what I thought in no uncertain terms. That's what you heard in that video."

"You said that he would be sorry."

"And I meant it. The world has had enough of this racist and sexist—" She cut herself off, then looked at the jury with genuine embarrassment. "I'm sorry. I do have a mouth on me. I get that from my beloved father. He raised me to be a straight shooter, and I am. The days when it was ok to make racist jokes—while insisting that you're not really racist—are over. Racist jokes are not acceptable. Racist slurs are not funny. Zero tolerance. That's the way racism ends. I took steps to make sure Callahan never again worked in city government and I have no regrets. Actions have consequences in this world. When people agree that this kind of behavior is unacceptable, racism ends."

Way beyond the scope of the question, but Jazlyn didn't seem to mind. Jazlyn had been subdued ever since Gloria Culpepper testified. Was it possible she was having second thoughts about this prosecution?

"And then there is the third victim. Dr. Jonathan Primo."

"A sloppy historian. An embarrassment to his university."

"What do you mean by that?"

"Benji explained this, and she knows more about it than I do. Benji got the records from Mr. Esposito's partner, a man named Hendrick, and Primo got them from her, violating about a million ethical rules. Just to prove how sloppy Primo's work was, he got the flow of money completely reversed. Thought he found money being received from Southside Imports when in fact it was funds going to Southside Imports, a short-term loan eventually repaid."

"Did you...have a grudge against Primo?"

"Well, I didn't love him to death." She actually winked toward the jury. And it seemed to work. She was regaining some of her natural charisma, re-becoming the Camila Pérez people saw on their television screens. He could be wrong, but he thought she was winning them over. Maybe.

She continued. "But I wasn't out to get him. And I certainly wouldn't have killed him. The truth would have come out eventually, probably during the investigation filed by the district attorney's office. His sloppy scholarship would have been exposed and I'd like to think he would've lost tenure and been kicked out of his university. There was no need for me to get my hands dirty."

"We've heard testimony indicating that you were in a program for anger management. True?"

"Very true. Actually, I did it twice."

"Why twice?"

"Because it didn't entirely take the first time. I was too young. I will admit it—I have the stereotypical Latin temper— which is not true for all Latinx, but it is true for me. Got that from my father, too. Sometimes it gets the best of me. Not for long, but still. I needed to get that under control, so I attended a week-long retreat in Phoenix. Call it immersion therapy or whatever you want, but I think it has made me a calmer, better person."

"And yet, we all witnessed what looked like an explosion of temper in that video."

She raised a finger. "That's where I disagree with you. That was not temper. That was me defending my people, my office, and myself. What is wrong with that? Would it have been better if I'd let the racist pig trample over me? If I'd cried instead of shouting? We need to redefine our gender-based expectations. If you had seen the entire video—the unedited video—you would agree with me."

All good so far, and the jury appeared to be buying it. Keep moving... "Your chief of staff also said you'd been arrested."

"That is true. But it was many years ago, when I was still a teenager. I was a handful." She glanced at the jury. "Maybe some of you were as well."

He caught a few smiles on juror faces.

"But this is no laughing matter. I got in a fight with my younger sister. Over a boy who probably cared nothing about either of us. She tripped on a curb, twisted her ankle. I grabbed for her but she fell hard on her right arm. Broke it. She was in a cast for three months. My parents were worried about my supposedly violent tendencies so they sent me to a hospital briefly, then to a live-in clinic to be examined. I think it was an overreaction, but I understand the need for parents to be careful. I have not been blessed with children yet—as many of you have—but I know I would love them with all my heart and would do anything to protect them. The doctors found nothing wrong with me and released me. The records of that and the arrest were sealed and subsequently expunged, but if they can be found, I have authorized my attorney to release them to the public. I want to be completely up front about this. No secrets."

He marveled at how well she explained even the most problematic details. He could only imagine how far that could take her—if this trial didn't end her career in one hideous fell swoop. "Do you have any idea who the fourth man in the oven was?"

"No. How could I?

"It does seem coincidental that you knew three of the victims."

"Why? I am the mayor. I have shaken half the hands in this city. I hope I have shaken them all before my term ends. I get around and I meet people. That is part of my job. Sadly, in today's world, that makes you a target." She twisted around so she could face the jury. "You've seen what they're saying about me on the internet?"

No one nodded, but there were some guarded smiles.

She pointed a finger at the jurors. "I know you cannot admit it, but you have. Why wouldn't you? You must be curious. You want to know what is really going on. Well, let me tell you something. While this hateful slander has increased since the murder charges were filed—it has been a part of my life since I entered the political forum."

"How have you dealt with it?"

"Not with anger, not most of the time. With patience, as much as humanly possible. This is what it is to be a public figure in today's world, where no one has privacy, and politicians have even less, and people can post lies on the internet to such an extent that the truth barely matters any more. One man calls me names. Another makes false accusations about campaign funds. This is my daily life. Barely enough to capture my attention. Certainly not enough to inspire me to do something so stupid as murdering four men in such a contrived and gruesome manner."

She made a 'V' with her fingers and pointed at her eyes. "Look at me when I say this. I did not commit this crime. I did not murder those men. I would not lie to you. Not now. Not ever."

CHAPTER FORTY-SEVEN

To Dan's amazement, Jazlyn did not cross-examine. Did she think Camila was too charismatic to leave on the witness stand? Did she not have any good questions?

He knew the answer to both of those questions was in the negative. Jazlyn was skilled enough to overcome charisma and to deliver a few zingers even in the worst of circumstances. If she didn't cross the defendant—it was because she didn't want to cross the defendant.

He rested his case. There was no rebuttal testimony, and Jazlyn's closing argument, though thorough, was not earth-shattering. She did her job and nothing more. She didn't throw in the towel. But he had the sense she wasn't trying too hard, either. There were no emotional appeals, no whining about the importance of law enforcement to keep us all safe. She summarized the facts and let the jury draw their own conclusions.

Under those circumstances, it would look weird if he talked too long during his closing. He didn't want to leave the impression that he was fighting for Camila's life. Better to leave the impression that he'd done his job, done it right, and they could all see that Camila was not guilty.

"Let's face it," he said to the jurors, "this case has been political from the get-go, and not just because the defendant is the elected mayor of this city. It started with allegations of campaign finance irregularities, and we still don't know for sure who got those rumors going. It expanded into murder, and even though nothing at the scene of the crime linked my client to these murders, the police decided almost immediately that she must be the perpetrator. They admitted they never seriously considered any other suspect. You have either seen or heard about the barrage of fake news slandering the mayor. Who paid for that? And how did they get it going so quickly? Time and again during this trial we have heard references to shadowy figures behind the scenes making important decisions. Who decided to investigate the mayor? Who decided to charge her? Who is so determined to take her down? Is it because of her Latin heritage? Or because she's a woman?" He paused a moment. "Or both?"

He paced slowly alongside the jury box. "One thing is certain. We don't know what happened here. Yes, my client knew these men and may have disliked some of them—but have you heard anything that qualifies as a motive for murder? For this grisly murder? Come on. I don't buy it and neither do you. It just doesn't add up."

Beforehand, Jimmy reminded him of the importance of personal connections. He wasn't permitted to single jurors out during closing. But he could show that he'd been paying attention when they were interviewed. "Most of you work in this city. You go to your office and do your job. You probably follow politics, but you don't live in that world. You've got your own world. You have kids in school. Two of you have kids in college. You don't have time to get involved in the minute details. And that's probably just as well—because politics is a dirty world. You've only seen a small piece of it in this court-room. But my client lives it. Every day."

He recalled some of Garrett's concerns, and his statistics,

and dropped them into the closing. "Camila has to deal with fake news and alternative facts and slanderous memes and baseless allegations. Even murder charges. Soon the only people who can hold office will be people who have lived such quiet, unaccomplished lives that no one can find anything to complain about. Is that really who we want running our country?"

He smiled a little. "But I want to focus on this case, these false accusations, and how flimsy the evidence is. Let me summarize. My client owned the bakery. She was preparing to tear it down. She had keys to the premises. Her prints were there. She knew three of the men involved and yelled at one of them after a racist tirade. And that's it. Nothing else ties her to this crime, much less gives her a motive to commit it. And you know what?" He paused, hoping the jurors would reach this conclusion for themselves. "That's just not enough."

He glanced back at Camila. "You have heard my client tell her story. With your own eyes, you have observed who she is, what she is. Does she seem like a stone-cold killer who drugs men, ties them up in an oven, and burns them alive? Or does she seem like a compassionate caring woman who could go far in this world—and thus poses a threat to those who want power only for themselves and others like them?" Another pointed pause. "You decide."

He spread his hands wide. "The judge will instruct you that to convict my client, you must find her guilty beyond a reasonable doubt. Has the prosecution met that standard in this case? Have they even gotten close?" He shook his head. "You know they haven't. And that's why you must find her not guilty."

He quietly took his seat at the defense table. While the judge read his instructions to the jurors, Camila patted his hand. She seemed content.

Maria slid a legal pad toward him.

GREAT JOB. JUST RIGHT.

He wrote back: ENOUGH?

She smiled a little. WE'LL SEE.

LESS THAN AN HOUR AFTER THE JURY WAS DISCHARGED TO deliberate, the foreperson sent the bailiff a note indicating they had reached a unanimous verdict.

"In less than an hour?" Camila said, nursing a hot tea from the downstairs coffee shop. "What does that mean? Is it good or bad?"

He shrugged. "Impossible to know. The OJ jury reached a verdict about as quickly—and they acquitted. The El Chapo jury took six days—and they convicted on almost all counts."

Maria cut in. "What he's trying to say is—no one knows anything. And trying to predict a jury is a fool's game, and he's no fool. So why don't we just go back into the courtroom and find out?"

Camila nodded. "Ready for the final chapter, Dan?"

"Yes. I just hope it's the one I'm hoping for."

She laid a hand on his shoulder. "Whatever the result, I want you to know that I think you did a fantastic job, and I appreciate it."

"I did my best."

"You did much more than that. I think you took it person-ally. I think you treated me like someone you care about, not just another client."

"Well…" His eyes looked into hers. "I do…care."

"Hold that thought. To be continued. Maybe."

THE JURY FILED IN SLOWLY. AT THIS POINT, OF COURSE, THEY could just shout out what everyone wanted to know. But that would be too easy. Instead, they had to go through all this procedural rigmarole. Draw it out. Make it a big drama. Whoever invented this process must've hated defendants. And their attorneys.

"Have you reached a verdict?" Judge Hayes asked.

A middle-aged woman on the back row rose. As he recalled, Mrs. Peterson worked at the local cinema and had a son she was putting through Georgia Tech. "We have." She handed a slip of paper to the bailiff, who brought it to the judge. Judge Hayes glanced at it, and without revealing a hint of a reaction, passed it back to the bailiff, who returned it to the foreperson.

Come on, he muttered under his breath. Just get on with it.

"On the count of murder in the first degree, we find the defendant...not guilty."

He felt someone squeezing his hand so tightly it cut off the flow of blood.

"On the count of murder in the second degree, we find the defendant not guilty."

The judge nodded. "So say you all?"

"Yes, your honor. This verdict was unanimous." The foreperson turned slightly, looking at Camila. "And we got there on the first ballot."

"Very well then. I thank you for your service. The jury is dismissed. Let me admonish you that although you are free to exercise your first amendment rights and speak to media—I advise against it." He turned to face the defense table—and smiled. "*Mayor* Pérez, you are free to go."

CHAPTER FORTY-EIGHT

JIMMY AND GARRETT RUSHED UP FROM THE GALLERY TO JOIN the group hug. Camila had tears in the corners of her eyes, which he realized was the softest emotion he had ever seen from her. Perhaps she was more worried than she let show.

"Killer closing," Jimmy said. "Seriously. One of the best I've ever heard."

He scuffed the floor with his shoe. "Aw, shucks."

Maria leaned forward and gave him a kiss on the cheek. "Way to go, slugger. You hit the ball out of the park. You beat the best prosecutor in the city."

He shook his head. "Jazlyn folded."

"What do you mean?"

"I can't quite put my finger on it...but I know I'm right. Her heart hasn't been in it today. She didn't have the authority to dismiss the charges but...she didn't kill herself, either."

"Why would she cave?"

"I'm not sure." Jazlyn had already left the courtroom. "Maybe it was Benji's testimony. Or Gloria's. But somewhere along the way...I think she realized this case didn't make sense."

Garrett extended his hand to Camila. "Congratulations. I'm glad this turned out the way it did."

Camila wiped an eye. "You? I thought you believed I was a liberal threat to the republic."

He shook his head. "No, I think we need more people like you."

"Even if I keep opening those shelters that break up families?"

Garrett drew in his breath, then slowly released it. "You know, I heard the testimony Ms. Culpepper gave about her sister, and all the families she's worked with in those shelters. And as hard as it is for a guy who thinks he knows everything to admit it...I may have been wrong."

Camila's lips parted. "Now I have achieved a victory."

"I think maybe we could all stand to evolve a little." Garrett slapped his partner on the shoulder. "Why are you still here, Dan?"

He did a double-take. "I work here."

"Did you not hear the judge? Camila is a free woman. And probably hungry after all those days of house arrest. I understand she isn't much of a cook."

Camila nodded. "Truer words were never spoken."

Garrett bounced up and down on his toes. "But I know someone who is..."

Was Garrett actually...matchmaking? Of course, some handmade gnocchi would hit the spot...

"Do you think Jazlyn will go after someone else?" Maria asked. "I mean, this was a horrendous crime."

"I doubt it," Jimmy said. "She lit out of here fast."

"That's unlike her. We usually chat..."

Camila shrugged. "You know the saying. Hell hath no fury. Right, Dan?"

His head suddenly jerked to one side.

"Dan, are you okay?"

His brain raced. "What—What did you say?"

"It's a famous quote. From Shakespeare, I think."

He shook his head. "Congreve. But the full quote—" His head twitched again. Neurons fired. "Oh no. Oh no."

Camila leaned closer. "What is it? Come on, spill."

A thousand mental images flashed before his eyes at the speed of sound.

Earring in the left ear. Pocket protector. Mismatched socks.

He shook his head vigorously. No, that wasn't it.

Tattoo on the neck. No jewelry. Blue eyes.

He was getting closer. But he hadn't made all the connections...

Sleepovers. Cell phones. Keys.

What was it? What was he missing? What had he been missing all along? Sometimes he was so stupid...

He heard words reverberating in his mind.

"An office filled with women, men needn't bother applying."

"Kept talking about needing to scrape together some Georgies."

"I don't have time for a private life."

His eyes widened. His hands shook.

"Dan? Speak to me, Dan. Tell me you're not stroking out."

"I—I—" He paused, then started again. "I've been a complete fool." He gulped for air. "But no longer. I'm having an epiphany."

Jimmy's eyes narrowed. "Is that like a conversion experience? Because I don't know if a defense lawyer will find religion helpful."

"I know who killed those men. In the oven. And I know why. It all makes sense—once you understand."

"Yeah," Jimmy said, "things usually make sense once you understand. Speak English, Dan."

He glanced at his watch. "We have to hurry." He grabbed his backpack. "Maria, Camila, can you come with me?"

Camila appeared completely lost. "Is this going to be dangerous?"

"Extremely."

She shrugged. "Well then. Out of the fire…"

Maria looked even more perplexed. "Are we rushing…to stop someone from skipping town?"

He shook his head, already halfway to the door. "No. We're rushing to stop the killer from taking a fifth victim."

CHAPTER FORTY-NINE

DAN PUSHED OPEN THE GLASS DOOR TO THE MAYOR'S OFFICE. Despite the fact that it was well past five, the door was unlocked.

He'd ditched his security team back at the courthouse. Nothing personal, but a big show of force could make what he intended completely impossible.

He stepped inside. He didn't see anyone. But he could hear the skrtich-skritch of pen on paper in one of the back offices. He followed the sound.

Acting Mayor Alex Denton sat at his desk, apparently hard at work. Was it always this easy for someone to get close to the sitting mayor? He'd seen security in the lobby, but he'd had no trouble getting past them.

He entered the office. Denton looked up.

"Pike? Wow, that was even faster than I expected."

"You expected me?"

Denton seemed uncannily calm. "I knew it wouldn't take you long to put two and two together."

"You were expecting me?"

"Sure." Denton leaned back in his chair. "I have friends in the courtroom. I knew what happened ten seconds after the verdict was delivered." He paused. "And I knew that once you'd finished one task, you'd start on the next."

"Which was?"

"Well, you got your client off the hook. Again. Man, you must have a hell of a batting average."

"That's beside the point. What do you imagine is my next step?"

"I didn't think you'd wait around long." He reached for his desk drawer.

"Why don't you just leave that closed."

Denton brought up his hands quickly. "You're the boss."

"Not in this office."

He grinned. "Anyway, since you got Camila off the hook, she's free to retake her office. I knew she couldn't wait to seize control."

His forehead furrowed. "That's what you're talking about?"

"Is Camila with you? It's ok, I've already started packing."

His brain was firing, synapses exploding faster than he could think. "That's why you believe I came here? To boot you out of Camila's office?"

"I'm just finishing up. Enjoying a last drink in the office." He grinned, then reached across the desk for a flask.

"Don't drink that!"

Denton looked at him as if he'd lost his mind. "Dude, it's just whiskey. I can handle it."

"Are you sure that's all it is?"

"I poured it myself."

"Have you left it alone? For even a minute?"

Denton pondered. "I did visit the little boys' room a while back."

He crossed the office, picked up the flask, unscrewed the lid, and sniffed. "Yeah, Denton, this isn't just whiskey. Don't drink it. Unless you want to have the best sex of your life."

"Uh...well..."

"And then die immediately afterward."

Denton's expression flattened. "You think…"

"Yeah. I do."

Behind him, he heard the soft tread of footsteps. "Damn you, Pike. Damn you all the way to hell and back again."

He pivoted on one foot. "Thought you'd be around here."

Benji emerged from the shadows. Holding a gun.

"Couldn't just mind your own business, could you, Pike?"

"Actually, this is very much my business."

"You got your client off the hook. It's over."

"Except it isn't. She'll always be under a cloud. Her career will go nowhere. Unless I can prove who really fried those men in the oven." He took a step closer, trying to keep his voice level, even though his heart was racing. He knew she was unstable, and a gun in the hands of an unstable murderer was not a promising situation. "You killed those men, didn't you? For your own selfish reasons. And then you framed Camila. Because you're insanely jealous of her."

"I am not jealous of her." Benji's face hardened. "I hate her."

"Same thing. Different word. You killed those men and now you're planning to take out Denton. Which you couldn't do while Camila was under house arrest and wearing an electronic ankle bracelet. You had to wait until she was free, so she could be the prime suspect."

"You don't know anything. You have no idea what happened."

"It's been staring me in the face all along, but your do-or-die devoted servant bit was so convincing it fooled me. For a while. People kept saying it was such a coincidence that Camila knew three of those men. But it wasn't a coincidence at all. The common denominator was you. You brought those losers into her life. You've been in relationships with all of those men. I'm not even sure who the fourth one is, but I'd be willing to bet you were in a relationship with him. That went badly. Did all four men jilt you?"

Her eyes narrowed to tiny slits. "They all used me. Every one of them. Then cast me aside, once they got what they wanted."

"People told me repeatedly that Nick Mansfield came to Camila on the rebound. I assumed that was a reference to his fling with Gloria Culpepper. But the timelines don't match up. She dated him more than six months before the murders. And during that time, he took up with you, right?"

Her lower lip trembled. "He said he loved me. He said we'd be together forever. Liar. All he wanted was money."

"Culpepper said he had debts. She called him a gigolo."

"He'd borrowed money from the mob. They were threatening to kill him."

"And you paid his debts."

"I sold my house for him! I sold my whole damn house! That's why I'm living in that disgusting apartment." Tears sprung from her eyes. "I loved my house. But I sold it. He took the money, but the second I introduced him to Camila, he dumped me. He had a new target in his sights."

"I'm sorry," he said genuinely. Denton didn't move. He seemed spellbound by the drama unfolding around him. "I'm sorry some men are complete losers. But that's no excuse for what you did."

"You'd feel differently if it happened to you." He wondered how her eyes could seem so cold and so wild at the same time.

"You dated Callahan too. That's why you recommended him when Camila needed a plumber."

"And how did he thank me? Threw a tantrum in the office. Turns out to be a racist pig who probably took the job just so he could give her a piece of his mind. Belongs to some militia group. Probably a hero to his racist friends now. And once he had what he wanted, he dumped me."

"You admitted you were in a relationship with Primo. That's how he got access to Camila's financial records."

"And as soon as he had them, he dropped me, just like the others. Selfish scumbag. I gave him my body. My greatest gift. And he treated me like trash."

"Why did you have those financial records?"

The corner of her lips curled. "So you don't know everything. You haven't figured out who the fourth man in the oven was."

"Why don't you enlighten me?"

She tilted her head to one side. "Why the hell not? You're not going to tell anyone."

Keep her talking, he told himself. She's probably wanted an audience to brag to for a long time. "Something to do with financial records?" He thought another moment, letting the connections form in his brain. Then he snapped his fingers. "Esposito's partner. The one who disappeared. Hendrick."

"You win the Daily Double. Nice job, Brainiac." Her eyes withdrew, as if she were looking inward. "Hendrick tricked me, used my connections to pull off this big land-fraud deal. Esposito's idea, but Hendrick oversaw the execution. I was willing to forgive him. I was willing to do anything." She pressed her free hand against her eyes. "Laughed at me when I said I loved him, told me he was only using me." Her throat rasped. "So I killed him like the other scumbags who treated me like garbage."

"Hell hath no fury indeed."

"I think Esposito figured it out. But he hasn't said anything, because his partner's disappearance gave him the opportunity to keep all the cash from the deal rather than splitting it. In fact, I think Esposito went to considerable lengths to make sure the police didn't identify that body."

Is that why Esposito changed his testimony so drastically? Did someone buy him off? Offer a cover-up in exchange for perjury? Who would have that kind of power?

Only one name came to mind.

"How did you finally figure it out?" Benji asked.

"The 'C' scrawled in blood was the best clue—and also the biggest piece of inadvertent misdirection. Everyone assumed that was a 'C' for Camila. Seemed the obvious conclusion. Except Nick Mansfield didn't know Camila owned that bakery. The key, I finally realized, was that Mansfield was a former banker. Unemployed, sure, but he had worked in that world for many years. He was a numbers person, a math major. He talked the talk. People told me he talked about making 100K per 'annie.' Needing to scrape together some 'Georgies.' To Mansfield 'C' was a Roman numeral. For one hundred. As in C-note. A hundred-dollar bill. A Benjamin. Or as he'd say—a Benji."

He took a step closer to her. "That 'C' really was a dying clue, best he could manage with the time he had, his rapidly weakening body, addled brain, and the limited amount of time and blood. But as best he was able, he was telling us you were the murderer."

Benji's gun pressed closer. "Aren't you the little smarty pants."

"Not nearly smart enough." He completed the narrative. "One by one, you lured the four men to the bakery. How'd you get Nick back there after he'd dumped you? Sex? Drugs? Money?"

"All of the above. I got even. I learned from my mistakes."

"You learned the wrong lesson. Sure, he was a complete Nickwad. But that didn't make what you did okay. You had some bad experiences. We all do. You're supposed to make it a teaching moment. Learn from it. Grow. But instead, you let it stick in your head. Change you in the worst possible way. You went Count of Monte Cristo when you should've gone Scarlett O'Hara."

"You don't know what you're talking about."

"You knew Camila bought the bakery. No doubt liberated

the keys from her and copied them. I bet you chose that date because you knew the mayor would be around opening that restaurant. You drugged three of the men before the christening ceremony and Nick after, tied them up, then turned on the oven and baked them to death."

"Poetic, don't you think? They burned me. So I burned them."

He stared at her, trying to understand. "Did you wait outside the oven and watch them die? Did that give you pleasure?"

"It did. And will again." She eyed Denton. "You're next."

Denton looked baffled. "Why me? We only dated twice. I liked you."

"You fired me. You replaced me with a man. Maybe afterward I'll come back for you, Pike."

"That's not the main reason you want to kill Denton. If Denton dies now, right after Camila is acquitted, everyone will assume she killed him. Vengeance against this threat to her power. Or maybe you'll spread fake news saying they were sleeping together. People will assume Camila committed all the murders, even if she was acquitted." He took a cautious step forward. "You are completely insane, aren't you?"

"Who's to say? Are you completely sane? Not from where I'm standing. You work for a guy you've never met, you live on a boat though you could afford a mansion, and you regularly engage in sports that could kill you. Sounds insane to me."

"Hardly the same thing."

Her eyes darkened. "None of us knows what we're capable of doing if pushed hard enough. Not until the time comes." She didn't lower the gun. "I never thought of myself as a killer. I never thought I'd hurt a fly. But how long can a woman go on being screwed by men who lie and cheat and say they love her? How long?" Her voice choked. "We say this is the era of women. Equal rights. Shattered glass ceilings. But what's changed? Even after all the MeToo and Time's Up, men still run this world, treat women like crap, and as long as they don't rape anybody, they get away with it."

"You're…exaggerating."

"Am I? Even that pissant Mansfield got away with robbing me blind."

"Because you let him."

She gritted her teeth and thrust the gun forward. "I did not *let* him!"

Denton raised his arms. "Pike, maybe we should not anger the lady with the gun…?"

But he continued. "You're a smart woman, Benji. You must've seen the signs. But you ignored them."

"Because I don't want to be alone my entire life. Because I want someone greeting me at the end of the day other than my cats. Because I want to be loved. Is that such a crime?"

"We all want that," he replied. "And that's usually when we make our stupidest mistakes." He needed to keep her talking. "But why frame Camila? She's not a man. She didn't hurt you. She made you her Chief of Staff."

"Which means I'm basically her glorified appointments secretary. I never had any real power or influence. She never listened to anything I said. Whenever she had an important decision to make, she'd turn to Esposito or Denton or Luis González. Some man."

"I'm sure that's not true."

"And she screwed Nick Mansfield. She took him from me."

"She didn't even know you'd dated him."

"Doesn't matter. All men want is sex."

"That's a cliché, and wrong."

She charged forward, gun still poised between them. "What about you, hotshot? I've seen the way you look at me, sizing me up. Want a moment of perfect pleasure?"

"It…would never work between us."

She moved uncomfortably close. "Are you sure?"

"Yeah. Because I'm a dog person…and you're a lunatic."

She brought the gun around and whipped him on the side of the head. He winced but remained standing. "She stole my man!" Her eyes were wide and wild.

He felt blood trickling down the side of his head. "That loser stole from you. You were better off without him."

"He was all I had!" She began to break down, tears streaming from her eyes. "All I had in the world…"

He hesitated, not sure what to do. "You know this is over, right? You're going to be convicted. Probably placed in a mental institution."

"You can't prove anything."

"I think I can. You've left a lot of footprints, once you know where to look. Like on your Fitbit."

"What?"

"We've had hackers working for us for some time now. We think Sweeney introduced malware that invaded all the computers in this office, and my office, including staff laptops. Which is how Garrett got into your computer while I drove over here. He accessed your online Fitbit records."

"You—*what*?"

"At the time of the murder, you were not, as you claimed, at home in bed. Your heart was racing, according to Fitbit. I assume that's because of the sex you had in the bakery lobby on the table with Mansfield. But you know when your heart raced even more? When you killed four men." He shook his head. "You've got a serious problem, Benji. You need help."

"You need to die." She stretched out her arm and aimed at his face.

"You can't get away with this, Benji."

No one had to look to identify that voice. Camila Pérez emerged from the hallway. "I heard every word, Benji. Your crime spree is over."

Benji laughed. "As if anyone would believe you. Or your

sleazy lawyer. Who cares what the jury says—everyone thinks you're guilty. The internet thinks you're a lying whore."

"I believe her. I won't be the only one." Maria stepped beside Camila. "And I also heard every word you said."

Benji laughed even louder—and less convincingly. "Another lawyer. Who no one will believe. You can't prove anything."

"I can."

This time, Benji had to turn—to find Jazlyn Prentice, the third woman standing outside the office. "I've had misgivings about this case for some time. And now I know why. It didn't make sense. Camila would never do this. But a mentally unbalanced woman who has been mistreated by men one time too many—now it makes sense. I'll be happy to prosecute the case against you."

"You have no case!"

"Are you kidding?" Jazlyn held up her cell phone. "I recorded every word you've said."

"You see what you're up against, Benji?" he asked. "Three strong women, working together, standing shoulder to shoulder. That's how the world changes for women. Not because of people like you. Because of people like them."

Benji darted toward the door, but Camila sidestepped, blocking her path.

Benji raised the gun. "I will kill you. Gladly."

"Are you going to kill all five of us?"

"Maybe," she said, snarling. "Starting with you, Pike."

He leapt forward and tackled her from the side. She fell forward but managed to twist around and grab his hair as she fell, pulling hard. He broke her grip, but she came back, pounding the side of his face with the gun. He shielded his face, but his sore leg buckled and they both tumbled backward.

He grabbed her arm and pounded it against the carpet. She did not drop the gun. He pounded harder, but she managed to hold on. She was trying to curl her wrist, to point the gun at him.

She fired. The report of the gun was shattering. He winced.

He looked around fast. The bullet went into the wall. No one was hurt.

He tightened his muscles and pounded again, as hard as he could.

Maria stepped forward and kicked the gun out of Benji's hand.

He exhaled heavily. "Thanks, partner."

Benji sat up suddenly, arms extended, shrieking. She scratched her nails down the side of Dan's face.

"That—*hurt*!" He pushed her hard against the wall. "Give it up, Benji. It's over."

She rocketed back with astounding speed, pushing him away, pushing free. He blocked her way to the door. She reached into her pocket and withdrew a pen, holding it like a dagger aimed at his face. "I'll poke your eyes out. Both of them!"

He clenched his teeth. "Crazier than anyone imagined."

She lunged, but he checked the assault. Behind her, Maria wrenched Benji's arm back. The pen dropped to the floor.

And still she struggled. Maria and Camila both wrapped their arms around her, then Jazlyn joined in, adding more strength. Benji screamed like a banshee, struggling to get free. With another cry, she lurched forward, breaking through the women's arms and launching herself again at the man blocking her path. "It's always some damn man, isn't it?" she cried. She leapt at him, trying to knock him over.

He caught her in midair and shoved her back. Her head slammed against the wall with a thud. "My mother told me to never hit a woman. But you've been wanting equal opportunities…"

"Allow me," Camila said, fist raised.

Her right hook was impressive. Benji fell to the carpet, dazed.

"I'll tie this bitch up," Maria said. "Someone call the cops."

"Already on it." Jazlyn had her phone pressed to her ear.

He touched the side of his face. She'd given him a good mauling. Denton crawled out from behind the desk, still looking shaky.

"Face hurt much, Dan?" Maria asked.

"I'll live. Thank goodness you were all here."

"We're only here because you figured it out." She removed the scarf from her blouse and used it to tie Benji's hands behind her back. "I don't know if I've mentioned this lately, Dan, but I am seriously glad you're on my side."

"And I'm seriously glad I have friends. Like you three women."

Camila beamed. "Who are more than just pretty faces?"

He nodded. "Much more."

CHAPTER FIFTY

DAN AND THE REST OF HIS TEAM SAT ON THE SOFA IN THEIR office lobby gazing at the large-screen television, which was bizarre, because there was nothing on the screen. Only a voice emerged.

"How's the face healing?" Mr. K asked.

"Not fast enough," he answered, touching the wounded area "Stings when I smile. Might leave a scar."

"I hope it does," Maria said.

"Thanks so much."

"It would give you kind of a roguish appearance. Like a pirate lawyer."

"Pirate lawyer? Is that a thing?"

"I thought we were all pirate lawyers," Jimmy murmured.

"I'm sure it will be fine," Mr. K said. "I've contacted a facial repair surgeon I know. He'll be calling you. I'm sorry that had to happen. But if it's any consolation, remember— you did save a life. Benji had already drugged Denton's flask."

"Do you think she was planning to have sex with him before she killed him?" Garrett asked.

Maria pulled a face. "Eew."

"Probably," Jimmy said. "She had a serious black widow thing going."

"What matters most," Mr. K said, "is that Benji is locked up and unable to hurt anyone. My sources tell me the DA's office will file charges later today. It's embarrassing for them—they have to admit they made a mistake when they charged Camila. There may even be an investigation into whether those charges were politically motivated."

"The best news," Garrett said, "is that Camila is back in the mayor's office. Where she belongs."

"Agreed," Mr. K replied. "And I don't think it will stop there. I was worried that even after acquittal, her reputation would be tainted. But now that someone else has been charged with the crime and we have a prosecutor as eyewitness to her confession, Camila seems completely exonerated. In fact, people are treating her as if she's a martyr, a Gandhi for women's rights, someone who suffered but emerged victorious. Don't you agree, Dan?"

"Yes, I think she has an extremely promising future. She told me she's been contacted again by the National Democratic Committee. They want to put her on a mini-tour. Speak on behalf of other candidates. Raise her profile. See that she's known for something other than being wrongfully accused."

Maria smiled. "Go Camila!"

"And," he continued, "as we all know, there's a Florida Senate seat being vacated next year. She could be taking a giant step from the mayor's office to something much bigger."

"Wonderful news," Mr. K said. He paused a moment. When his voice returned, it was lower than before. "But you need to warn her. Winning this case doesn't mean all opposition has disappeared. There are still people out there who consider her dangerous. A female Hispanic Democrat is someone to stop. Before she gets to the White House."

"I know who you're talking about. Sweeney. The same man who hired someone to abduct me and try to run me over.

The same man who launched the fake news campaign. Which was such a good idea, we had one of our hackers launch one against him. Get this—turns out Sweeney is the head of an international cult of Satan-worshippers."

"Except…I'm not sure that isn't true," Jimmy said.

"I sent Sweeney a message. When he takes down all the crap about Camila, we'll take down the stuff about him. I think he'll give in."

"Glad to hear it," K replied. "But Sweeney isn't the only white male running scared these days. People like Camila will see many rough patches ahead. Many battles yet to fight before we become a more inclusive society."

"But that's why we're here, isn't it?" Dan said, leaning forward. "That's why you created this whacked-out Charlie's Angels law firm. We're your angels, tackling the cases that need us but might be impossible for a lawyer who has to make a living. We do the dirty work, and you stay out of the crosshairs. No one even knows who you are."

"I know who he is," Maria said. "I may not know your name, K. But I know who you are. And I'm very glad to be one of your angels." She raised a cup in salute.

"Thank you, team. That's good to know. Because as it happens, I've got a new case for you. Take the weekend, then come back Monday morning ready to work. It involves a mysterious disappearance, then reappearance. Dan, I think this one is squarely in your wheelhouse."

"Because it requires brilliant trial skills?"

"No." Mr. K cleared his throat. "Because it's completely bizarre."

DAN FELT THE SEA SPRAY SPLASH IN HIS FACE. THE WEATHER was perfect, not too warm, not too cold. The ocean water was brisk and there was just enough wind to make kitesurfing interesting. He'd invited the whole team out for instruction and adventure. All three showed—plus a couple of additions.

Camila slid her arms around his waist. "Thank you for inviting me. I needed this."

"I'm glad you could come. You looked good out there."

"Are you kidding? I have the coordination of a mollusk."

"It was your first attempt."

"And possibly my last."

"Don't say that. It gets easier every time. Exercise is good for you."

"I am all in favor of exercise." She hugged him tighter. "But I think I would prefer a different form."

He arched an eyebrow.

Garrett helped Jimmy get into his gear and mount the kite. "Am I doing this right?"

He flashed a thumbs up. "You look like a pro, Jimmy."

"I think I can get up into the air this time."

Garrett laughed. "He thinks he's Superman."

Dan shook his head. "Aquaman. Much cooler. And we are in the water."

He heard footsteps splashing behind him. "Did you two know you have a couple name?" Maria smiled. "That means it's official."

"What is?"

"You two. Believe me, the 'shippers think you're adorable."

Camila frowned. "We've been seen in public exactly once."

"And the press is already calling you two 'Danila.'"

Dan pondered. "Better than Camiel."

"Oh, you just want your name to go first."

Jazlyn waded up behind them. "Hey, thanks for inviting me out today. I was surprised—but pleased."

"I should've suggested it a long time ago." He held out his hand. "Friends?"

She took his hand and grinned. "Just don't tell anyone."

He jerked his head around. "Holy moley. Jimmy just took off."

They saw the kite skitter across the surface of the water. Jimmy lasted an impressive eight seconds before spilling over.

They cheered. "Not bad at all. Especially for a first attempt. Jimmy, you've been hiding your talents."

Jazlyn whistled. "Maybe he is Aquaman."

Camila grimaced. "If he starts talking to fish, I'm out of here, Dan."

He grinned and wrapped an arm around her. "We all have something to contribute." He leaned over and planted a kiss on her salty lips. "But not that. That would just be weird."

EPILOGUE

SWEENEY SAT BEHIND HIS DESK. THE PANORAMIC VIEW OF THE city afforded by his penthouse windows hung like a halo behind his head. He thought it was important that they meet after hours. He didn't want any witnesses. Just what was in that bag. "Do you have it?"

"Of course I do."

"Then stop screwing around. Give it to me."

The man in the blue uniform withdrew a small silver flask sealed in a plastic evidence bag. And put it in Sweeney's hands. "Still don't know why you wanted me to take this. Hardly seems worth the risk."

"That's because you have no imagination." He held the flask up to the light. "No one saw you take it?"

"Of course not. I did it just like you told me."

"And it has her prints on it?"

"It does now. But who cares? She's been exonerated."

"But he hasn't."

"He?" The man thought for a moment. "You mean the lawyer?"

"Indeed."

"He hasn't been charged with anything."

"Yet." He placed the flask inside his desk. "You've done good work. You will be appropriately rewarded."

"Not necessary. I'm just glad to be on your team. I think what you're doing is important. Someone has to stop what's going on out there before this country is completely ruined."

"That's what I like to hear."

"A lot of us admire what you've done in the past and— well, we just hope you won't stop."

"I will never stop."

"I'm speaking for a lot of people when I say you shouldn't let this little setback slow you down. We hope you'll make a comeback."

"Oh, I will come back." Sweeney's hands tightened into fists. "With a vengeance."

DAN'S RECIPES

Want to try Daniel Pike's cooking? Here's his recipe for Spaghetti Aglio e Olio.

Bear in mind that Dan makes his own pasta using dough he has prepared from scratch, but you can also use a pasta maker, which is suprisingly easy, only takes about fifteen minutes, and is almost as good. Dan uses a Philips pasta maker, but there are many good ones on the market. If you must use store-bought spaghetti, remember that not all spaghettis are equal. Look for plain semolina-flour noodles (not whole wheat). Rao's Homemade is excellent.

Ingredients:

1/4 pound spaghetti

extra virgin olive oil (with a spicy flavor profile, if you like the heat)

3-5 garlic cloves, sliced, and if you like, garlic confit

1 tablespoon dried chili flakes

plain breadcrumbs

1 pinch Italian parsley

1 lemon (use the zest)

kosher salt

Instructions:

1) Bring a large pot of salted (but don't overdo it) water to simmer, then add spaghetti. Cook for a minute or two less than normal, until the pasta bends but is still "al dente (firm)."

Note: If you bring the water to a boil, it will cook quicker, but it will be hard to obtain the ideal texture.

2) In a separate saute pan, heat the olive oil and put the sliced garlic in the oil. Don't burn the garlic!

3) Remove the saute pan from the heat and add the red pepper flakes. Stir well. Let the chili flakes and the garlic infuse the oil.

4) Put the saute pan on low heat. Add some of the pasta water and the pasta. Saute quickly so the sauce will coat the spaghetti. Taste. If the spaghetti is too firm, saute longer with a little added water and mixing. When you're finished cooking, stir in garlic confit, if you're using it.

5) Sprinkle with bread crumbs, and/or if you like, drizzle a little extra olive oil and sprinkle with parsley. Add lemon zest. Serve hot.

ABOUT THE AUTHOR

William Bernhardt is the author of forty-eight books, including *The Last Chance Lawyer (#1 Amazon Bestseller)*, the historical novels *Challengers of the Dust* and *Nemesis*, two books of poetry, and the Red Sneaker books on fiction writing. In addition, Bernhardt founded the Red Sneaker Writers Center to mentor aspiring authors. The Center hosts an annual conference (WriterCon), small-group seminars, a newsletter, a phone app, and a bi-weekly podcast. He is also the owner of Balkan Press, which publishes poetry and fiction as well as the literary journal *Conclave*.

Bernhardt has received the Southern Writers Guild's Gold Medal Award, the Royden B. Davis Distinguished Author Award (University of Pennsylvania) and the H. Louise Cobb Distinguished Author Award (Oklahoma State), which is given "in recognition of an outstanding body of work that has profoundly influenced the way in which we understand ourselves and American society at large." In 2019, he received the Arrell Gibson Lifetime Achievement Award from the Oklahoma Center for the Book.

In addition Bernhardt has written plays, a musical (book and score), humor, children stories, biography, and puzzles. He has edited two anthologies (*Legal Briefs* and *Natural Suspect*) as fundraisers for The Nature Conservancy and the Children's Legal Defense Fund. In his spare time, he has enjoyed surfing, digging for dinosaurs, trekking through the Himalayas, paragliding, scuba diving, caving, zip-lining over the canopy of the Costa Rican rain forest, and jumping out of an airplane at 10,000 feet.

In 2017, when Bernhardt delivered the keynote address at the San Francisco Writers Conference, chairman Michael Larsen noted that in addition to penning novels, Bernhardt can "write a sonnet, play a sonata, plant a garden, try a lawsuit, teach a class, cook a gourmet meal, beat you at Scrabble, and work the *New York Times* crossword in under five minutes."

ALSO BY WILLIAM BERNHARDT

The Daniel Pike Novels

The Last Chance Lawyer

Court of Killers

Trial by Blood (November 2019)

The Ben Kincaid Novels

Primary Justice

Blind Justice

Deadly Justice

Perfect Justice

Cruel Justice

Naked Justice

Extreme Justice

Dark Justice

Silent Justice

Murder One

Criminal Intent

Death Row

Hate Crime

Capitol Murder

Capitol Threat

Capitol Conspiracy

Capitol Offense

Capitol Betrayal

Justice Returns

Other Novels

Challengers of the Dust

The Game Master

Nemesis: The Final Case of Eliot Ness

The Code of Buddyhood

Dark Eye

Strip Search

Double Jeopardy

The Midnight Before Christmas

Final Round

The Red Sneaker Series on Writing

Story Structure: The Key to Successful Fiction

Creating Character: Bringing Your Story to Life

Perfecting Plot: Charting the Hero's Journey

Dynamic Dialogue: Letting Your Story Speak

Sizzling Style: Every Word Matters

Powerful Premise: Writing the Irresistible

Thinking Theme: The Heart of the Matter

The Fundamentals of Fiction (video series)

Poetry

The White Bird

The Ocean's Edge

For Young Readers

Shine

Princess Alice and the Dreadful Dragon

Equal Justice: The Courage of Ada Sipuel

The Black Sentry

Edited by William Bernhardt

Legal Briefs: Short Stories by Today's Best Thriller Writers

Natural Suspect: A Collaborative Novel of Suspense

CPSIA information can be obtained
at www.ICGtesting.com
Printed in the USA
LVHW041224070721
692085LV00010B/1275